HONEST TO

DOG

A GOLDEN RETRIEVER MYSTERY

BY NEIL S. PLAKCY

Neil S. Plakcy

Reviews for the Golden Retriever Mysteries:

Mr. Plakcy did a terrific job in this cozy mystery. He had a smooth writing style that kept the story flowing evenly. The dialogue and descriptions were right on target.

--Red Adept

Steve and Rochester become quite a team and Neil Plakcy is the kind of writer that I want to tell me this story. It's a fun read which will keep you turning pages very quickly.

--Amos Lassen – Amazon top 100 reviewer

We who love our dogs know that they are wiser than we are, and Plakcy captures that feeling perfectly with the relationship between Steve and Rochester.

-- Christine Kling, author of *Circle of Bones*

In Dog We Trust is a very well-crafted mystery that kept me guessing up until Steve figured out where things were going.

--E-book addict reviews

1 – FALLING APART

"I am totally screwed." I ended my phone call and put the cell on the kitchen table, then leaned my head down to my chest. My golden retriever, Rochester, rose from his place by the sliding glass doors and came over to me, resting his head in my lap.

Lili walked into the kitchen and sat beside me. "What's the matter, Steve?"

I reached down to stroke Rochester's golden head, then looked up. "That was Professor Finkle's wife. He's in the hospital with a perforated bowel, and he won't be able to lead the personal finance seminar for me this weekend."

"He's in more trouble than you are," Lili said. "A perforated bowel is serious."

"I know, and I feel bad for the guy. I'll even send him flowers. But now I'm going to have to cancel the grand opening and first seminar at Friar Lake."

I'd been offered the chance to manage a brand-new conference center for Eastern College, my alma mater, and had spent the past eight months supervising the property's conversion from a nineteenth-century abbey. Because so many people like me in their early forties, and older, were recognizing the need to focus on investing to ensure a financially secure retirement, I had chosen to offer a weekend seminar on the topic for my inaugural program.

Eastern was a liberal arts college without a lot of business courses, but I'd been able to recruit Fred Finkle, who taught economics. He'd won many awards for his teaching, and I knew he had the ability to take arcane material and make it interesting. Then I had worked my butt off to advertise the program and prepare for the launch. And all I'd put together was going to fall apart because of Professor Finkle's perforated bowel.

"Can you find someone else to run the program?" Lili asked. "There must be other faculty who could do it." Lili was a professor of visual art and chair of the fine arts department at Eastern, and sometimes I looked at her, her auburn curls cascading around her heart-shaped face, so beautiful and smart and funny, and marveled that she was willing to love me.

"Not with Finkle's expertise," I said. "And his wife said he's knocked out from all the drugs, so he's too sick to suggest anyone from outside who could help."

"Can you run it yourself, working from his notes?"

"Honey, my degree is in English," I said. I'd taught courses in that discipline at Eastern as an adjunct, and I was decent at it because I loved the way words could be used, and I was able to convey that enthusiasm to students, to help them correct their grammar and clear up their muddy thinking. But the world of finance was completely foreign to me.

Maybe it was the word "foreign," but I remembered my old friend Tor, a Swedish-born investment banker in New York. We'd been friends since our grad school days at Columbia, when he was in the business school and I was getting my MA in English.

"I'm going to call Tor," I said to Lili.

"Excellent idea. I'm going upstairs to relax. Call me if you need me."

As she left, Rochester sprawled at my feet, and I dialed Tor's number.

He answered right away. "Hello, Steve. I was just thinking about you. My children are obsessed with having a dog since they have heard so much about the amazing Rochester. Perhaps we will come out to the country one weekend soon."

Tor's speech retained an endearing formality, even though he'd been in the US for over twenty years.

"That would be fun. Not this coming weekend, though, because my first program at Friar Lake is supposed to start."

"Not good for us either," Tor said. "I leave tomorrow morning for a conference in Chicago."

"Crap," I said. "I was hoping you could help me out with the program." I explained my bind. "I don't suppose you know someone who could jump in, do you?"

"Let me think for a moment."

There was silence on Tor's end as I contemplated the disaster ahead of me. My programming would go down in flames, I'd be fired and have to go back to cobbling together a living from part-time teaching.

"There is one man I know," Tor said eventually. "He worked here for a while but left us to move to your town, where his ex-wife and children live. His name is Douglas."

I wrote that down. "First or last name?"

"First. Last name Guilfoyle. I will spell it for you while I look in my contacts for his information."

I wrote the name down. "Here it is," Tor said. "I will email you his information."

"You don't have a personal number for him, do you?" I asked, looking at the clock. It was after six on a Wednesday evening, so doubtful the guy would be at work.

"Personal cell. Here it is." He read it out to me.

I thanked him profusely and hung up. Why did I know Douglas Guilfoyle's name? Had I met him through Tor at some point in the past? Though I trusted Tor, I Googled Guilfoyle and I found Guilfoyle's information on LinkedIn. He had an MBA from Michigan, and had spent nearly twenty years in public finance, the arm of an investment bank that handles issuing bonds for governments, including a short stint at Tor's firm. In January he had joined a firm called Beauceron Capital Partners in Stewart's Crossing.

I checked out the company's home page, which featured an impressive looking black dog with tan paws, one of the European shepherd breeds. The caption beneath the picture read, "The

Beauceron is an ancient herding dog native to France. It is faithful and obedient, with a tireless work ethic. We at Beauceron Capital Partners work hard and faithfully for our clients."

After skimming through employee bios and the company's investment philosophy, I was convinced it was legitimate. I dialed the number Tor had given me, and when Guilfoyle answered, I introduced myself as a friend of Tor's.

Before I could get any farther, he said, "I'm sorry, but I'm just about to take my kids and dog out, so I can't talk now."

"You're in Stewart's Crossing, right? Where do you walk your dog?"

"The Delaware Canal, behind the Drunken Hessian restaurant."

"Would it be all right if I brought my dog out there and we walked together? I need to talk to somebody quickly. I'd appreciate it."

"I suppose. If you don't mind my kids hanging around. We'll be there in about fifteen minutes. You can't miss us—we have a Yorkie with a pink bow on her head."

I told him that I'd be with a golden retriever, and we hung up. Then I looked out at the courtyard of my townhouse. Daffodils Lili had planted were beginning to bloom, and what was left of the sun was nearly as yellow as the flowers. Even if Douglas Guilfoyle couldn't help me, a nice walk with Rochester could clear my head.

I called upstairs and told Lili I was going to take Rochester to the canal for a walk. At the magic word, my happy golden began dancing around the kitchen like a manic kangaroo. He was almost three years old, but in many ways he was just a big puppy, though he was almost ninety pounds of fur, tongue and muscle.

He was a rescue dog originally adopted by my next door neighbor. After she was killed, he came to live with me, and gave my life a sense of purpose when I needed one.

Once upon a time, I was married and living in Silicon Valley, working as a technical writer and developing my computer skills while my wife and I tried to start a family. After her first miscarriage, she indulged in retail therapy that put us in a financial hole for the next year. When she miscarried a second time, I hacked into the three major credit bureaus and put a red flag on her credit cards so she couldn't bankrupt us again.

That stunt got me a year in a California prison and a two-year probation, which had ended recently. It also dealt the final blow to my marriage. The last I'd heard from Mary was that she was remarried, had been promoted, and had a baby son. I was glad she'd gotten everything she wanted, but had no desire to see her or talk to her again.

I returned home to Stewart's Crossing without a full-time job, family or close friends nearby. After years spent in what became a childless, loveless marriage, I had forgotten what it was like to care for someone else—and to receive affection in return. Once I adopted Rochester, I had to get up every day and feed and walk him. I had to make sure he had shelter and toys and the comfort that came from being part of a pack. More than anything else, it was Rochester's unconditional love that brought me back to the world of the living.

He brought me his leash in his mouth, and I loaded him into my ancient BMW for the ride down to the park which ran along the Delaware Canal, through the center of town. Barges had once brought coal down from upstate Pennsylvania to the port at Bristol, but when rail replaced mule barges, the canal had been abandoned. In the 1960s, the county had converted the towpath beside the canal to a linear park. It was a great place to let Rochester run off excess energy.

I parked and we walked down to the towpath. A big, sodden log floated alongside us, and Rochester got down on his front paws and barked at it. "Don't worry, puppy, it's just a log." I was afraid he might try and jump into the water, which was deep and fast-moving after recent rains, so I tugged him down the path.

With the log behind us, I let Rochester off his leash and tossed a Frisbee for him. The towpath was paved with reddish gravel, and the new grass along the canal bank was a bright green. Daisies and lilacs bloomed on the verge, beneath a thicket of trees that sheltered us from the back yards of houses. Though we were in the middle of town, it was like we'd pushed the real world away, and that was just what I needed.

Rochester galloped down the bank after the Frisbee, but when he caught it, instead of returning it to me, he settled down for a chew. I often called him my golden thiever, because once he grabbed something it was his. I strolled over to where he rested on the grass and sat down beside him, one hand ruffling his golden fur.

The sun was setting, casting bright glints and long shadows on the water. As I looked up and down the towpath for Douglas Guilfoyle, my thoughts went back to the upcoming program at Friar Lake. It would be a nightmare to contact everyone who had signed up and refund their money. What if someone had made flight arrangements? Would we be expected to reimburse them for their airfare? How could anyone trust Friar Lake – or me—if the very first program was cancelled?

I had struggled through years of uncertainty, fighting against prejudice because of my criminal record, to earn the responsibility and the financial security that came with it. Did I have it in me to begin that fight all over again, if Friar Lake went down in flames?

2 – OLD CLASSMATE

A female Yorkie with a pink bow in her topknot came trotting toward us from around a slight bend in the canal, and Rochester popped up. If that was Guilfoyle's dog, then where was he? She seemed friendly, going down on her front paws in the classic play position, and Rochester nosed her. Then they began to run around in circles.

From the distance, a chorus of voices called, "Pixie! Pixie!"

The dog heard her name, and took off in the opposite direction. Rochester followed her for a few feet, but she darted into the underbrush and he stopped. He barked once, but when the little girl dog didn't respond he came back to me.

I looked down the canal bank and saw a heavyset man of about my age approaching with two kids – a boy of about sixteen, a girl a few years younger. Had to be the Guilfoyles.

"You shouldn't have let her off the leash, Ethan," the man said.

"She always comes when I call her," the boy said. "It's just because you're here. She doesn't like you anymore." He was rail-thin with straight, dark blond hair that fell over his forehead and a typical teenage slouch. If I were his father, I'd make him wear a belt to keep his jeans up on his slim hips instead of sliding down to show off the waistband of his briefs.

"You're mean, Ethan," the girl said. She looked like her father, with round cheeks and baby fat and the same curly dark hair. She wore a tight pink polo shirt and khaki slacks that were so new they still had the packaging creases.

Rochester popped up as the boy answered, "Shut up, Madison."

"Both of you focus," the father said. "We have to find Pixie."

I stood up as Rochester rushed down the bank in the direction the little dog had been headed. "You must be Douglas Guilfoyle. I'm Steve Levitan." I held out my hand, and we shook. "Pixie ran into the azaleas over there." I pointed to where Rochester was nosing at a hedge of pink flowers coming into bloom. He barked once and then sat on his haunches.

"Call me Doug," he said as the four of us I hurried down the bank to where Rochester sat.

Through the new leaves I could see the little Yorkie's pink bow. "Looks like she got stuck in there," I said.

I peeled back the bushes and Doug peered in. "Yeah, she got into some kind of corner, but it doesn't look like she's caught on anything."

Pixie started yapping, and Rochester yawned and sprawled on the ground beside me.

"She doesn't do reverse," Ethan said.

"I know that, Ethan," Doug said. "Your mother and I only split up a year ago. I haven't forgotten anything about you, or Pixie."

I pried the bushes aside so Doug could reach in for the little dog. Once he had her in his arms, she began to squirm. Madison hooked the leash to her collar and her father put the dog on the ground. Pixie tried to run away, twisting the girl's arm.

"Give her to me," Ethan demanded. When his sister complied, he jerked hard on the leash and the dog yelped.

I don't like to see anybody mishandle a dog, but I wasn't going to jump into this family dynamic. Rochester, though, stood up, ready to protect his brand-new friend.

"Don't hurt her," Madison said.

"Pixie, heel!" Ethan said, and the little dog obeyed. "We're going to walk her, Dad."

He and his sister took off down the canal bank. "Be careful," Doug said. "Don't get too close to the water."

"The water isn't too deep here," I said.

"Yeah, but I can't swim, and I have a morbid fear of water from back when I was a kid." He took a couple of steps back from the water's edge to make his point.

Rochester slumped back down on the bank beside me. "So, you must be Tor's friend Steve," Doug said. "When I told him I was moving down here he mentioned you." He took off his glasses and rubbed the bridge of his nose, and something about that gesture reminded me of why he looked so familiar.

"Dougie!" I said, remembering his college nickname. "Freshman year at Eastern, we both lived in Birthday House." The rumor goes that the money for that dormitory was donated by a very wealthy alumnus named Hoare. The college demurred at naming a dorm Hoare House, so the man made his donation on his birthday.

"Jesus, nobody's called me Dougie in years," he said. "Wow. We haven't seen each other for a donkey's age. How do you know Tor Svenson?"

We talked for a couple of minutes about the past. Doug hadn't aged well – I didn't remember him being so heavy, and there was more gray in his hair than in mine.

"Remember the night we all got arrested?" I asked.

One spring night just before final exams, Dougie and I were playing a drinking game in the student lounge with a bunch of buddies. By the end of the game, we were all smashed. Dougie suggested we should race around the outdoor fitness course around the perimeter of the lawn — naked.

Hey, it seemed like a good idea at the time.

About a dozen of us stripped down in the lobby and left our clothes in a big, sloppy pile, then took off outside. We were halfway through when the cops arrived. I guess we'd woken up some of the nerds in the dorm who thought sleep was important for success at final exams.

"I remember," Doug said. "We did some crazy shit back then." He looked down the bank and saw his kids playing with their dog. "You stayed in the area all this time?"

"Grew up here, lived in New York and California for a while, then came back after my divorce with my tail between my legs to start over."

"Yeah, I'm trying to start over myself," he said. "After our divorce, my ex moved down here from Westchester County because she has cousins here. I followed them all because I want to stay part of my kids' lives. But we're having a rocky time of it, and my ex isn't making it easy for me, either."

He sighed. "Ethan hates my guts and Maddie's just confused. But I'm in it for the long haul. Not going to let them go."

I saw the way he looked at his kids as they returned along the towpath, and I hoped he'd be able to manage the reconciliation he wanted. Rochester roused himself and ambled down the canal bank toward the kids and the Yorkie.

Maybe my golden and I could help Doug, especially if he was able to take over the seminar at Friar Lake, and we rekindled our friendship. The first step, then, was to recruit Doug's help. "Are you busy this weekend?" I asked, as we stood up. "I need somebody to lead a seminar on personal finance, and Tor suggested you might be able to."

He thought for a moment. "Catherine has the kids this weekend, so I'm at loose ends. All I'd be doing is sitting around my apartment."

"Hold on. Did you marry Catherine Hollister?" Catherine had been an English major, like I was, and we'd been in several classes together. I remembered that she'd been dating Dougie senior year.

"Yeah. As soon as I got my MBA. We moved to New York and I went to work in public finance, and Catherine got one of those secretarial jobs in publishing that they pretend is an editorial one."

"I considered one of those myself," I said. "Couldn't type fast enough, though."

"She quit when Ethan was born, and for fifteen years I worked my ass off to support the family, traveled nearly every week for business. Didn't notice my marriage was falling apart until it was too late."

"That's a shame."

"The divorce was a big wake-up call. I realized I didn't want to keep making the same mistakes, so I hunted for a job that would let me move down here with them, a job where I didn't have to travel so much. Finally got one with Beauceron, but it's all on commission, so I've got to work my tail off to build up a client base."

"Then this seminar could work out for you," I said. "There will be a lot of people interested in how they can better manage their investments. Maybe you can pick up some of them as clients."

"That would be good," he said. "I need to start generating some revenue. Catherine's alimony and the child support is bleeding me dry." He shook his head. "The other day Maddie told me Mommy has a boyfriend. I didn't say anything to her, but I hope it's true. If Catherine remarries then I'll be free of the alimony."

"I can pay you for the weekend," I said. "I remember being in your situation and I know that every little bit helps. Why don't I email you the handout and presentation that the professor who was going to lead things put together? We can talk after you take a look at it."

"Sure, I'll give it a look." He gave me his business card as Rochester romped back down the bank toward me, followed by Pixie, Ethan and Madison.

"My new boss Shawn and I bonded because both of us went through bad divorces," Doug said. "At least he got to keep his dog. Big boy, comes to work with him every day."

"What kind of dog?"

"A Beauceron, of course," he said. "French version of a German Shepherd."

Rochester rushed up to me, and I scratched beneath his chin. "Hey, boy, did you have fun playing with Pixie?"

"Your dog is big," Madison said.

"But he's cool," Ethan said, and for the first time he smiled. "My mom says we can't get a big dog because they drool and shed too much."

"Once I'm settled down here maybe I'll get a dog," Doug said. "When you come over on weekends you can play with him."

Ethan's face darkened. "Whatever."

Helping Doug reconcile with his kids would be a big job. But I wanted to give it a try, and I knew Rochester could help. Doug would be doing me a huge favor if he took on the investment seminar, so I'd owe him.

I resolved to think about what I could do as soon as my first program at Friar Lake was finished.

3 – Fine Tuning

The next morning it was warm enough to roll the windows down on the way upriver along the Delaware, and Rochester got to stick his head out into the spring air, barking at a flock of geese in a flooded field along the river. Then I turned inland and climbed the winding road to Friar Lake.

The former abbey was an impressive property, with a Gothic-style chapel and a cluster of dormitories and other buildings built of native fieldstone. Its hilltop location provided a vista of fields and forests down to the Delaware. A lot of work had gone into the restoration, and it was almost finished, with just a few punch list items remaining.

As I parked next to the gatehouse where my office was, Joey Capodilupo crossed the lot and hailed me. He was a tall, good-looking guy in his early thirties, wearing neatly pressed jeans and an off-white fisherman's sweater. An Eastern College ball cap was on his head backwards, the rising sun logo glinting in the early morning sunlight.

Joey had worked for the construction company as project superintendent, and when most of the work had finished he had joined the College staff to manage the physical aspects of the property. "Small problem," he said, as he walked up. Rochester stood up on his hind legs and nuzzled Joey's crotch.

"Down, Rochester!" I was energized by having recruited Doug Guilfoyle. "Problems solved are my specialty," I said to Joey. "Come in to my office."

We walked inside, and I shucked my light jacket and sat at my desk, in front of the big window that looked out at the property. The buildings and grounds looked terrific, ready to accommodate a group of eager students. "What's the problem?"

"Our temporary certificate of occupancy expires tomorrow. The building inspector who needs to sign off is out sick, and I'm not getting any traction with anyone else in that office."

"The last time we talked you said we were good to go with the first seminar. Why didn't you tell me that there could be problems?"

"I was maybe a bit too optimistic," he said. "We had a couple of little issues we had to tidy up. But they've been finished since last Monday, and I kept hoping the inspector would get better and come back to work."

"Our first guests are arriving tomorrow evening and we can't let them on the property if we don't have a certificate of occupancy," I said, my adrenaline level rising. "What can I do to help? You want me to drive over to the township office?"

"I tried that yesterday. Couldn't get past the secretary."

"Show me what needs to be signed off, and then I'll try my hand at some calls."

I hooked up Rochester's leash, and we walked outside. The deciduous trees were in full leaf by then, and bright green shoots of daffodils and tulips poked through the dirt beside the entrance to the chapel. Birds chirped in the distance. Above us a jetliner flew silently through the sky.

Joey led me through each of the open issues on the TCO. I'd learned a lot about construction during the renovation phase of the project, and the terms he used no longer were such a foreign language.

I left him at the classroom building, what had been the monks' workshop, and walked back to my office.

Friar Lake was my first real management position, and every day I had to learn a new skill. I'd been lucky to get a part-time teaching job at Eastern after my return to Bucks County, and after a couple of semesters of that, I'd been able to parlay my skill with databases into a job in the alumni relations office. All those experiences had helped me function in an academic environment and led to my assignment at Friar Lake, where I had a million-dollar budget and a twenty-acre facility to manage, as well as a slate of programs to create and execute.

It was important to me to succeed at Friar Lake so that I could feel my life was continuing on a forward trajectory. But right then, with yet another crisis looking, it sound overwhelmed by the responsibility. I could imagine seminar registrants arriving the next day to find some kind of "unfit for occupancy" sign plastered across the front gate.

Rochester must have sensed my mood, because he nuzzled me once I sat down at my desk, and I spent a couple of minutes playing with him. I'd learned in the past couple of years that petting a dog could reduce ward off depression, lower blood pressure, and boost immunity, and Rochester was a champ at providing the unconditional love I needed.

I could have called the college's president to ask for his help, but I didn't want to give up without trying myself. I called the number Joey had given me, where the secretary couldn't help me, and told me the director of the department was unavailable.

I thanked her politely. I had one more idea. I had met the township manager a few months before, when we hosted a ground-breaking ceremony at the Friar Lake, and he'd been delighted that the abbey was going to have a new life after the monks who lived there had moved on.

Though as an educational institution, Eastern College was exempt from property taxes, it pumped a lot of money into government coffers, from payroll taxes to college spending to the cash spent locally by students, faculty and staff. There had already been some buzz, led by the presence of the conference center, about an upscale residential development coming to what had been an undeveloped area of the township.

After a couple of minutes on hold I was able to speak to the manager and plead my case. "As you can imagine, if we have to cancel our first program, that threatens the viability of Friar Lake as a conference center," I said. "Someone has to sign off on extending our TCO, or better yet, on our permanent certificate of occupancy, before our first guests arrive tomorrow evening."

"Let me make some calls," he said.

I thanked him and hung up. Next on my agenda was Doug Guilfoyle. "Have you had a chance to look over the materials I sent you?" I asked.

"I have. It looks pretty comprehensive. How many students do you have coming?"

"Thirty-two." Personal finance was a hot topic for our target audience, professionals in their forties and fifties who had capital to invest for their retirement. I had advertised the program extensively, in Eastern's alumni magazine, in the *New York Times* and other publications. I was delighted to have that many people sign up for a program with no prior track record.

"Awesome. Would it be okay to invite my boss to stop by? He went to Eastern, too, and it would be a good opportunity for him to see me in action."

"Sure. You can have him come to the opening reception tomorrow night—cocktails at six, followed by dinner." I ran through the rest of the weekend's agenda with him. "We have a whole complex here, including a kitchen and dormitories. I have a private room and bath set aside for you for both Friday and Saturday nights."

Soon after, I heard from the township manager. "I spoke to the director of building and zoning and he's going to come out himself first thing tomorrow and if everything's kosher you'll get your CO."

I thanked him profusely and hung up, then pumped my fist into the air. Two problems solved – or at least on the route to being solved. But given that this program had started to feel jinxed, I worried what else could happen.

Joey was in the classroom building fiddling with an air handler. I told him what I'd learned. "You're sure everything is fixed, right?"

"Just doing a little fine tuning here," he said. "Don't worry, be happy."

Words to live by. I was still nervous for the rest of the afternoon, but no other crises arose. As we drove home that evening, Rochester had his head out the window, his golden fur flying back like Tibetan prayer flags, and I wished I could be as happy and carefree as he was. Even after I took him for a long walk around the neighborhood, I kept pacing around the townhouse, worrying about the seminar, with Rochester right on my heels.

"Steve, you're getting on my nerves," Lili said finally. "I need to focus on these papers and your agitation is distracting me. Why don't you call Rick and see if he wants to get a beer with you? Have dinner with him, relax, come back when you're mellower."

Rick Stemper was a detective with the Stewart's Crossing police department. We'd been acquaintances back in high school, and then become friends after I returned to town, bonded by bitterness over our divorces.

I was about to protest that it was my house – but it was Lili's home, too, since she'd moved in with me six months before. I called Rick, and he said that he'd had a bad day and could use a beer and a burger, too. We arranged to meet at the Drunken Hessian, a bar in the center of town.

I remembered what Joey had said, and repeated it to Rick. "Don't worry, be happy."

He snorted, and I laughed. Maybe the inaugural seminar would go off without a hitch. Fingers crossed.

Neil S. Plakcy

4 – COCKTAIL HOUR

I parked at the back end of the lot behind the Drunken Hessian, where it butts up against the canal. The path on that side was much narrower than the one across the canal, and erosion of the bank made it more dangerous, so Rochester and I stuck to the other side for our walks.

I stood there for a moment in the fading light, looking at the water and remembering seeing Doug Guilfoyle and his kids there the day before, until I was startled by the beep of Rick's horn as he pulled in beside my car.

Rick and I were the same age, though his hair was grayer and thinner than mine. In his favor, he was in better shape, probably no heavier than he'd been in high school. He had a high-energy Australian shepherd, and he and Rascal ran every morning. Too bad Rochester was more of a meanderer than a runner.

We walked inside the bar, which hadn't changed since we were teenagers – the same scarred wooden booths, neon beer signs in the window. We settled in a wooden booth at the back, the table etched with decades of initials, and ordered a pitcher of Yards Brawler, a microbrew made in Philadelphia that the Drunken Hessian kept on tap.

"So what's got you so agitated that Lili kicked you out of the house?" Rick asked.

I told him about the problems at Friar Lake.

"Sounds like you have it all under control," he said. "What's the big deal?"

"Do you ever worry that you just can't handle everything on your plate?" I asked. "I've never done this kind of job before. I can't anticipate what can go wrong because I have no experience, and so everything that happens blindsides me."

"You'd be surprised at the variety of crime that pops up, even in a small town like Stewart's Crossing," he said. "I can go from giving roadside sobriety tests to investigating a break-in to pulling in some kid from the high school for drugs."

I knew a lot about the variety of crimes Rick investigated, because I'd helped him out a few times. I held up my mug and said, "They say variety is the spice of life."

We clanked our glasses together at that, then ordered burgers and fries. "Before I forget, Sunday is Justin's birthday. Tamsen's having a party for him and you guys are invited."

Tamsen was the woman Rick had been dating, and Justin was her young son. "How old's he going to be? Nine?"

"Yup. I admire Tamsen so much – he's a very active kid and it's tough for him growing up without a father." Tamsen's husband had died in the Iraq war when Justin was very young.

"It's good that he has you," I said. "You having any thoughts about making the arrangement permanent?"

"You mean marrying Tamsen? It's still early days yet. We haven't even been dating a year. Though Justin has started to ask if I'm going to be his new dad."

From everything I'd seen, I knew that Rick needed someone to take care of, and while Tamsen was smart and independent enough to be a good match for him, she needed his help with Justin, who worshipped Rick. A marriage would work out well for all parties involved. As long as there was love under it all, that is.

***

As I'd told Doug, there were a couple of rooms in the Friar Lake dormitory set aside for staff, and I was going to be staying in one of them for the weekend, and I'd have to take Rochester with me, too.

I often called him my Velcro dog, because he stuck beside me, following me around the house and the office, even if I just jumped up for a minute. It might have been his background as a rescue dog, and then the death of his previous owner, my neighbor Caroline Kelly. He probably felt he had to keep an eye on me at all times to make sure nothing happened.

Friday morning I put together a bag of clothes and toiletries for the long weekend, as well as food and toys for Rochester. Lili seemed happy to have a couple of days to herself, and she had planned a beauty salon appointment and dinner with a couple of her friends from the faculty. We kissed goodbye and she wished me luck with the program.

My day began with a frantic call from my friend Gail Dukowski, who ran the Chocolate Ear café in Stewart's Crossing. I'd convinced her to branch out into catering and provide the food for the weekend. We had a full kitchen at Friar Lake, but she had to buy all the raw materials and transport them up to the property, then hire additional staff to help with preparation and serving, while still running her café.

She'd gone out on a limb for me, and because she recognized it was an opportunity to expand her business. "I arranged to borrow a van from another restaurant, but the chef just called me and said he smacked it up last night. What am I going to do? I have a kitchen full of food and no way to get it up to Friar Lake. I already cut my profit to the bone for you, and if I have to rent a van I'll be losing money and I can't afford to do that. Do you have one up at the college I can borrow?"

I looked out the window, where I saw Joey Capodilupo sweeping the walkway in front of the chapel, and I had an idea. "How big a van do you need?" I asked.

She gave me the details and I called my friend Mark Figueroa, who ran an antique store in the center of Stewart's Crossing, a few blocks from Gail's café. I'd hired Mark to help with the design and furnishing of Friar Lake, and I knew he had a van he used to make pickups and deliveries.

During the time we'd worked together, I'd fixed him up with Joey, so he owed me. It took a bit of wheedling, including a promise to take him and Joey to dinner, but he agreed to drive over to Gail's café bring the food up to Friar Lake.

The director of building and zoning came out an hour later, and Joey and I walked him around the property, showing him the way each of the outstanding items had been handled. Rochester was right behind me, taking every chance he could to mark buildings, trees and bushes as his territory. I felt like he did, proud of this facility I had helped bring together.

The inspector agreed that all the issues had been resolved, and signed off the paperwork we needed. Once that was done, Rochester and I returned to my office in the abbey gatehouse, and Mark arrived soon after with Gail and the food, and I spent the afternoon answering phone calls and handling minor crises. When each one came up, I stressed again, but Rochester's presence brought me back to earth each time my adrenaline skyrocketed.

When I was in prison, I had no control over my life whatsoever. Rules dictated when I ate, slept, worked at my job in the library. I'd been adrift for a while afterward, learning to be responsible for myself again. Then taking on Friar Lake had added a whole new level, and I'd experienced occasional panic attacks when problems had come up. I'd solved that by becoming a micro-manager, retaining control over everything.

But now that programming was about to launch, I had to step

back and let other people do their jobs. Trust Joey to keep the property running, Gail to feed us all, Doug to lead the seminar. It was hard to relinquish that control and I fought the panic that came when I remembered my powerlessness in prison.

This was different, I kept reminding myself. I'd found good people to help me, and I hard to trust them. At four o'clock, the part-time student I'd hired to help out arrived, and we set up the registration table, where she began checking in the first participants to arrive.

I kept Rochester in my office, pacified by treats and rawhide bones, though he was eager to get out and be part of what was going on. When Doug Guilfoyle showed up, I hooked up Rochester's leash and the two of us walked him over to the dormitory building.

The monks who lived at the Abbey of Our Lady of the Waters, as Friar Lake had been called back then, were housed in narrow cells with a communal bathroom at one end. Our renovation of the dormitory building had created a series of hotel-type rooms with en-suite bathrooms. We had retained many of the details of the original building, including the hardwood floors and stucco walls, and each room got a narrow floor-to-ceiling window that looked out at the grounds.

Mark had done a great job with the furnishings. Since the rooms were fairly narrow, we had incorporated the closets and cubbyholes the monks had used instead of buying armoires for each room. That way, we had managed to fit a double bed, night stand, desk and chair.

Instead of televisions, which were big, expensive and probably not going to be used much, we had stocked each room with an iPad connected to our T1 line, and access to cable movies and television shows.

Doug and I went over a couple of details, and he must have sensed my nerves, because he said, "Don't worry, Steve. I read through all your professor's notes and I know exactly what I'm going to do. It's going to be a great program."

I told him I appreciated his help, then led Rochester down the hall to the room where he and I would be spending the weekend. My room was like Doug's, only my view was of the hillside and the lake. I sat on the bed and Rochester jumped up beside me, and I petted him for a few minutes, then gave him a rawhide bone to chew.

"I'll bring you something yummy from dinner, puppy." I scratched him behind the ears, but he was more concerned with his bone.

Gail had sectioned off the nave of the abbey chapel for cocktails with a pretty, if incongruous Japanese screen, and as I arrived a young guy in a white shirt and black slacks was setting up an array of liquor bottles, with wine and beer in coolers to the side. I'd found a CD of Gregorian chants, and I set up the audio system to play it at low volume, then opened the front door and began welcoming people inside.

Most of the crowd looked like they'd come directly from work, lots of dark business suits and shiny loafers. They all had name tags with their first names in big letters, then last name and home city in smaller type below. All Eastern alumni had their year of graduation as well.

I slipped behind the screen to check the dinner setup in the apse. Seven round tables of six were set with glasses, plates and silverware. Napkins in light blue, one of Eastern's colors, had been folded into the shape of cardinals' hats, to match the abbey setting. Joey had hung an Eastern banner behind the speaker's podium along with the Eastern flag hanging limp on a pole beside it.

Through an open curtain, servers buzzed around the impromptu kitchen. Confident everything was under control, I returned to the cocktail party, where Eastern's president, John William Babson, had just arrived. He was tall and rawboned, and when he spoke about the college he bubbled with enthusiasm. He had deep green eyes and dark curly hair, and that evening he was wearing a snazzy Italian suit that made me feel underdressed in my khakis and Eastern College polo shirt.

"Looks terrific," he said as we shook hands. "Congratulations. This center is going to be one of the jewels in Eastern's crown." He looked around the room. "Where's Fred Finkle? I need to talk to him."

"Still in the hospital," I said. "You didn't know?" I told him about Finkle. "I called the hospital this morning and he's recovering comfortably. But don't worry, I've got a great replacement for him. His name's Doug Guilfoyle, and he went to Eastern with me."

"You think he manage?"

"This is just the kind of thing Eastern trains us for, isn't it? To handle every situation life throws at us?" They were his own words, so I figured he'd agree.

Babson laughed. "You've been listening to my speeches for too long, Steve." He looked at the crowd. "Now, point me toward any alumni I can talk to about fund-raising."

I sent him on his way and then looked around for Doug. It would be time to move in to dinner soon and I wanted to make sure to introduce him to Babson before then.

I felt a thrill of anticipation. My first program was about to begin. The baby I'd been nurturing for eight months had come to term, and finally I'd have a birth to celebrate.

Neil S. Plakcy

5 – MOST LIKELY TO

I couldn't find Doug anywhere. I looked through the crowd in the chapel, then went back to the dormitory to see if he was still in his room. Not there, nor was he in the classroom building. Was he lost somewhere on the property? Maybe he'd tripped and fallen in the woods? Had he gotten cold feet and run off?

Then I spotted him at the edge of the parking lot, engaged in some kind of heated discussion with another man. As I got closer, I recognized his boss, Shawn Brumberger, from his photo on the Beauceron website. He wore a well-cut dark suit, a starched white shirt and a blue Eastern College tie patterned with yellow rising suns. His short dark hair was tinged with gray and artfully arranged to cover a bald spot.

Shawn's face was red and he was leaning in close to Doug, poking at him with his index finger. Was he angry that Doug had agreed to lead the seminar? What if Doug had to walk out now in order to keep his job?

Whatever it was, I had to get in the middle of it. I needed Doug in the chapel, getting to know the participants, and Babson wanted to speak with Shawn and begin the delicate dance that might lead to Shawn making a donation to his alma mater. Nothing good could come of letting this argument fester.

As I approached, Doug noticed me and pivoted away from Shawn. "Hey, Steve, I want you to meet my boss," he said. He turned back to Shawn as if they hadn't just been arguing and said, "Steve's the guy I told you about, who invited me here to speak to all these potential clients."

Shawn and I shook hands, and the three of us walked back to the chapel, where I led them over to President Babson. After I introduced them, Babson said, "Thank you for lending Doug to us for the weekend. I'm sure he's going to do a terrific job."

"He was a great catch for us," Shawn said. "Nearly twenty years on Wall Street. What he doesn't know about municipal bonds isn't worth knowing."

Babson didn't seem to notice the fake camaraderie—but then, he hadn't just seen them arguing so heatedly they almost came to fisticuffs.

"Eastern alumni are the best hires you can make," Babson said. "We pride ourselves on providing a well-rounded liberal arts education that will help our graduates succeed no matter what path they take."

I'd heard Babson's patter so often it washed over me, but Doug and Shawn smiled and nodded at each other. Whatever had gone on between them earlier appeared to have washed away, but I was nervous that another fight might erupt, so I hovered on the edge of the conversation until Doug and Shawn separated, each of them speaking to seminar participants.

I made sure the bar was running smoothly, then shook hands and introduced myself to a lot of folks, asking them what they hoped to learn from the weekend and pushing together the singles who stood alone like wallflowers at a high school prom. I snuck back to my room for a few minutes to feed Rochester and make sure he had water, and promised to come back after dinner and take him for a long walk.

Then I found Gail in the kitchen. She wore black slacks and a white blouse with black kitchen clogs and a bright green apron embroidered with the name of her café, The Chocolate Ear. Her blonde hair had been twisted into a French braid and she looked elegant and in control. "How's everything going?" I asked.

"All set. You can help me move the Japanese screen so people can sit down." She left the apron in the kitchen and the two of us walked across the courtyard to the chapel. Servers scurried around us carrying platters of frisée salad, and once the water glasses were filled and the salad plates set, we invited everyone to take their seats.

Babson and I had agreed we'd split up so that he, Doug and I could meet as many of the participants as possible. I joined a pair of couples, two well-dressed women in their sixties and a guy about my age. We chatted over the salad, then chicken cordon bleu, roasted heirloom potatoes and fingerling carrots. As I expected, all of them were concerned about whether their investments would keep up with inflation, looking for tips on how to balance their portfolios and handle the risks involved.

Neil S. Plakcy

After the dinner plates were taken away, I snuck back to the kitchen and assembled a doggie bag for Rochester. I went out the back door of the chapel and delivered Rochester his treats, then returned to the table for a slice of moist chocolate cake layered with white, milk and dark chocolate mousse.

I kept looking around the room. Doug and Shawn were both engaged in avid conversations at their tables, and it looked like whatever had angered them earlier had dissipated. But I couldn't help wonder what that was, and worrying that it might have some impact on Doug's ability to deliver a great program.

As we were finishing dessert, Babson stood up and gave a brief speech about his plans for Friar Lake, that it would be one of the premier academic conference centers of the east coast. Then Doug spoke for a few minutes about what people could expect the next day. He asked them to come to the morning session with a list of places where they got financial information, and told a couple of stories from his Wall Street days.

We reopened the bar in the nave of the chapel, and though many of the guests went to their rooms, a dozen stuck around over snifters of brandy and tall glasses of Irish coffee. Gail had to open the café early the next morning, so she'd left one of her assistants to close up. When Doug and I were the last two left, we walked outside into the cool darkness, the sky above us spangled with stars.

"So what have you been doing since graduation?" Doug asked me.

I told him about the work I'd done, how I'd taught myself HTML and moved into web development. "Then Mary had her first miscarriage and ran us into credit card debt with some retail therapy."

"That's tough," Doug said.

"Yeah. Around that time a guy I worked with passed on some hacking software to me, and I picked up some extra cash doing some freelance projects."

"You're a hacker?"

"That's what the state of California calls me," I said, trying to make light of my conviction. "I might have gotten off with a slap on the wrist as a first offender, but I broke into some companies that took offense."

I took another sip of my brandy and told him the rest of the story – the year in prison, the two years on parole.

"You sure wouldn't have been the guy in our class voted most likely to go to prison," Doug said. He was quiet for a moment, and I worried that he was going to judge me because of my criminal background. Instead, though, he said, "You know about computers, right? Since I was able to help you out here, maybe you could return the favor."

"Just ask," I said. "I need to take Rochester out. You want to come with us and tell me what you need as we walk?"

He agreed, and we went back to my room to retrieve Rochester. He was sprawled on his side on the floor, snoring and making small whimpering sounds. I squatted down beside him. "What's the matter, boy? You all right?"

In a flash, he was up from his after-dinner nap and jumping around me, licking my face and hands. "Come on, let's go for a walk," I said, grabbing the fur around the back of his neck for balance so I could stand up. I hooked up his leash, grabbed a flashlight and a plastic bag, and the three of us walked outside.

"What do you think I can help you with?" I asked, as Rochester tugged me forward.

"I've only been at Beauceron for a couple of months but I'm worried that there might be something not quite kosher going on," Doug said. "I need to keep this job because I need to stay close to my kids, and this is the only job I could find in the area. But at the same time, I could lose my license if I'm know about criminal activity and I don't report it."

Was that what he and Shawn had been arguing about?

The night was quiet and almost spooky. Friar Lake was located at the top of a low mountain a few miles from the Delaware River, surrounded by farmlands and a couple of new suburban developments. Beyond the stars above, the only light came from the couple of street lamps and a few windows in the dormitory. We walked on a paved path that ran beside the woods, which were dark and deep.

"What is it that you think I can help with?"

"At Beauceron, we have a number of our own funds that customers can invest in, and one of them is an equity Real Estate

Investment Trust, also known as a REIT. We take investor capital and use it to provide first and second mortgage loans to commercial operators—apartment houses, shopping malls, that kind of thing. A lot of the properties are risky and they pay us high interest, which we pay out to our investors. It's our best-performing fund by far – double-digit returns, which in this economy is phenomenal."

"Sounds too good to be true." Rochester stopped, nosing around the base of a maple tree with a gnarled trunk. The air smelled fresh and humid.

Doug took a moment to collect his thoughts. "After Catherine and I sold the house in Westchester, I lived in Hoboken for a while. Last week I went up there to talk to a guy I knew who might be a client, and on my way back, I was driving down US 1 near Newark airport, and I remembered that our REIT had invested in a property near there. I thought it would be fun to drive by and see what was generating all this revenue."

We started walking again. "What kind of property?" I asked.

"A strip shopping center called Route One Plaza, anchored by a grocery store at one end and an electronics outfit at the other. But when I got there, both the big stores were shut down, and there were only a couple of small businesses still struggling in the middle."

"So a bad investment," I said.

He shook his head. "Not according to our books. We're still carrying that property as income-generating."

"Could there be something you don't know about?" I asked.

"Maybe there's a bankruptcy trustee who's keeping up the payments or something like that."

He shook his head. "I checked, and the limited partnership that owns the center isn't even paying the property tax. There's already a tax lien for more than the land is worth."

Rochester finally found the spot he'd been looking for, and popped a squat to do his business. I juggled the flashlight and the plastic bag, and it wasn't until I was finished that Doug continued.

"Here's the thing," he said. "I need some help going through the list of properties that the fund invests in and checking each one out. I don't have the computer skills to do all that research, and I'm so busy scrambling for clients I don't have the time either. Is there any way you can help me out?"

We stopped again beneath a lamp post, and I looked at Doug. "What are you going to do with this information?" I asked. "Report them to the authorities? If the company closes down you'll be out of a job anyway. So why not just quit if you think there's something criminal going on?"

"Shawn is pressuring me to bring new investors into our funds, particularly the REIT. So there's a chance I could get arrested, too, if there's illegal activity. But like I said, I can't afford to walk away right now."

He took a deep breath. "I keep hoping that maybe I'm wrong. Maybe that shopping center is generating income—it could be that the leases have to be paid even if the store closes. Or maybe it's an outlier, and I'm getting upset over nothing. It took a long time to get this job, and if I quit, I'll fall behind on alimony and child support, and everything I've worked for will go down the drain."

I knew how he felt – I'd experienced the same doubts and fears when I learned that Fred Finkle wasn't going to be able to run the seminar.

"The atmosphere at Beauceron is very competitive," Doug continued. "Everybody seems to be chasing after the same investors, and nobody is willing to talk about the actual quality of the product. You're the only guy I know who has the ability to get in there and see if there's something wrong. Please?"

I'd been in trouble in the past, and I appreciated everyone who'd given me a helping hand. It was my turn to pay forward those old favors. "It looks fishy, I agree. Once this seminar is over I'll have some time. If you send me the data, I can look it over for you."

By then we had circled back to the entrance to the dorm. A few lights were on in the newly renovated bedrooms but it looked like most of our guests had already gone to sleep.

"That would be awesome," Doug said. "I'll even give you my ID and password so you can see everything I do."

I shook my head. "You shouldn't do that, Doug. I mean, yeah, we knew each other years ago, but you don't know that you can trust me." I didn't add that if there was something bad going on at Beauceron, I didn't want my name or ID to be connected to it. My two-year parole had finished only a few months ago, but I knew the court wouldn't look kindly on a convicted hacker getting involved in any kind of dodgy business.

I opened the door to my room and let Rochester off his leash. I stepped inside and got a pad and pen from the desk. "Write down your ID and password here. That way there's no digital trail showing that you gave the information to an outsider."

My curiosity had gotten me into trouble in the past, snooping around in places online where I wasn't supposed to be. Now I'd volunteered to use someone else's ID and password to view a company's confidential files. I'd never studied law, but I'd done enough work helping others in prison with their appeals, and reviewing the conditions of my own arrest and then parole. I didn't think I was breaking any laws by helping Doug, but I couldn't be sure.

I knew that I couldn't use any information I discovered for my own benefit—that would fall under the insider trading statutes. And I was reasonably certain that anything I found couldn't have my name attached to it, or it would be inadmissible in any court case, and put me on a legal hot seat.

I owed Doug a favor, so I'd help as much as I could. But I'd have to be careful not to destroy everything I'd built since my return home.

6 – Protected Information

Doug and I met up again at the after-dinner bar on Saturday evening. I'd been so busy during the day I hadn't had a chance to sit in on his sessions or talk to the students. "How do you think it went?" I asked.

"There was a big variance in the level of knowledge. Sometimes I had to go slowly to explain things to people with no background, and I could see some of the knowledgeable people getting restless. But overall, I think people got what they paid for."

He drained the last of his brandy. "You think we could look at the Beauceron files together?"

I had been on the run all day and I was tired but I could see how worried Doug was. "Sure. Come down to my room when you're ready."

A few minutes later Doug arrived at my room, carrying his laptop. "I want to show you where you can get the information about the REIT," he said. "Our annual report lists all the properties, but it doesn't break out the income individually. That's all in spreadsheets on our server."

While he opened his laptop and logged in, I yawned, but once he had access to all the company files I perked up. Something about seeing protected information always does that to me. "Why don't you download a zip file with the information you want me to look at," I suggested. "Then we don't have to stay logged on to the Beauceron server for too long, which could raise someone's suspicions."

He looked at me wide-eyed. "You think someone is monitoring our access to the company server?"

"I'm sure there are data logs being kept," I said. "Whether someone is analyzing them or not is hard to say."

I showed him how to create the zip file, and once it had downloaded we shut off the connection to Beauceron and he transferred the file to my laptop with a flash drive.

As I ran the extraction program, Doug sat beside me, stroking Rochester's head. When a list of folders was displayed on my screen, he leaned forward. "Each of these folders represents a single property," he said, pointing at the screen. "Inside each one is all the information we have on the property we've provided a mortgage for, identified by ID number. This is where we keep records of property appraisals, copies of the mortgage loans and deeds, real estate taxes and so on. We have our own in-house system of ranking the quality of the loans, something Shawn put together. What is the risk involved in the property? What are the income projections, outside factors, and so on."

He clicked open the folder for the shopping center near the Newark airport. "One of the conditions for the mortgage is that the borrower keep us up to date on tenants, leases and rental income.

Here's a spreadsheet that tracks all that." He pointed at the screen. "See this store? Jose's Dominican Market? It was closed when I drove past. There's no way the owner is still paying rent. I'll bet that's the case with almost all the other tenants."

"And if they aren't paying rent, and the LLC that owns the property is bankrupt, then these income figures can't be true," I said, pointing at the revenue that was supposed to be coming in.

"Exactly."

I sat back in my chair. "This property is in trouble, and the spreadsheets aren't telling the true story," I said. "You think there are other properties with similar problems?"

"I do. These are high-risk mortgages, remember. That's how come Beauceron can charge them such a high interest rate. I'm afraid that there are a lot more properties in our portfolio in similar trouble. And that means that there's no way we can legitimately be paying out such high returns to our investors."

He sat back in his chair. "Can you figure out which other properties in the portfolio are in trouble?" he asked. "I know computer guys. You must have some way to automate the process."

I shook my head. "What you need is someone to compare the Beauceron numbers to reality. But you can't know what the truth is without doing a lot of other research—the way you went to that shopping center in person."

My hands were resting on the keyboard, and Rochester leaned his head up and nudged my elbow. Probably to remind me that he was there and wanted me to pay attention to him – but instead, I accidentally hit the combination of keys that took me to the very bottom of the file.

A hyperlink sat in the final cell of the spreadsheet. "Any idea what this is?" I asked Doug.

He leaned in close, then shook his head. "No idea."

I clicked the hyperlink and Excel tried to open another spreadsheet, one that wasn't in the batch Doug had downloaded for me. I was curious, so I logged back into the Beauceron server using Doug's ID and password, then tried the hyperlink again.

This time, a window popped up asking me for a password to open the file. We tried Doug's password, and it didn't work. "This may be a key to what's going on," I said. "Let me see if I can download the file without the password."

No luck.

"That's got to be important," Doug said. "Why else would it have its own password? Can you figure it out?"

"The password request means that the entire Excel document is encrypted with the RC4 stream cipher—a standard way to protect a document. If whoever set this up allowed the cipher to create the password, then it could be very difficult to figure it out, because it's randomly generated. And someone could be monitoring access to this file, too."

I looked at him. "Do you have a tech guy on your staff? One who updates your computers, monitors tech traffic and so on?"

"We did. But Shawn fired her a couple of weeks ago, and the guy who's doing the job now is nowhere near as smart."

"Then you might be safe. But even so, whoever created the file might know that you've tried to see it. You need to come up with a story in case anyone asks."

Doug's eyes opened wide. "A story? What kind of story?"

"Keep it simple. You saw what happened with the first file, right? I accidentally went to the end of the file, saw the link, and clicked on it. That's reasonable and innocent."

"And that's all we can do? We can't actually see the file?"

"I didn't say that. Most people use their own simple passwords rather than remember, or write down, a complex series," I said. "I have a password cracker program at home that can analyze the contents of the file, discover where the password is stored, and then run a series of tries to figure it out. Even then it could take a long time."

"But you can try?" he asked. "I'm sure there has to be a clue there. Why go through all this stuff unless there's something to protect?"

"It could be just that Shawn's extra careful," I said. "He's a smart guy, right? So he probably knows that it's important to protect your data."

I remembered the argument Doug and Shawn had been having the night before. "You were fighting with Shawn about something last night," I said. "Before we went in to the cocktail hour. Can you tell me what that was about?"

"I tried to ask him about the shopping center and how it could be generating revenue when it looked so run down. He got in my face and told me it wasn't my business."

I blew out a breath. "Then you need to be extra careful. From now on, don't do any snooping under your own ID. Let me do the work."

"But you'll be careful, right? Getting fired would be bad, but going to prison would be a lot worse. I can't imagine what would happen to my kids if I got arrested."

"I know exactly how bad prison can be," I said. "I guarantee you I'll be careful."

Doug left, and I shut down my laptop. While I watched the system go through its routines, I let my mind wander. Back in college, I'd gone to Vermont with some friends over Christmas break to learn to ski. I remembered one trail in particular. It started out with a gentle slope, and I was moving downhill in an easy slalom. Then suddenly the terrain got steeper, and I was going much faster than I was comfortable with. I tried to remember what I'd learned about using turns to slow down, but quickly I was out of control and I ended up tumbling down, hitting a tree, and popping the bindings off my skis. I was lucky I hadn't been hurt.

Even so, the adrenaline rush had hooked me, and I kept on skiing whenever I could. It was the same thing with hacking. All the trouble I'd gotten into hadn't made me stop – it had just made me more cautious.

What did that say about my personality? My parole officer had often said that I thought I was smarter than anyone else, that I was savvy enough to skirt around rules, and that kind of hubris was what kept convicts on a cycle of repeat offenses. I'd have to make sure I kept that hubris in check as I snooped.

Neil S. Plakcy

7 – PARTY TIME

Sunday morning I was up early, walking Rochester and then making sure everything was in order for the concluding brunch. Doug made a few brief remarks, sending folks off with some action items they could accomplish that would move them forward in their path to financial understanding.

I announced I'd be emailing them all a link to a survey, and thanked them all for joining us. As they filtered out, Doug came up to me. "You're going to look into that password protected file today?"

"I'm going to try," I said. "But honestly, right now I want to go home and take a nap." I patted him on the shoulder. "Don't worry, I'll look into it. I promise."

As I locked up the center, Rochester by my side, I felt a surge of pride. I'd overcome all the obstacles, large and small, and put on a great program. I had come back to Bucks County an ex-con who couldn't go back to my computer-based career, and through hard work and a relentless desire to rebuild my life I'd pulled together all my skills in writing, program development, management and conflict resolution to turn myself into the manager of a conference center.

Of course, the golden retriever by my side had been a big part of that transformation. Without his love I couldn't have made the progress I had. I reached down and scratched him under his neck, running my hands through his golden ruff. "You know I love you, puppy, don't you?" I asked.

He gave me a doggy grin and licked my fingers. Then we drove back home.

Lili greeted me at the door with a flat package wrapped in "happy birthday" paper. "Sorry, it's all the paper we had in the house," she said. "Congratulations on putting on your first program. I knew you'd be a success!"

She leaned forward and kissed my cheek.

"You didn't have to get me a gift," I said.

"I know. But this is a big moment and I wanted to celebrate it."

Rochester kept nosing at the package, so I walked inside, put my rolling suitcase down and ripped open the wrapping paper. Inside was a T-shirt that read, "I have the golden touch," above a drawing of a golden retriever who looked just like Rochester.

"This is so adorable," I said. "Can I wear it to Justin's party?"

"If you want. But I figured you'd want to save it for dog-walking."

That would probably be better, and after I'd unpacked and thrown my dirty clothes in the washer, we got ready to leave. "You have the gift for Justin?"

"I asked Tamsen what he'd like and she said an iTunes gift card, so I picked one up yesterday. And that reminded me it's my sister-in-law's birthday next week so I stopped at Mark's antique shop yesterday and found this great Tiffany charm for her, in its original little blue bag. I'll have to show it to you later."

Tamsen and her son Justin lived in a fifties-era split level a few blocks from where I'd grown up in the Lakes neighborhood of Stewart's Crossing, so it only took us ten minutes or so to reach it. As Lili, Rochester and I walked up the driveway, we heard the squeals and screams of kids at play in the back yard. Rochester must have smelled his friend Rascal there, because he pulled ahead, dragging me along like the tail of a kite.

Rick answered the door, wearing a bandanna, a striped shirt and vest, and brandishing a plastic knife. "Ahoy, mateys, welcome to the party," he said, and I couldn't help laughing.

"Laugh now, buddy. Grab a hat and an eye patch or Justin will make you walk the plank. And the whole pirate theme should make you feel right at home."

I had a brief flash that reminded me of the password cracking I needed to do for Doug, but Lili was already digging through a big box of props and costumes. She handed me a blue and white checkered bandanna for Rochester, who had his paws up on Rick's waist, sniffing him for clues to Rascal's location. I tied the bandana around his neck and let him rush forward into the house in search of his matey. A cascade of barking let us know they had met.

"There's another dog here," Rick said. "A little Yorkie named Pixie."

"Doug Guilfoyle's dog? Is Doug here?"

Rick shook his head. "Don't know who that is. The dog came with Tamsen's cousin and her kids."

I processed that information as I put on a tri-cornered pirate hat with a plastic skull and crossbones on the front, then stuck a plastic dagger into my belt and looked at myself in the hall mirror. I looked properly piratical. Maybe I should dress this way whenever I needed to snoop around online.

Lili wrapped a long red scarf around her waist and clipped on big gold-colored hoop earrings. Then Rick led us to the kitchen, where Tamsen and her sister Hannah were laughing and drinking wine.

Tamsen was the kind of beautiful woman who could pose for magazine ads – healthy and wholesome looking, with shoulder-length blonde hair and a broad smile. She wore a blousy white top and a black bustier with a red handkerchief stuck in the top. She made a very sexy pirate wench and I had to remind myself that she was Rick's girlfriend, and that I was damn lucky to have Lili by my side.

Tamsen and Hannah were both tall and slim, though Hannah's hair was darker and she wasn't quite as pretty as Tamsen. She was dressed more demurely as well, in a high-necked white blouse and white jeans, with a red handkerchief that matched her sister's.

"Thanks for coming," Tamsen said. She kissed both of us hello. "We need some more adults here to balance out all those wild kids."

"They aren't so wild," Rick said. "It's the dogs who are crazy." He pointed through the sliding glass doors to where the kids were playing in the back yard. Rascal and Rochester appeared to be trying to mug one of the little girls. "I'd better get out there."

As he hurried out, a slim, dark-haired woman came inside, wearing blue jeans and a black T shirt with a skull and crossbones on it. "Wine," she said, staggering theatrically. She had the perfectly groomed and manicured look of a pampered wife, from her perfectly cut hair to her French manicure, down to the leather slip-ons on her feet. Living with Lili had taught me that the simpler the shoe, the more expensive it was.

Tamsen handed her a glass. "This is my cousin Catherine. Cath, this is Rick's friend Steve and his girlfriend Lili."

Suddenly everything clicked. Doug had said that his ex-wife had cousins in Stewart's Crossing. Doug's dog and his kids were here. And the woman across from me was the woman he'd dated through college, who I'd shared a few classes with. She was twenty years older, but I could still see the girl she'd been.

"Steve Levitan," I said, as I reached out to shake Catherine's hand. "You and I went to Eastern together."

"Really?"

I guess I wasn't so memorable. Tamsen turned to help her sister take a platter of miniature pizzas from the oven as I told Catherine about a couple of classes we'd shared, and she smiled and said that she believed me, she just didn't remember me.

I wondered if I should mention having just spent the weekend with Doug, but he'd said that Catherine was making things difficult, so I'd wait until she said something.

Hannah picked up the tray of miniature pizzas, then turned to her cousin and Lili. "You guys want to help me pass out these pizzas to the ravening hordes?"

After the three of them left, I joined Tamsen at the counter, slipping on to a stool next to her.

She picked up her wine glass. "It's funny, I knew that Cath and Doug both went to Eastern, but I never connected them to you."

"Obviously your cousin has forgotten me," I said. "If I recall correctly, she was completely focused on Doug back then."

Tamsen drank some wine, then put the glass back down on the counter with a sharp noise. "Well, she isn't any more. She's pretty angry that he quit his high-paying job on Wall Street and now he's having trouble paying alimony and child support."

"You can't blame him for wanting to be near his kids," I said.

"Oh, no, I don't blame him at all. I'm very sympathetic. I've seen what it's like for Justin to grow up without a dad around and I wouldn't wish that on Ethan and Maddie."

"What brought her here, anyway? Why didn't she stay up in Westchester county?"

"She's an only child, and when we were growing up, she was like another sister to Hannah and me. Doug traveled a lot for his job, and she'd come down here with Ethan and Maddie for long weekends. After the divorce, she thought it would be good for Ethan and Maddie to grow up around family."

She sighed. "Catherine's my cousin, and I love her and I see how much she loves her kids. But she has issues. A lot of people here in town commute into Manhattan, you know, and she's been trying to keep up with them when instead she needs to scale back, spend less money on manicures and haircuts and facials. I keep pointing her toward part-time jobs, and I've even offered to train her in my business."

"But?"

"But she's been working on a children's book, and she's sure she's going to be the next J.K. Rowling. She insists that she has to finish the book before she can even consider getting a job. I've tried to explain that Rowling was living on government assistance when she wrote the first Harry Potter book but it hasn't sunk in yet."

She shook her head. "And then she's been seeing this guy, very sweet, but in my opinion he's feeding into her dreams in a way that's not very realistic. He writes kids' books, too, but even though he's published a bunch of them, he has to teach at George School to make a living."

"Has she published anything?"

"Not yet. She asked me to look at a few chapters of her book last week, and in my opinion, it wasn't ready yet but anything I tried to suggest she shot down." She sipped her wine again. "Not that I'm an expert, but I read whatever Justin does, and I couldn't see him having the patience to wade through all this historical detail about a Lenni Lenape girl around the time of the American revolution."

"I took a creative writing class with her at Eastern back in the day, and she was touchy then, too."

"Divorce is so difficult," Tamsen said. "Sometimes I think that if I had to be on my own again with Justin, I was lucky to be a widow instead of a divorcee." She sipped her wine. "Look at Rick and Tiffany. They're just the opposite of Doug and Catherine. She doesn't want to let him go."

"Really?" That was news to me. As far as I knew, Rick and his ex had broken up on bad terms and he'd been quite bitter about her. I'd never met the woman myself, but I'd heard enough stories about their marriage to have formed an opinion.

"After she broke up with her latest loser, around the beginning of January, she drunk-dialed Rick to cry on his shoulder. He didn't tell you?"

I shook my head.

"He told me, because he said he didn't want to keep any secrets from me. That they had been part of each other's lives for a long time, and he didn't want her to feel totally alone."

"He's a good guy," I said. I was impressed not only with his honesty, but with his ability to see past the bitterness of his divorce. But that fit what I knew of his character.

"I know. Justin worships him, and they're really good together. And I'm pretty fond of him myself." She smiled, and stood up. "Come on, let's go see if the kids left us any of those pizzas."

We walked outside, where a dozen kids in different kinds of

pirate costumes romped around the yard. I recognized Justin and his cousin Nathaniel, Hannah's son, and Ethan and Madison Guilfoyle. The other kids were strangers to me.

Rick was acting the role of pirate captain, putting on a voice and marshaling a scavenger hunt around the yard. Rochester and Rascal chased poor Pixie until she took cover in an azalea bush, and then they stood there barking at her until she came out so they could chase her again.

Catherine came up to me. "I'm sorry I didn't remember you right away," she said. "I've tried to put Eastern and the rest of my past in a drawer and lock it away. But we were in Professor Parker's creative writing class together, weren't we?"

"We were," I said. "You wrote a story about waiting for someone at 30th Street Station in Philadelphia, didn't you? I remember something about pigeons roosting in the ceiling. It was beautiful."

"I always had a knack for description," she said. "Now I'm trying to remember what you wrote."

"I was in love with Ernest Hemingway back then," I said. "I was working on a story about an American spy being held in a Mexican jail. Parker asked me if I had ever been in jail. Or in Mexico. And I said no."

"Oh, I remember!" she said. "He went into one of his rants about how we should only write about what we know."

I wondered if she remembered my story, or just Parker's rant.

"He said that since we were such callow youths we should write about childhood." She laughed. "Took me long enough to follow that advice."

I realized now I finally had the experience I needed to write that story about the man in the Mexican jail – though I had no interest in reliving my own incarceration.

We talked about the children's book Catherine was working on, a historical novel about a young Lenni Lenape girl living on the banks of the Delaware at the time of first contact with Europeans. I tried to channel Parker's fusty manner. "Have you ever been a young American Indian girl, Miss Hollister?"

"Here's what we both should have said to him back then. I don't need to have lived the story of my characters. I just need to be able to imagine how they live and act, and put that down on paper."

I nodded. "Excellent reply. The French call that *l'esprit de l'escalier*, thinking of what you should have said after a conversation is over."

"Exactly! Although in this case that conversation has been over for almost twenty-five years."

We heard Madison screaming excitedly and looked out to the yard. The kids had each been given a map that showed the location of various pieces of pirate booty. Madison had found the special one, a small pirate chest filled with candy and toys. After she got over her excitement, she generously shared it with the other kids. What a nice kid. Her mother could probably learn from her behavior.

When the party broke up, Lili and I drove home with Rochester, and it was very nice to be back in my own house. When Lili moved in, we gave away my dad's lumpy old couch and bought a new one, with rolled arms and plump cushions, and a big plaid comforter to protect it from dog hair. We'd replaced my dining room chairs with hers, and she'd filled the walls with her own photographs, and work she'd collected in her travels. The photo over the dining room table, a blurry shot of Parisian lovers in the rain by a photographer Lili admired, was the first big gift I'd given her.

The shelves were a mix of her souvenirs and books, and my books and the golden retriever picture frames, little statues and cute signs I'd begun to collect after Rochester came into my life.

The subject of all that adoration nosed me, reminding me it was time for his walk. I hooked up his leash and Lili and I walked outside. "Tamsen said something interesting this evening," I said as we walked. "Rick has been back in touch with Tiffany, his ex."

"Really? Why?"

"She broke up with her latest loser, and I guess she's feeling like she made a couple of wrong moves. You know Rick. He has to have somebody to take care of."

April weather had returned, clouds pushing away the cold front that had been hanging around, and I looked forward to lots of spring walks with Rochester. One of the great things about River Bend, our gated community, was that the streets curved, making for pleasant walking, and the central lake was shaded by old oaks, with a few cast-iron park benches where I could relax and watch the domesticated ducks poop all over the sidewalk.

That evening, as the three of us walked toward the lake, I kept thinking about the twists and turns my life had taken. I took Lili's hand as we walked, grateful that I had her beside me. "I feel sorry for people who have bad relationships with their exes," Lili said unexpectedly. "Do you ever think about Mary and wonder what she's up to?"

"The last time I spoke to her was right after I got out of prison and moved back here. She shipped some stuff to me, and then she called to let me know she was getting married again."

"And how did you feel about that?"

I crossed my arms over my chest and tried to remember. "I was still angry at her, but I was polite and congratulated her. Inside, I was thinking 'fine, let somebody else put up with your *mishegas.*'"

Lili laughed. *Mishegas* was Yiddish for craziness or nonsense, and both of us often studded our speech with similar expressions we'd learned from our parents. Even though we had grown up in very different circumstances, our shared culture was one more thing that brought us close.

"I admit that I Google both my exes now and then," Lili said unexpectedly. "Adriano and Philip. Just out of curiosity. Maybe just that I want to know if they're still alive."

"They're part of your life," I said. "Trying to ignore or forget those years isn't healthy. That's what I worry about Doug and Catherine. I hope they can find some way to get along, if not for their own sakes then for the kids."

Poor Doug. His life had taken a sharp turn when Catherine divorced him, and now he was stuck at a job that might put him into bad trouble. I hoped I'd be able to give him a helping hand, the way so many people had done for me.

Neil S. Plakcy

8 – INNOCENT AND TRUSTING

Early Monday morning, my phone pinged with a text from Doug. He wanted to know if I'd been able to break the password on that hyperlinked spreadsheet we had looked at on Saturday night. I texted back that I'd get on it that day, and before I left for work I dug out the laptop that had belonged to Caroline Kelly, my late neighbor. Two years before, when Rochester and I began searching for her killer, my computer use was closely supervised by my parole officer, so I had appropriated her laptop and installed a number of illicit software programs on it, ones that had gotten me into trouble in the past.

I had used them on several occasions since, always convincing myself that my intentions were good in trying to bring criminals to justice without harming anyone innocent. In order to help Doug, I needed to see the contents of that hyperlinked spreadsheet, and the only way I knew to download it without the password was to get into the Beauceron server at the file level.

I considered myself a hacker – in the classical definition, originated by MIT, I was a guy with an interest in how things work, and how to tinker with them. A generation ago, I might have been a ham radio operator or one of those hobbyists who met in garages to share news about those new-fangled computer things.

Neil S. Plakcy

A cracker was someone whose purpose was to break into systems by circumventing security measures, usually with malicious intent. While I'd done a bit of cracking in my day, I'd never done it to steal anything or harm anyone. Because I was not a programmer and couldn't create my own tools, just use ones written by others, some people might consider me among the script kiddies—a pejorative term referring to hackers who don't care how the tools work, just want to use them, usually to play around online.

Since I was over forty, it was silly to consider me a kid. But I wasn't about to go back to school for programming, either. So I trolled around the dark web, a series of overlay networks which use the public Internet but require specific programs, configurations or authorization to access. That's where I found the software I needed to do what I wanted.

A year before, Eastern had upgraded the Wi-Fi network at the campus library due to the profusion of students bringing their own laptops in to for a quiet place where they could write papers and do research. I could have high-speed Internet access there and use my hacker software to mask my IP address.

As I headed to Friar Lake, I thought about the thrill that launching my first adult education seminar had provided. It was a great feeling, to know that I had worked hard at something and then made a success of it. But when I compared that to the adrenaline rush of breaking into protected sites online. No doubt, hacking was a whole lot more exciting.

I made a quick stop at Friar Lake to drop Rochester off with Joey and then drove to campus, where the lawns between buildings were scattered with students. At the first breath of spring, students at Eastern swing into warm-weather mode. It can be fifty degrees outside, and they'll shuck their Canadian down parkas, their Doc Martens, and their hip-hanging jeans for t-shirts, shorts and flip-flops. I used to do that, but now that I'm over forty, I have this thing about not putting myself at risk of pneumonia. Quirky, I know, but that's me.

At the massive glass and stone library, I found a secluded corner of the first floor and opened my laptop, then initiated the software that I used for port scanning and information gathering. I mapped the network at the library and got a list of all the ports on user computers that were available for me. The first couple I checked belonged to students—I could tell from the names of their hard drives, and the homework files they kept on them.

I stopped at one where the hard drive was simply called C: and where the dozens of files were kept on the desktop instead of organized into folders. A quick survey indicated the computer belonged to a professor who taught Latin and ancient history. I recognized the man's name—he was elderly and often snoozed through college-wide meetings.

Ah, the older generation. So innocent and trusting.

Long ago, I'd had a boss who wouldn't let the receptionist use the intercom system at the office to page employees, because he felt that it interrupted our concentration. It was from that I'd learned the term flow, to mean when I was so caught up in what I was doing that time passed without noticing it. Hacking did that to me, and it was a giddy feeling.

I used Telnet, a network protocol software, to connect to his computer and determine what software it was running. Once I knew that, I'd be able to tell which of my hacking tools would give me easiest access.

I felt a momentary pang of conscience. What I was doing was against the law—breaking into a company's internal server, with a plan to download a file of possibly proprietary information without permission.

As I usually did, I justified my actions. I was only doing this work at Doug's insistence, because he was worried that the company was doing something illegal. I wasn't going to use the information I found to make a profit or to cheat anyone. Of course, it was doubtful that law enforcement would believe me, and as a repeat offender it was possible I'd be sent back to prison.

It was extremely doubtful that anyone would notice I'd visited the Beauceron server, and even if my intrusion was noted, it would take a lot of fancy footwork on someone's part to track my IP address back to the Eastern library. From there, it would be almost impossible to connect Caroline's laptop to the hack—unless someone was already looking at me, and got a search warrant for my equipment and my files, the way the police had done in California.

With all those protections in place, I proceeded.

Cyberattacks usually require that the targeted computer have some pre-existing system flaw, such as a software error, a lack of antivirus protection, or a faulty system configuration, for a hacker to exploit.

My elderly colleague's computer was running an older version of Internet Explorer with some known vulnerabilities, and I was able to use one of those flaws to take control of it. I doubted he'd even notice that I was running programs in the background. I just had to hope he was there in the library for a while, or I'd have to start all over again.

I sent a series of messages to the Beauceron server, looking for a way inside, hoping it had either been misconfigured, or that it lacked up-to-date security software. Computer servers are such complicated pieces of hardware that there can be many, many settings that have to be enabled precisely.

It took close to an hour to get access to the files on the Beauceron server. As soon as I was in, I navigated my way to the location of the hyperlinked file. Because I was able to get access to it at the directory level, I didn't need the password to download it. Once I saw it had been saved on the laptop, I severed my connection to the server and released my control of the elderly professor's computer.

I felt jittery and nervous. There was no turning back now—I'd broken the law, and having that downloaded file on the laptop was the kind of evidence that could send me back to prison, this time for a lot longer than a year. Every time I heard someone move around me I worried it was some cyber cop who was there to arrest me.

The password cracker program I had didn't require Internet access to run, so I didn't need to stay at the library. I closed the laptop so quickly the lid banged, and a couple of nearby students looked over. Then I hurried to my car, the laptop hot in my hand. I couldn't wait to drop it on the seat next to me.

The drive back to Friar Lake calmed me a bit. I'd protected myself well, and now everything I needed to do was off line, with no chance of anyone discovering me.

The only vehicle in the Friar Lake parking lot was Joey's truck, and the property was strangely quiet after all the activity of the weekend. I dropped the laptop in my office, then got Rochester and took him for a walk around the property.

Maybe it was his presence, or the residual sense of peace that hung around the old abbey properties, but my nerves dissipated as we walked. This was my domain, these ten mountain-top acres and a cluster of buildings old and new. I had shepherded their transformation into a modern conference center and successfully launched the first of a series of programs. Life was good.

Rochester slumped on the floor beside my desk as I set up my laptop and opened a program called Snap, Crack and Pop, a silly takeoff on the Rice Krispies slogan. The splash screen looked old-fashioned, with very simple windows and amateurish icons. But I knew there was a powerful intelligence inside it, hidden behind the façade.

Snap, Crack and Pop figured out that the password on the file was a series of twelve numbers, letters and special characters, like question marks and parentheses. It began generating possible combinations, and the display on the screen was dizzying, as one after another was rejected.

It was hypnotic, watching that constantly changing display, and made my pulse race, as it often did when I was close to breaking in somewhere.

My cell rang with Rick's "Hawaii Five-O" ring tone, and Rochester jumped up. For a moment I worried that Rick knew what I was doing and had called to check on me. That was just paranoia, though.

"Yo-ho-ho and a bottle of rum," I said, as Rochester nuzzled my knee.

"I could have used that rum after the party," Rick said. "Those kids wore me out. I don't see how Tamsen manages day to day."

"She's a mom. AKA a superhero." I reached down and scratched behind Rochester's ears, and he opened his mouth wide.

"Got that right. Anyway, I need to pick your brain. Can we get together tonight?"

"Sure. You want to bring Rascal over for dinner?"

"I'd rather not talk about what I have to say in front of Lili," he said. "Maybe you and I could meet at the Drunken Hessian?"

"Lili teaches a Monday night class, so I'm free," I said. "I just have to feed and walk the hound before I can go out."

We agreed on six o'clock, and I hung up. What didn't Rick didn't want to say in front of Lili. Was it something about her? I couldn't imagine he'd know anything about Lili that I didn't know. Then I remembered Tamsen saying that Rick had been in touch with Tiffany. Perhaps that's what he wanted to talk about, and he didn't want to confess something in front of a woman who knew his girlfriend.

That was almost as troubling. Tamsen was a great woman and a good match for Rick. She was smart and successful and beautiful – a lot like Lili. But there was also something vulnerable about her, the way she had lost her soldier husband to war, the way she was raising her son on her own.

In being Rick's friend for last two years, I'd discovered he was the kind of person who wanted to do good in the world. He was a cop because he believed in his work. His first wife was a mess, and Rick had taken care of her for years. Now he had a chance with Tamsen, who appeared to be a lot more together than Tiffany, yet still could use Rick's help.

What if he'd screwed up somehow? Cheated on Tamsen with Tiffany? That would be a disaster. It wasn't what I'd expect of him, but we were only human, after all, and I knew how easy it was to slip up and do the wrong thing for the right reason.

I forced myself to look away from Snap, Crack and Pop and

focus on my to-do list. Yes, it appeared that the seminar had been a great success. But how did the participants feel? What did the numbers show? Was the advertising I'd done worthwhile, had we had enough food—or too much? Did the seminar, and the upcoming slate of programs I'd shown off, enhance the image of Eastern College among the participants?

I had a lot of numbers to crunch before I could be certain that I'd made the right moves. I set up the seminar survey, emailed thank you notes to all the seminar participants, filed my expense reports and filled out the forms to get Doug paid.

By the time I finished that, Snap, Crack and Pop had discovered the password to open the spreadsheet, displaying it superimposed over the graphic of an open padlock. I turned back to the laptop, double-clicked the file, and then pasted in what my program had found.

I don't know what I was expecting – that there was a virus in the file that would crash my computer? That alarms would go off? But the only thing that happened was that the spreadsheet opened, and it looked perfectly normal.

But it had been hyperlinked back to the file Doug and I had looked at, the spreadsheet for the run-down shopping center near Newark airport. Why? I opened the original file in a second window side-by-side with the first and began comparing the two. All the headings were the same, as were the dates along the left side. The only difference was in the data.

Starting about a year before, the income from the property recorded on the protected sheet dropped to zero, while on the public spreadsheet it continued to grow.

So whoever created that spreadsheet didn't want the real figures to be visible. Why not? It couldn't be for tax purposes—you'd want to hide income, not losses. And if shareholders in the fund saw that the property was making money, they'd expect to see their returns go up.

I never went to business school, but I'd written a number of annual reports in my career and I had a basic understanding of the kind of documents a company had to release. If Beauceron was hiding losses, there had to be a reason for it. Maybe Doug would know. I'd show him what I'd found, and let him decide what to do.

I texted Doug and asked him to call me when he could talk. I drummed my fingers on the desktop while I waited. I'd just had a major breakthrough and there was only one person I could share it with. Too bad he was probably too busy to get right back to me. I carried my cell phone with me as I took Rochester for a walk around Friar Lake. Now that the construction was complete, and all the contractors and workmen gone, I felt isolated up there on top of the mountain. I missed the activity of the Eastern campus and wondered how I would manage on my own all the time.

Then Rochester tugged forward in search of a fascinating smell, and I remembered I wasn't alone at all.

I was driving home when Doug finally called me. "Sorry I

couldn't get back to you earlier. Things are scary here, and I was in a meeting all afternoon with Shawn where he kept asking me strange questions my internet use and file access, though he didn't say anything about linked spreadsheets. What did you come up with?"

I told him about finding the duplicate spreadsheet with the real data. I waited, but he didn't say anything.

"This seems like something you should report to the authorities," I said finally. "It could be an anomaly, but my guess is that it's a way to hide money, or hide the fact that there isn't any money coming in."

"I'd like to I see it for myself. I'm on my way to pitch a prospective client and I don't know when I'll be finished. Can we meet for breakfast tomorrow morning?"

I suggested Gail's Chocolate Ear café in the center of Stewart's Crossing, and Doug agreed to meet me there at seven-thirty. I was surprised that he didn't ask for more details over the phone, but perhaps I hadn't conveyed enough urgency.

My bigger problem, though, was how I was going to get through dinner with Rick Stemper without bragging about my successful hack.

Neil S. Plakcy

9 – UNOFFICIAL INQUIRIES

When I got home, I fed and walked Rochester, then took a few minutes to log in to the hacker support group I had joined a few months before. All of us had gotten into trouble at one time or another for computer hacking, and being part of the group gave me an opportunity to talk about temptation and backsliding.

One of the regular members, Brewski_Bubba, was online at the time, and I opened a chat window with him. I didn't know much about him, other than that he was a Southerner, a beer lover, and a guy who'd gotten in trouble for credit card fraud.

After we went through the preliminaries I told him that I'd hacked into a server that day in order to download a file. "It was a favor for a friend," I typed. "So yeah, illegal, but he works there, so he figured he ought to have access to it."

"Sounds like you're rationalizing," he replied.

"Yeah, I am. What's scariest is how easy it was and how good it felt. Do you think we'll ever be over this need to hack?"

He typed in one of those emoticons I didn't quite understand, a face with weird eyes and a tongue sticking out. "Doubt it," he wrote. "Did you cover your tracks?"

I explained the way I'd taken control of the other computer, used the college's Wi-Fi and so on. "Shouldn't be any way to get back to me."

"Don't tell him how you did it or what parts were illegal," he wrote. "If he gets caught for something you don't want him to rat you out."

I agreed that was a good idea, then logged off and drove down to the Drunken Hessian. It was a three story building in the old Colonial style, wood-framed with a chimney along one side and a door in the center of the façade, leading out to a broad porch. Three dormer windows stuck out of the high-pitched roof.

A plaque outside said that an inn of some kind had been on that spot since the Revolutionary War, and the décor hadn't much changed, except for the introduction of indoor plumbing. The sign depicted one of the Hessian soldiers whom Washington had surprised at Trenton on Christmas day, looking like he'd had quite a few too many.

The promised cold front was on its way and I shivered as I stepped out of the car. I hurried into the warmth of the bar and spotted Rick at a booth in the back. I slid in across from him and asked, "What's so hush-hush that you didn't want to talk about it in front of Lili? It's not about her, is it?"

"Not at all. I'm just embarrassed. It's awkward enough to talk about it with you."

"If you're having embarrassing problems you should see a

urologist."

"Nothing like that, dufous," he said. The waitress appeared and we ordered a pair of Yard Brawlers, the beer we'd had the other day, and both decided to opt for the grilled chicken Caesar salad – too many burgers make middle-aged men fat.

"So," I said, when the waitress was gone. "Is this about Tiffany?"

He looked up at me. "How did you know?"

"Hey, I'm Joe Hardy, aren't I?" I had helped Rick with a couple of cases, and while at first he'd teased me as one of those amateur sleuths from cozy mysteries, eventually I'd worked my way up in his esteem to being the younger of the Hardy Boys, Joe to his Frank. "Tamsen mentioned that you'd been in touch with Tiffany, and I figured that might be something you didn't want to talk about in front of Lili."

"And I always thought the dog was the brains of your operation," he said. Rochester had a knack for finding clues, and though Rick had resisted at first, he'd eventually come to accept my dog's talents.

"Ha-ha. Or should I say woof-woof?"

The waitress brought our beers. I tipped my glass to his and said, "To problem solving."

"Yeah," he said, "To problem solving."

"So what are we solving here?"

"Tiffany. I can't seem to get her out of my hair."

"What's wrong now?" I knew she was the kind of woman who was attracted to danger junkies. She had married Rick because she liked the thrill of his being a uniformed patrolman, the chance that he might not survive a day at work. When he moved up to detective, she had lost interest and left him for a fire fighter. That hadn't worked out, and she had moved through a series of bungee jumpers, parachute jumpers, and petty criminals since then.

"Tiffany is the kind of girl who always falls into bad situations." Rick held up his hand. "I know what you're going to say. She married me."

"Actually, I think that was the one good thing Tiffany did. But go on."

"When I spoke to her in January, she was waitressing at the bar of a fancy restaurant in North Jersey, and she had just broken up with some loser," he said. "That's the last I heard from her until she called me this morning, freaked out. She tends to do that, you know. I only hear from her when there's some kind of drama going on."

He took a sip of his beer. "This morning, she was totally freaked out. Apparently a few weeks after we last talked, she met a guy who got her a job working for a doctor in Union City processing insurance paperwork. The Feds raided the clinic where she works first thing this morning and confiscated all the computers and the patient files."

"Medicare fraud?" I asked.

"She didn't know, or she wouldn't tell me." He looked down at the table, etched with decades of initials, hearts and plus signs.

"You know you're not Tiffany's husband any more. She's not your responsibility."

"She'll always be my responsibility. I'm Catholic, remember?"

His need to take care of people went deeper than religion, but I didn't say that. "What can I do to help?"

"I can't make any official inquiries about this case, because I don't want anybody to think I'm interfering, or that I might be passing information back to Tiffany. But I have to know what she's up against in order to advise her."

"I may be able to find some background for you without breaking any laws. I have access to a whole lot of databases through Eastern so I might be able to find complaints against the doctor's office, newspaper articles, that kind of thing."

The waitress delivered our salads. "She made a big jump, from waitress to doctor's office," I said, as we began to eat. "She have any training for that?"

He shook his head. "Only that she speaks Spanish. She's been learning the insurance part on the job."

"You know the name of the doctor?"

"Rolando de la Fe. He has a family medicine practice."

I pulled out my phone and opened the notepad app. I wrote down the information. "Any danger they could arrest her?" I asked.

"That's what I need to figure out. Until I understand what the investigation's about, I can't grill her on what she did."

I'd been grilled a few times by Rick myself, and I didn't envy Tiffany the experience.

When we finished dinner, Rick insisted on paying. "I appreciate your help, Steve," he said. "You're the only person I can ask about this."

"Hey, it's what Joe Hardy would do for Frank, right?" We fist bumped. "Hardy Boys forever."

He laughed, and we walked outside.

"Seriously, Rick, you've got to break this pattern with Tiffany if you expect things to work out with Tamsen. And I don't have to tell you which one of the two you should stick with."

"I know. If I can get her through this all right, I'm letting her know we're done. I need to do it, for Tamsen, and for myself."

"Sounds good." The wind chill was fierce, so I hurried to my car, turned the heat on blast, and drove home. Rochester was so glad to see me that he jumped on me and sniffed my groin. Well, actually he did that all the time, even when I'd been gone for only a few minutes.

"I'm home," I called, and Lili answered from upstairs that she was grading papers.

That was my signal to stay on the lower level. I petted Rochester and told him he was a good boy, and to make up for my absence I sat on the floor with him and rubbed his belly.

When he was temporarily satisfied, I opened my laptop and typed "Dr. Rolando de la Fe" into my search engine. I realized it was the second time that day that I'd been asked to snoop into something—but at least this time everything was legal.

A lot of links popped up about the doctor and his clinic, the Center for Infusion Therapy. The most recent was a tiny blurb in the local section of the *Newark Star-Ledger*.

> *Three offices of the Center for Infusion Therapy were shut down on Tuesday afternoon by agents of the Federal Bureau of Investigation.*
>
> *Infusion therapy, the process of intravenous delivery of medication to patients who do not require hospitalization, has come under increasing scrutiny by Federal regulators. In several notorious cases, patients have been charged for medications they did not receive, and Medicare and Medicaid have been billed for services that were neither medically necessary nor delivered.*
>
> *Federal agents declined to comment on the raid or on possible wrong doing at the CIT, which has offices in Newark, Union City and Hoboken. Eduardo de la Fe, managing director of the company, declined to discuss the company's operations.*

From the clinic's home, page I learned that it had been founded in 2001, and provided intravenous medication for a range of illnesses, specializing in cancer and HIV. Their "caring staff" could provide in-home or in-office care, and everything was fully covered by Medicare, Medicaid, and most private insurance policies.

There was no clue in what I read that might lead to an FBI raid.

Neil S. Plakcy

The pictures on the website looked like they'd come straight from a stock photo supplier, but that wasn't a crime. Smiling health care workers in colorful uniforms and smocks, and a range of ages and skin colors on patients who looked grateful for the life-saving ministrations they received. No nurse trying to find a vein in an elderly woman's withered arm, or cleaning up vomit from a patient the meds didn't agree with.

I clicked on the "about us" link and read that Dr. de la Fe had graduated from medical school in Havana in 1961. After living under Fidel Castro's rule for a few years, he left Cuba to study at the University of Miami, where he gained the credentials necessary to practice in the US. He had set up his family medicine practice in Union City in the early 1960s. That had to make him at least eighty, awfully old for a practicing physician.

I wasn't surprised that he'd ended up in Union City. A college friend of mine had grown up there, and had bragged that it was nicknamed Havana on the Hudson because of the large Cuban-American population. There had to lots of business for a Cuban émigré doctor and a Spanish-speaking staff.

A number of nurses were listed by name and credential, but the only other full bio was for the operations manager, Eduardo de la Fe, the doctor's son. He had a degree from Rutgers in business administration and had helped his father found the clinic, after working in customer service positions. His belief, in Spanish and in English, was "The Patient Comes First" or "*El Paciente es lo Primero.*"

Yeah, the patient was the first one to get ripped off, followed by the insurance companies and then the government.

I sat back and stared at the screen. There had to be some information out there about the raid. I doubted that I could find the smoking gun, but I ought to be able to find out more about what was going on at the clinic.

Rochester came over to me with a stuffed golden retriever toy in his mouth. He looked so cute that I had to stop what I was doing, grab my phone and snap a picture. I'd post it to Facebook, to a golden retriever group I belonged to.

Of course. Social media. I got up and gave Rochester one of his treats, and told him what a good boy he was. "You always know what I'm thinking, don't you, boy?"

He was too busy chomping on the treat to answer.

I sat back at the computer and opened up Facebook. I tried "Tiffany Lopez." I got 242,000 hits and realized that though I'd seen a photo of Rick and Tiffany at his house, I hadn't paid much attention to what she looked like.

I changed my search to "Tiffany Lopez Stemper," and found Tiffany's Facebook page. The first photograph was one of an elderly man being led from an office building with his hands cuffed behind him. The words "Center for Infusion Therapy" were visible behind his bent head. "OMG, this is where I work!" Tiffany had written beneath the picture.

I'd never met her in person, so I looked closely, starting with her timeline photos. She'd obviously been a fan of TBT – Throwback Thursday – because she had put up a lot of pictures of herself when younger, including one from her marriage to Rick.

He and I had been out of touch for about twenty years after high school graduation. In the wedding photo he looked the way I remembered him from high school – skinny, serious. She had a heart-shaped face and shoulder-length dark hair in loose curls, and she'd been very pretty back then. The intervening twenty years hadn't been kind to her. Her cheeks were plumper in her later pictures, and she had a scar along her hairline that showed up about a year after her divorce from Rick. And as she got older she wore more eye shadow and lipstick in brighter shades.

She hadn't protected her profile, so I was able to read everything she'd posted. She had graduated from a Catholic high school in Philadelphia, she was "in a relationship," though it wasn't specified with whom, and she liked Jon Bon Jovi, Bruce Springsteen, and Southside Johnny and the Asbury Jukes. She had about a hundred "friends," she was a fan of the New Jersey Jets and a bunch of those housewife reality shows. And she had dozens of "check-ins" at bars and restaurants and concert venues all over North Jersey.

She listed her job as "Insurance Case Manager" at the CIT, and I was pretty sure that was a bloated way of saying she processed claims.

It was tedious sifting through posts about every happy hour, photos of her Latin clubs, and status updates from bars and restaurants around Union City, but I soldiered on. I was surprised at how frank she was about her job on Facebook – didn't she realize that her boss could read her posts?

In one update, she'd mentioned processing Medicare claims for "wrinklies," though at least she didn't have to look at them, because the patients didn't actually come into the office. She noted that her boss, a Colombian-American woman named Maria Jose, had told her to give her name as Yoani if patients called to complain, because that was the name of the woman who'd worked there before her, who had been fired.

As a snooper, I liked the sound of that. Maybe this woman who'd been fired would have something more to say about what was going on at the clinic. I searched for "Yoani" on Facebook and got too many results, mostly about a Cuban blogger named Yoani Sanchez, but when I added "center for infusion therapy" I found the right one—a woman in her late 20s who listed the CIT as a past employer.

Yoani Rodriguez was had made a number of posts about irregularities at the CIT after she was fired. She pointed out that there weren't physical or electronic charts for many patients who had been billed, just a Social Security number, and sometimes she had to rely on the Internet to find the information necessary to process the claim. And those patients who did have charts and who had seen the doctor, back when he was actually treating patients, often called to complain that Medicare had been billed for services they hadn't received.

So that was the genesis of the problem. Patients had complained to Medicare about services they didn't receive, so the agency had begun an investigation.

I sent Rick an email with the information I'd found. At least he could ask Tiffany if she'd seen the same things as Yoani, and what her role had been in processing claims. Did she know there was fraud going on? Had she participated in it? If she had, she could be in a whole mess of trouble.

It seemed like whenever people asked me to use my skills, it was to dig up difficult information. Which reminded me that I had some notes to pull together before my breakfast the next day with Doug Guilfoyle, where I'd be the bearer of even more bad tidings.

10 – LADY GAGA

Tuesday morning I walked Rochester, then slipped out of the house while he was chowing down at his breakfast. The Chocolate Ear café was bright and cheery, with framed art deco posters of French food labels hung on yellow walls. Doug sat at a table in the back and waved. I ordered a café mocha and a chocolate croissant, and then joined him.

"Thanks for meeting me," he said, his voice low under the French pop music playing quietly in the background. "What did you find?"

"You were right about that strip shopping center, Route One Plaza. I was able to crack the password for that hyperlinked spreadsheet, and the numbers there are very different—probably a lot closer to the truth. But I don't understand why Shawn is keeping that property on the books. Why not just write it off?"

"Do you know what a Ponzi scheme is?" Doug asked.

"Sure. When a company offers unreasonably high returns on investments, but they can't sustain those returns from operations so they start paying original investors from the money new investors bring in instead." I shook my head. "It's surprising scammers can still get away with that today."

"There are greedy, gullible people," he said. "Look at all the people who invested with Bernie Madoff. They had to have known those returns weren't reasonable, but they turned a blind eye because they were making money."

"Are you suggesting that if there's no income from these properties, Beauceron is paying the original investors with money from new ones?"

He nodded.

"Shawn's got to know he'll get caught eventually," I said.

"Hubris is a funny thing," Doug said. "I saw it all the time on Wall Street. Guys think they're smarter than everybody else, that they'll never get caught."

Yeah, I'd felt that way myself. And that reminded me of the FBI raid on the clinic where Rick's ex-wife worked. Whoever ran it had probably had the same hubris.

"I'd love to stay at Beauceron until the end of the month when I get my commission check. If I quit now, I walk away with nothing. How bad do you think the fraud is?"

"I've only looked at the one spreadsheet so far," I said. "But it looks like there are a lot of other sheets in that hyperlinked file."

"Can you do some more checking?"

If Shawn was breaking the law and there was a chance Doug could be held culpable, then he needed to quit the job and move on as quickly as possible. One screwy spreadsheet could be explained or rationalized, but a pattern would mean bad news all around.

"I'll do what I can," I said.

Doug hadn't been able to eat much of his breakfast sandwich, and threw the rest of it away as we left. After I picked up Rochester at home, I had to drive to work with the windows closed and the heat on, which meant Rochester couldn't stick his head out the window. He wasn't happy, especially as he had his eye on a big flock of Canada geese on a barren field to the left. He kept trying to step on me to look out my window and I had to push him away.

My mind was on Doug and his problems so I wasn't paying enough attention to the road. It probably hadn't been paved or widened since the Kennedy administration, and it was always a challenge to avoid the potholes. Every time I swerved left to avoid one, I ran over the rumble strips between the double yellow lines and my car shook. By the time we got to Friar Lake my head hurt and so did the rest of my body.

I parked and let Rochester out of the car, and he ran around like a wild animal for a few minutes, until he returned to me, panting happily. As I walked into my office, my phone was ringing and I had to scramble to grab it. "Steve, John Babson here. You've heard of the Bucks County League of Entrepreneurs, haven't you?"

"Not specifically."

"Well, they're a great group, do lots of civic outreach. And the folks behind it are prominent entrepreneurs who ought to know about the great work we're doing at Eastern."

That was Babson's shorthand for "rich people we need to suck up to."

"The League sponsors a Kids Code program that teaches middle-school kids how to program computers," Babson said, and I froze. Did he want me to volunteer with them? It would be ironic to ask someone who'd been jailed for computer crimes to teach kids about programming, and I was sure I wouldn't pass a background check due to my felony conviction.

"The office building where they're scheduled to run a session on Friday has just had a power blowout, and they need a new space pronto. The gal in charge called me, hoping we could spare a computer equipped classroom for the day. But ours are all booked, and this would be a great opportunity to show off our new jewel."

"You want to let them use Friar Lake?"

"I know a sharp guy like you can make it work," Babson said. "Let me know if you run into any roadblocks. I'll have Sheila send you all the information."

He hung up before I could come up with any arguments. I hadn't even taken my coat off. "Come on, boy," I said, rattling Rochester's leash. "We've got to go back out and find Joey."

Since Joey managed the physical facility at Friar Lake, it was up to him to make sure that we were ready for the flood of kids and adults on Friday. The "gal" Babson had mentioned, a woman named Yesenia Cruz, called me as Joey and I walked the property, and when I told her it looked like we'd be able to accommodate her group she said she'd come right over to see the facility.

About a half-hour later, she showed up at my door. She was in her early thirties and had skin the color of light coffee and dark curly hair pulled back into a ponytail. She wore a pink polo shirt, faded blue jeans and sneakers.

"Thanks for letting us use your facility," she said. "I was worried we'd have to cancel our training session and I know the kids would be so disappointed." She had a light Spanish accent, pronouncing 'worried' more like 'wooried,' which was charming.

"It's our pleasure to help out. I wish they'd had courses like this when I was a kid," I said. "When I graduated from high school we were just beginning to use DOS-based clones in classes, and they couldn't do much beyond word processing, games and some limited programming. I didn't get my first computer until I was in college."

"I grew up in Cuba," she said, "and I was lucky to be part of an accelerated program. I was surprised that there wasn't something like that for my kids anywhere here in Bucks County, so I started Kids Code."

"It shouldn't be much trouble to get things set up," I said. "Do you need any special software installed on the computers?"

We walked around the property, and it was fun to have some to geek-speak with. Even so I was eager to get back to Doug's spreadsheets, and I was pleased to wave goodbye to Yesenia just before lunch.

While I ate my sandwich I used my laptop to open each of the spreadsheet files Doug had given me, and list which ones were connected to individual spreadsheets in the main hyperlinked file. There were about a dozen of them. Another twenty had no links. Did that mean they were still making money?

I called Doug to ask if he wanted me to do anything more, but the call went to voice mail and I didn't want to be specific, so I just left him a message to call me. When he hadn't returned the call by the time I left for home, I called again, and once more my call went right to voice mail. Hey, if he was too busy to talk to me, then maybe he was working things out at Beauceron – or putting his exit strategy into play.

Lili and I had dinner together, and I was glad that I had the middle-school program to talk about because I was reluctant to tell her that I was snooping around on behalf of Doug and Rick. I should have told her that I'd broken into the Beauceron server to get that file for Doug, but that would have opened a whole can of worms. Since I wasn't hacking on my own behalf, I said nothing.

My cell rang as I was slotting the last of the dishes into the dishwasher. "I spoke to Tiffany again," Rick said. "She's calmed down a lot, says her new boyfriend knows what's going on and not to worry."

"Oh, really? And how would he know?"

"She wouldn't say. His name is Alex Vargas, but that may not be his real one. From everything Tiffany has said, he's the kind of guy who ought to have a record. I can't do anything official to look into him because he's not the subject of any investigation. And I'm so accustomed to using police records that I don't know enough about where to look for anything outside those. You think you can check him out for me?"

"Sure. You know how old he is?"

"Tiffany says he's younger than she is. All that I know besides that is that he was born in Newark and he lives in Hoboken now. Tiffany doesn't want to tell me anything else. I think she's afraid of him."

"When I was a kid my dad had cousins who lived in Hoboken," I said. "Kind of a lower middle-class neighborhood back then. But it's a hipster town now. All those artists and musicians who get priced out of Manhattan and Brooklyn."

"This Alex guy is some kind of artist, but of the scam variety," Rick said.

"I'll see if I can find anything out there in social media about him," I said. "According to Tiffany's Facebook status she's in a relationship, so he may show up on her page."

After dinner, Lili went upstairs and I sat down to investigate, beginning once again with Tiffany 's Facebook page. She had obviously been sufficiently freaked out by the FBI raid the day before that she hadn't posted anything new to her wall.

I checked her photo albums. In the most recent photos she was with a dark haired guy with tattoos circling around his pumped biceps. Was that Alex Vargas? The way she cuddled up to him indicated he was more than just a casual friend.

I put "Alex Vargas" in quotation marks to narrow down my search results. I got a lot of hits for a singer by that name, but he looked nothing like the guy with Tiffany. The same for a first round draft pick for the Houston Astros, and a fat, bald guy who sold insurance in Passaic.

It took me nearly a half hour of sifting through results before I gave up. Nothing matched the details of the guy Tiffany was dating.

Maybe he used his full name. I tried "Alexander Vargas" but I came up blank again. I gave up and went back to Tiffany's Facebook page. Maybe there was a clue there.

Alex only faced the camera in one photo – in the rest he was turned toward Tiffany. I copied that photo, cropped it, and uploaded it to Google's image search to see if I could find a match. No luck. The picture was too blurry.

Rochester came nosing over to me. "How are you, puppy?" I asked him, and I scratched under his neck. He put his front paws up on my thigh and sniffed at me. I petted him, and he rested his head against my laptop keyboard. Before I could pull him away, one of Lady Gaga's songs began to play. "I know that you may love me, but I just can't be with you like this anymore, Alejandro."

"Of course!" I said. "Rochester, you're a genius!" I tugged him down and shut off the music. I didn't bother searching Facebook again, because if Alejandro had a page there I was pretty sure Tiffany would have linked to it. Instead I Googled "Alejandro Vargas."

I checked the image results first, since I had an idea of what Tiffany's new boyfriend looked like. Sure enough, I found a photo tagged with his name that matched the ones on Tiffany's page. So Alex was just a nickname for Alejandro.

Using the name Alejandro Vargas, I found a very interesting article from a small town paper in North Jersey from about a year before. The Vargas I was looking for had been arrested for drug possession. The situation had arisen after a neighbor called the cops because he was playing his music too loud, and when the cops arrived, they found a group of men who appeared to be high on drugs. The tenant, Alejandro Vargas, was on probation and pursuant to the terms and conditions of his probation, the cops were allowed to conduct a search of his apartment.

In that search, they discovered nearly twenty pounds of marijuana, as well as hash oil, THC pills, THC-laced chocolate bars, and THC infused bottled lemonade, much of it packaged for resale and commercially labeled. THC was the chemical in marijuana responsible for its intoxicating effect, but I hadn't known you could put it in lemonade, of all things.

For a moment I imagined the guy with the tattooed biceps behind a lemonade stand with a bunch of dopers lined up. Then I went back to the article. Vargas had been arrested for possession of marijuana for sale and booked into the Morris County Jail on $20,000 bail.

I couldn't find any follow up to the arrest, but I emailed Rick the link to the article.

Lili came downstairs then. "You've become a Lady Gaga fan?" she asked. "I heard that song play."

"Just an accident," I said. "Rochester and I were fooling around and his nose hit the keyboard." I was about to skip the rest of the explanation, but then I remembered how Rick had been so open with Tamsen about speaking with Tiffany. I needed to be as honest with Lili.

"But it led me to something." I stood up and shut down the laptop, then stretched. "Want to walk Rochester with me and I'll tell you about it?" I asked.

As we walked, I explained that Rick had asked me to look into Tiffany's new boyfriend, and that Rochester had led me to the name Alejandro. "You don't mind that I'm snooping around, do you?" I asked her.

"Rick asked you to," she said. "And it's not like you're hacking, right?"

I took a deep breath. "Well, not for Rick," I said. "You remember the guy who took over the seminar for me, Doug Guilfoyle?"

"He asked you to do some hacking?" She stopped under a street lamp, her hands on her hips. "For what purpose?"

"It sounds like he's in trouble at work," I said, and realized that Tiffany was in the same situation. I sketched out Doug's problem. "All I did was download this spreadsheet that might explain the irregularities he's worried about."

Rochester pulled forward but I reined him in.

"Why couldn't he download it himself?" Lili asked.

"It was password protected."

"So someone at Doug's company created a spreadsheet and then put a password on it to keep other people from seeing it. You cracked the password, didn't you?"

The anger in her voice was so evident that even Rochester heard it. He sat on his butt to wait out the storm.

"I'm not going to lie to you. I did."

"And isn't that illegal? The kind of thing that could get you sent back to prison?"

My first instinct was to defend myself, to explain all the precautions I'd taken to protect myself. That I'd only done it to help Doug. But all I said was, "Yes."

"You promised me, and Rick, that you'd talk to one of us before you did anything that might be remotely considered against the law. You didn't talk to him, did you?"

"No."

I felt terrible. I'd gone ahead and done what I wanted without thinking of the people around me and how they'd react.

"Did you find anything in this protected spreadsheet that could help your friend Doug out?"

"I did. I'm not sure what he's going to do with the information because he needs to stay with his job til the end of the month in order to collect his commissions. After that I don't know if he'll just quit, or quit and then report the problem to the authorities."

Lili started walking again, and Rochester and I followed her, Rochester tugging ahead as if his life depended on getting to that next smell before it evaporated into the air.

"I do understand you, you know," Lili said after a while. "You wanted to help Doug. Just like you're helping Rick by looking at Tiffany's new boyfriend."

I didn't say anything.

"And if there's a Ponzi scheme going on at Doug's company then a lot of people could be losing money and getting hurt."

That was what I'd felt as well, but I had the sense that Lili wasn't finished yet, so I didn't say it.

"I hope you covered your tracks well," Lili said, as we reached the big lake at the center of River Bend. "I'd miss you terribly if you went back to prison."

"You're not angry?"

"Of course I'm angry. You've done something that could damage our relationship. But getting angry isn't going to change you, and honestly, if you weren't the kind of guy who'd do anything he could to help others, I don't know that I'd feel as strongly about you as I do."

I reached for her hand, and she took mine and squeezed. "Just be careful, Steve."

"You and Rochester mean more to me than anything else," I

said. "I promise you I will try as hard as I can to make sure that I don't do anything that would hurt either of you. Which includes my going back to prison."

"Don't make promises you can't keep," she said, but she leaned in and kissed me anyway.

Neil S. Plakcy

11 – FLOATER

I still hadn't heard from Doug Guilfoyle by the time I left for Friar Lake on Wednesday morning. I kept thinking about him and his problems, though, as I traveled the twisting road upriver, passing luxury developments that had begun to pepper the landscape with huge houses and three-car garages. From everything I'd read, family size was shrinking—almost all my friends had only one, maybe two children. Who needed all that space? When I was growing up, most kids shared bedrooms or bathrooms, and families lived in tight quarters. Would all this space help them get along? Or not?

According to Doug, the house he and Catherine had owned in Westchester County was as much of a mansion as any of these. Now she'd taken a step down to an ordinary suburban split-level, and he was in a crummy rented apartment. How many of those families along the River Road would end up in similar circumstances?

And where was the money coming from to pay for the big houses, luxury cars and expensive vacations that everyone around me seemed to enjoy? Illicit schemes like the one that was going on at Beauceron? For the first time since I lost my software job in California, I was making a decent living, but I'd never be able to afford a million-dollar home or even to replace my aged Beemer with a brand new model.

Didn't I already have enough to think about? It was like I told Rochester when he was too eager to sniff a passerby or play with a new dog. Mind your own business.

I'd only been at Friar Lake for a few minutes when Rick called me. "Hey, did you get that article I sent you about Alex Vargas?" I asked before he could say anything.

"Not yet. I've got bigger problems right now. You know a guy named Douglas Guilfoyle?"

"Doug? Why do you want to know something about him?"

"Just answer the questions, Levitan."

The way Rick used my last name indicated business. "Sure, I know Doug. We went to Eastern together, and he helped me out with a program at Friar Lake last weekend." I didn't think it was necessary to add that he'd asked me to look into fraud at the company where he worked.

"That explains why there was a contract with your name on it in his back pocket," Rick said. "No wallet, so that paper is the only ID he had on him."

"Huh?"

"A woman out running this morning spotted something floating in the Delaware Canal south of the Ferry Street bridge. She thought it was a dead animal until she got closer. Then she called the cops."

"Hold on," I said. "Are you saying that Doug Guilfoyle is dead? But I just had breakfast with him yesterday."

"That's when you saw him last? Speak to him after that?"

My mind was racing as I explained about the calls to Doug he hadn't returned. Doug was dead? How could that be? His poor kids. "How did he die? Did he drown?"

Rick didn't answer. Instead he said, "I need some background from you as soon as possible. At the station?"

"I can be there in a half hour." I hesitated, then asked, "Have you called Catherine yet?"

"Catherine who?"

"What do you mean, Catherine who? Catherine Guilfoyle. Doug's ex-wife. Your girlfriend's cousin."

"Holy shit. I just met the woman on Sunday and never got her last name. You mean this dead guy is the ex she was bitching about?"

"He's not just a dead guy," I said. "His name is Doug Guilfoyle. In college everybody called him Dougie."

"Sorry," Rick said. "You're right. Obviously you knew Mr. Guilfoyle, and I need to know him as well as you do in order to figure out what happened to him."

"I'll fill you in on what I know when I get there. In the meantime, call Tamsen."

I let Joey know I was going out and asked him to keep an eye on Rochester again. Then I drove back down the River Road, thinking about Doug Guilfoyle the whole way. My stomach felt like acid, and every time I remembered an incident from college I started to tear up.

I'd have to tell Rick about the hacking I'd done on Doug's

behalf. If there was a Ponzi scheme going on at Beauceron, Doug's nosing around could have marked him for death. Rick would probably be just as angry at me as Lili had been the night before, but I'd have to man up and take whatever he wanted to throw at me.

Could Catherine have killed Doug? She'd probably get a big life insurance payout that would make up for the alimony and child support she'd been getting from Doug. What if he'd told her he might be losing his job, and the money would have to stop for a while? She must have known he couldn't swim.

But maybe I was over-dramatizing, as Rick often accused me of. Perhaps Doug had he been mugged, had his wallet stolen and either slipped or been pushed into the canal? I tried to remember if there had been similar incidents in town. The *Boat-Gazette*, our local weekly newspaper, listed all the incidents from the police blotter. Most of the ones I could recall were domestic incidents, noise complaints and traffic accidents, interspersed with the occasional house break-in.

Could his death have been a suicide? He'd been depressed about his divorce, and the difficulty of rebuilding a relationship with his kids. Afraid of losing the job at Beauceron and destroying the new life he'd worked so hard to build. Had he been sad enough to kill himself? Maybe he'd left his wallet in his car, or maybe it had floated out of his pocket when he was in the water.

There was also the possibility it was just an accident. Doug had told me himself that he couldn't swim. What if he'd fallen into the canal and been unable to climb back up onto dry land? The previous week, I'd seen the high water level and the fast current.

My brain was still buzzing with questions when I got to the police station, in a squat, one-story building from the 1970s built in the poorer neighborhood of town, at the corner of Canal Street and Quarry Road. I slipped my driver's license under the receptionist's window and told her I was there to see Rick, and waited in the dingy, 60s-era lobby until he came out and led me back to his scuffed wooden desk in a big bullpen area.

The questions began to fall out of my mouth before I could stop myself. "Doug told me he couldn't swim. Do you think he fell into the canal? Or was he pushed in?"

"Hold on, cowboy. You go first. Tell me everything you know about this guy."

I figured the part about running around Birthday Hall naked when Doug and I were seniors wasn't relevant, so I skipped ahead to Tor's recommendation that Doug handle the seminar at Friar Lake.

I went through my meeting by the canal with Doug, his kids and his dog, and how Doug had told me he couldn't swim. Rick was busy taking notes. "We talked about our divorces and how he'd come down here to be close to his kids, but Catherine was making things difficult for him."

"Tamsen says Catherine has a different take on that," Rick said. "I called her right after you made the connection for me. I'm meeting Catherine later today so she can identify the body, and I'll get her side of the story then. But go on."

"We talked about the presentation he was going to give, and then when we were up at Friar Lake over the weekend he asked me to look into the company he was working for, Beauceron. He was worried there was something suspicious going on and that if he got caught up in it he might lose his securities license."

"Define 'something suspicious' for me," Rick said, and I could see the air quotes around the words.

I related Doug's concern about the strip shopping center, and my discovery that Beauceron was keeping two sets of spreadsheets.

"How'd you find that out?" Rick asked.

Here was my chance to come clean. But if I'd broken the law to get the information, then it couldn't be used in the investigation. "Doug gave me his ID and password."

Rick snorted. "Giving you a password is like opening the henhouse door to the fox."

"Don't be a jerk. Remember, you asked me to look for information on Tiffany and the raid on her company for you."

He held up his hand. "Sorry. That was out of line. You *are* a good person to look into that kind of thing, because you know what's right and what's wrong."

I flinched, because I knew I was withholding information from Rick, and that put my ability to distinguish between right and wrong in question. But I soldiered on.

"I met Doug for breakfast yesterday morning at the Chocolate Ear, and he was pretty worried about what I found. He asked me to see how many other linked spreadsheets there were, and I did a bit more checking. I called him a couple of times yesterday to tell him what I found, but he never answered his phone and the only message I left was for him to call me."

I leaned forward. "Do you think maybe he was killed to protect what's in those files?"

"Until the ME tells me otherwise, I have to assume this is either an accident or suicide. Especially since you just told me he couldn't swim." He looked down at his notes. "Did he seem depressed after your breakfast? Possibly thinking of taking his own life?"

"I don't know," I said. "It was pretty clear he was going to have to leave Beauceron and look for a new job, and he was worried about paying his alimony and child support. I know he was stressed but I don't know if he was upset enough to consider suicide. And he'd just given up his career on Wall Street and relocated down here to be close to his kids. I don't think he'd abandon them."

"One thing I can tell you after years on this job is that you never really know what somebody else is thinking," Rick said.

Was there something in the way that he looked at me that implied he knew I'd been hacking, and that I wasn't telling him?

He looked back down at his notes. "Is there a Mr. Beauceron?" he asked. "Somebody I should speak to about Doug?"

"A Beauceron's a kind of dog, a French version of a German Shepherd. The managing partner is a guy named Shawn Brumberger. He was at the cocktail reception at Friar Lake last weekend. I saw him and Doug arguing but I never got the chance to ask Doug what they were fighting about."

I spelled Shawn's name for him, and then he pushed back his chair and stood up. "Thanks for coming in. This has been helpful."

"Tamsen said that Catherine's dating someone new," I said. "You should ask her about him. And Doug told me that if Catherine remarried, he could stop paying alimony."

Rick remained standing. "I know. Thanks for coming in." He nodded his head toward the door. "Do I need to show you the way out?"

"I'll try not to let the door hit my butt as I go," I said.

12 – FINANCIAL RECORDS

For the third time that morning, I drove along River Road, and once again my brain was occupied with thoughts of Doug Guilfoyle. The poor guy had been so determined to reestablish a connection with his kids that he'd turned his life upside down, leaving a successful career on Wall Street and taking the job with Beauceron.

It reminded me of my own situation, when I left prison and returned home to Stewart's Crossing. I'd been fortunate that the chair of the English department, who'd taught me as an undergraduate, took pity on me and hired me as an adjunct. President Babson was willing to overlook my police record and trusted me to run Friar Lake.

What would I have done if I hadn't had those chances? If I hadn't adopted Rochester, or become friends with Rick, or met Lili? Imagine all the good things Doug Guilfoyle could have done if he'd had the good luck I had.

I went back over in my head every interaction I'd had with Doug, from our first meeting by the canal to our breakfast the day before. Was there anything else I could have done? Something I could have done differently? Should I have quizzed him more about his mental state? Tried to see if he was suicidal? Reached out to him more?

Was someone at Beauceron tapping Doug's phone calls or monitoring his computer usage? Doug had zipped up and downloaded all those property spreadsheets on Saturday night at Friar Lake, and that log-in from a different IP address might have triggered an alert. I hadn't considered it seriously at the time, assuming that Beauceron was a small operation and that Doug's suspicions might have been unfounded.

A few minutes after that, I had used Doug's ID and password to log in to the Beauceron server from my own laptop, and tried to follow the hyperlink in the first spreadsheet to the second one. I'd discovered it was protected and that I couldn't download it without the password. Had there been some kind of flag on that protected spreadsheet that set an alert?

Then on Monday morning, I'd broken into the Beauceron server and downloaded the file from the root directory. I'd carried out the hack from the Eastern library, feeling pretty confident that even if the server noted my incursion, the raid couldn't be tracked back to me. But suppose someone at Beauceron knew that Doug was asking questions about the REIT and its payouts, and connected those questions to the download of the spreadsheet?

In that case, then I might not have been as anonymous as I thought. If someone was able to trace the incursion back to the Eastern library's IP address, that would raise the question of who

Doug knew at the college – which would lead directly to me.

All my other work had been offline, even when I opened all those other spreadsheets to check for hyperlinks. But I didn't know what else Doug might have done. I did recall him saying when he asked me to meet for breakfast that Shawn had been asking him a lot of strange questions.

Should I have grilled him more about those? If I'd pressed him more, could I have convinced him to act quickly? Would that have saved his life?

When I parked at Friar Lake, Rochester left Joey's side at the edge of the parking lot and raced across the pavement to me. He jumped up and down as if I'd abandoned him there for days. It took several minutes of tummy rubs, sweet endearments and a jaunt around the property for him to forgive me.

I tried as best I could to recreate the conversation Doug and I had and typed it into an email to Rick. "I have the spreadsheets if you, or some fraud investigator, wants to see them," I wrote.

After I sent the email, I realized Rochester wasn't in his normal position on the floor by my desk. When he wasn't around me, I knew he was up to mischief. "Rochester!" I called. "Where are you, puppy?"

I found him in the gatehouse lobby, where a stack of glossy brochures about Friar Lake had fallen to the floor. I'd written the text and Lili had taken the photos, as well as incorporating historic ones from back when the property was an abbey called Our Lady of the

Waters.

Rochester's head was resting on one of the brochures, open to a list of alumni donors to the project. "I can find you a better pillow," I said to my dog, as I tugged the brochure out from under him.

Shawn Brumberger was an Eastern graduate, I recalled, as I wiped a glob of Rochester's drool from the page. Could I find anything about him in our records, or online, that might indicate a predilection toward crime?

From the alumni database, I learned that Shawn was nearly fifty, about five years older than Doug and I were, and he had majored in economics, though without distinction.

Looking back through his file, I discovered that his first job after he graduated from Eastern was as a stockbroker with a firm called Best Capital Advisors, in Long Island City, New York. I looked up the firm, and discovered that it had been the subject of a fraud investigation in the late 1970s. I clicked through a bunch of links until I found the details of the fraud. BCA had been a "boiler room," a high-pressure call center. Brokers called people on "sucker lists" of potential investors and tried to convince them to buy high-risk stocks.

Shawn had stayed at BCA for two years, then gone to NYU for an MBA in finance. While he was there, a Federal investigation had shut BCA down, and I couldn't find any evidence that Shawn had been implicated in the probe. But clearly working at BCA had been Shawn's introduction to financial fraud.

He had interned at an investment bank during the summer between his two years at NYU, and then returned to that firm for a full time job after graduation. He had climbed the corporate ladder in fund management, and five years before he had left a position with a big Wall Street firm to found Beauceron. After some industrious digging I found that he'd been divorced at about that time, and remarried soon after. I wondered if the job shift and the divorce and remarriage were connected, and remembered Doug mentioning that he and Shawn had bonded over their bitter divorces, the way Rick and I had.

Doug had been saddled with crippling alimony and child support payments. Maybe Shawn was in the same boat, and couldn't afford to write off those bad debts at Beauceron.

How could I find out if he was having financial trouble without hacking somewhere? I went back over everything I'd found, and in a profile in a glossy magazine I found a mention of his kids. Shawna Brumberger was in her final year at SUNY Binghamton, and Shawn Jr. was a freshman at Westchester Community College in Valhalla, New York.

I shook my head at that. You had to have a pretty big ego to name both your kids after yourself.

If either of Shawn's kids had applied to Eastern, there might be something about Shawn's finances in their applications. I didn't have authorization to access our admissions database, so I called Sally Marston, the director of admissions, who I'd worked with in the past.

"You have a minute to talk?" I asked.

"This is a momentary lull in the craziness," Sally said. "Offers went out April first, so we're waiting to see what our yield is and how far we have to dip into the wait list."

I didn't want to tell Sally my real reason for looking into Brumberger, so I spun a story about meeting him and trying to determine if he was worth courting as a fund-raising prospect. "Can you see if either of his kids applied here? If they might have been looking for financial aid? That could tell me if he's got money or not."

Sally said she could look, and I gave her Shawn Brumberger's name and class year. "Daughter's name is Shawna, and the son is Shawn Junior."

"We don't hold onto detailed records once a class is admitted," Sally said. "There's been a big boom in Freedom of Information requests from students who want to see their admissions folders, so President Babson decided that it would be safer for us to destroy the materials rather than have something embarrassing come out. But I can look up these names, see if they applied and if they filed the government forms for aid."

I thanked her and hung up. While I waited I did some searching on Shawn and both his ex-wife and his current one. There might be details that could add to the puzzle I was assembling.

Shawn's ex, Barbara, lived in Westchester County in a house appraised at $5.2 million. He had transferred the deed to her for a dollar a few years before, most likely as part of the divorce settlement.

Barbara Brumberger did not appear to have a job, though she was on the committees of numerous charities. She was a plump woman in her early fifties with a pretty face and well-coiffed hair, and I found a lot of photos of her at events, wearing ball gowns and what looked like a diamond necklace and matching earrings.

I also found photos of Brumberger and his second wife, Svetlana, at similar charity events in Pennsylvania. She was a stunning beauty, a couple of inches taller than Shawn in her high heels and blonde bouffant, and she wore diamonds that looked bigger than Barbara's.

Sally called back. "Shawna Brumberger, the daughter, applied to Eastern three years ago, but her grades and her scores weren't very strong. She was wait-listed for admission but ended up going somewhere else. Shawn Junior was admitted last year, but his FAFSA was incomplete so we weren't able to offer him any financial aid, and he never matriculated."

"What does that mean, his FAFSA was incomplete?"

"The FAFSA is the common financial aid form for all college admissions," Sally said. "It could be that his parents refused to list their income, or provide copies of their tax returns. Unfortunately, we can't make an aid decision without it."

I thanked Sally and hung up. Why would a kid with wealthy parents apply for financial aid at all? Was it because his father refused to pay for his education? Maybe Shawn Junior had taken his mother's side in the divorce, and his father held a grudge. Or maybe Shawn Senior didn't have the money. But then why not fill out the form?

I remembered my college admissions process, when I first got to see my parents' financial information—how much each of them earned, how much they had put away for my education, and so on. Maybe Shawn wouldn't fill out the forms because he didn't want his son, and by extension his ex-wife, to know that he was broke. Or that he was depending on the illicit income from Beauceron to pay his bills.

Was Shawn Brumberger the kind of guy who could commit murder? I'd witnessed the angry exchange between him and Doug at Friar Lake. It wasn't hard to believe that he was cooking the books at Beauceron—it seemed like every Wall Street company had some kind of scam going on. But murder was a big step from cheating investors, wasn't it?

It all came down to motive. What was Shawn's motive in stealing money? To maintain his lifestyle? To protect his reputation? Were either of those strong enough to motivate him to kill?

13 – OPEN SOURCE TOOLS

I was on my way home that evening, Rochester by my side, when Rick called. "I have Doug Guilfoyle's laptop here, but it's locked down," he said. "Catherine says she has no idea what the password is, and neither does the secretary at Beauceron. I could send it off to a computer geek in Doylestown but I figured why wait when I have a geek at my disposal."

"You want me to crack his password?" I asked. "Isn't that illegal?"

"Get with the times, pal. Law enforcement is allowed to pursue digital evidence in the form of emails, internet history, documents or other file, as long as they're relevant to the investigation. I just can't ask you to use illegal tools."

"I have some open source digital forensics tools that a lot of agencies use. I can download the current version of the package at the station and show you how to use it, if you want. I just need to drop Rochester at home and then I can come over to the station."

"You can bring him here. He and the desk sergeant have a love affair going."

That was certainly true. A couple of times I'd had to take Rochester with me when I went in to speak with Rick, and I'd left him with the sergeant, who always kept some treats in his drawer for the department's K-9 officers.

When we got to the station, I went through the same routine—driver's license and verification that I was expected, though the officer at the window did look curiously at Rochester.

We were buzzed in, and as soon as Rochester saw the desk sergeant, he started jumping up and down with delight. I left my dog happily chewing a biscuit and crossed the room to Rick's desk, where he had a fairly new laptop open in front of him.

"So does this mean you think Doug was murdered?" I asked.

"Too early to make a judgment," Rick said. "There may be evidence on this laptop of his mood, for example, which could support suicide. But I can't get past this password window."

I directed him to the website where he could get the open source password-cracker, and while we waited for it to download, he continued. "Guilfoyle had a high blood alcohol count, but the ME says that doesn't mean he was drunk when he went into the water. Apparently your body manufacturers alcohol after you die, and that process gets accelerated when a body becomes waterlogged."

That was bad news. I could imagine Doug drowning his sorrows somewhere, then feeling maudlin enough to give up.

"I interviewed a waitress at the Drunken Hessian," Rick said. "She saw Guilfoyle drinking that night with another man. She pulled the tab for me – it was paid on the Beauceron corporate credit card."

He shook his head. "I love dogs as much as the next guy but I still think it's dumb to name a whole company after one."

"You mean we're not going to form Rochester and Rascal Investigations someday?"

"Highly doubtful. Anyway, I checked with the boss and he said they had a couple of beers to talk over things at work. He last saw Guilfoyle in the parking lot – Guilfoyle said he was going for a walk to clear his head before he drove home."

"Does that mean that Shawn was the last person to see Doug alive?"

"So it appears."

"Did he say anything about Doug's state of mind? Was he depressed?"

"We talked about that for a while. He said that Mr. Guilfoyle hadn't been bringing in enough new clients, and that he, Brumberger, wasn't sure they'd be able to keep him on. That obviously that was bad news to Guilfoyle. He was upset about being able to continue supporting his family. Brumberger was very upset at the idea that Guilfoyle might have committed suicide. That he should have stayed with Guilfoyle until he sobered up."

Or Doug confronted Shawn, and Shawn killed him. "Do you believe him?"

"No reason not to right now. And Guilfoyle's blood alcohol count was .09, which is enough in Pennsylvania to get you a $300 fine and six months' probation if you get caught behind the wheel."

"A good reason to go for a walk," I said. "But why along the canal? It's dark back there. He could have just walked up and down Main Street."

"He wouldn't have wanted to risk being picked up for public intoxication," Rick said.

"That's a crime? Just walking down the street drunk?"

"We can arrest you, if you're so drunk that you pose a threat to yourself or to other people. And with so much alcohol in his system it's doubtful he was thinking logically anyway."

"Did you look at that information I sent to you? About Doug's suspicions?"

"I did. But what Brumberger said makes a lot more sense, that Mr. Guilfoyle was drunk, that he was upset. I'm leaning toward either suicide or a simple accident right now."

"I don't believe Doug would commit suicide, no matter how maudlin he was feeling. He was going to have his kids this weekend. He was determined to reestablish his relationship with them. I can't believe that he would have killed himself."

"You never know what somebody else is thinking," Rick said. "There was some slight evidence of head trauma, so he might have hit his head on a low-hanging branch and lost his balance."

"Or that somebody hit him in the head and knocked him in the water."

Rick looked at me. In the past I'd let my imagination run ahead of the facts. And though there were a bunch of people with a motive to kill Doug, there was no evidence yet to show that his death was murder.

"What did Catherine say when you spoke to her?" I asked. "Did she think Doug might have committed suicide?"

"We didn't get into it over the phone. She was upset, and I'm planning to talk more to her after she identifies the body."

The password cracker program completed its download, and I showed Rick how to use it. We entered as much data about Doug as we knew – his birthday and those of his ex-wife and kids, his anniversary, kids' names, even the dog's name, Pixie. We connected Doug's laptop to Rick's computer with a cable, and then started the program.

Doug's password was pretty simple to crack, as most human-generated ones are. His kids' names, Ethan and Maddie, with numbers replacing certain letters—3thanMadd13. I could have figured that out without the software but I wasn't going to brag.

"Thanks," Rick said. "I can take it from here."

"Hold on, cowboy," I said. "Wait, isn't that something you say to me?"

Rick pursed his lips at me.

"I have a couple more things to show you. You know that you can view the metadata of the files, right? When a document first appeared on a computer, when it was last edited, when it was last saved or printed and which user were involved."

He nodded. "Got it."

"These tools can also recover hidden or deleted files. Why don't

I show you how to do that before I head out?"

"I bow to your superior knowledge."

I took over the keyboard and initiated a bunch of commands, and eventually a list of deleted files popped up, most of them emails. I retrieved them, and then pushed the laptop away. "My work here is finished."

He thanked me, and I picked up Rochester from the desk sergeant. Out in front of the station, he sniffed a bush and left some p-mail for his official investigative colleagues.

"What do you think, boy?" I asked him as we walked to the car. "Was Doug's death a suicide, an accident, or murder?"

Rochester had no opinion on the matter.

When we got home Lili was in the kitchen preparing dinner, and I poured out Rochester's chow while she added some water to the pot of risotto on the stove and stirred it. The smell of mushrooms and asparagus rose in clouds around her.

"Bad news today," I said, as I put down the bowl for Rochester. "Remember my college friend, Doug Guilfoyle? The one who helped out at Friar Lake last weekend?" I took a breath and added, "The one who asked me to download that file for him."

"What's the news? Did someone find out he got into that file and fire him?"

"He's dead."

Lili stopped stirring and turned to look at me. "Dead? What happened?"

"Rick isn't sure, but Doug's body was found floating in the canal this morning by a jogger. He'd been drinking at the Drunken Hessian with his boss and went to walk off the buzz. It's not clear if he fell in the water, was pushed in – or jumped."

Lili dished out the risotto and we sat down to eat. "Rick called you about him?" she asked.

Between bites, I explained about the contract in Doug's pocket that had identified him, how I'd given Rick some background that morning. "Then this evening, Rochester and I stopped by the police station and I showed Rick how to use some free public software to crack the password on Doug's laptop. He's trying to see what Doug's state of mind was before he died."

"Do you think Doug was depressed enough to commit suicide?" she asked.

"I don't know. I know he loved his kids and wanted to be part of their lives, but it looked like he was either going to get fire, or have to quit his job and start over again, and he might have thought it was just too much."

"Poor guy," Lili said.

"I know. And Ethan and Maddie – they both were upset by the divorce, and now they won't have time to work things out with their dad."

"Maybe we'll go over to Catherine's house this weekend," Lili said. She finished the last bit of rice, mushroom and asparagus on her plate, then crossed her silverware over it. "They aren't Jewish so they won't be sitting shiva, but I'm sure they could use some friends around, especially because they haven't lived here very long and probably don't know a lot of local people beyond her cousins."

"Sure," I said. "Though I doubt Catherine will need much comforting. That is, unless Doug didn't leave her enough insurance."

"Steve! That's mean."

"It may be, but it's true. You heard her talk about Doug. And didn't Tamsen tell you Catherine was seeing someone? If she remarried, she'd lose her alimony, and she might have to get a real job instead of screwing around trying to write a children's book about a Lenni Lenape girl."

"I don't like the way you always see the worst in people," Lili said, crossing her arms over her chest.

"I like Catherine," I protested. "I've known her as long as I've known Doug, though clearly I wasn't in touch with either of them until very recently. I'm not accusing her of anything. But things could get uncomfortable between Rick and Tamsen if Rick thinks Catherine had anything to do with Doug's death."

"I'm going upstairs," Lili said. "I have some papers to read. You can clean up."

The subtext was clear; I ought to stay downstairs. At least Rochester was willing to stay with me.

14 – CAT AND MOUSE

I paced restlessly around the living room, Rochester on my heels, thinking about Doug, worried that there was nothing more I could do to help him. I picked up the book I was reading but I couldn't focus on it, and when I turned the TV on there was nothing I wanted to watch. I was idly flipping through channels when Rochester left me to go upstairs.

I gave up and shut the TV off as Rochester came trundling back down the stairs with something in his mouth. He came up to me and dropped it at my feet, as if he was a cat with a dead mouse.

It was a small bag in the color I immediately recognized as Columbia blue—a light shade that was on most of the communications I got from my graduate alma mater.

It was also the same shade as Tiffany bags and boxes—and that's what Rochester had brought me, a small drawstring sack that read Tiffany & Co. I picked it up and a small silver dragonfly charm tumbled out.

That must be what Lili had bought for her sister-in-law. But why would Rochester bring it to me? Was he saying I needed to buy Lili a gift? Take him outside to catch dragonflies?

I looked at him and he cocked his head. "What?" I asked.

He woofed once, and I looked down at the bag. "Of course," I said. "Tiffany. What a smart boy you are." I reached down and scratched behind his ears, and he opened his mouth wide in a doggy smile.

He followed me to the dining room, where I opened my laptop on the table. He sprawled on the floor beside me as I went online. I was curious to know more about the office where Tiffany worked, particularly about infusion therapy. I Googled the term and discovered that it was a lot cheaper and more convenient to deliver IV antibiotics and other medications in an outpatient setting, rather than requiring the patient to be hospitalized. It was used particularly when a patient's condition was so severe that medication couldn't be delivered orally.

I was surprised at how many conditions could be treated that way, from dehydration to congestive heart failure to cancer. Many of the patients who needed such treatment were elderly, which meant they were on Medicare, while others were often covered by conventional insurance plans. The welter of regulations, agencies and companies involved made billing errors common, and opened the possibility of fraud.

Dr. Rolando de la Fe and his son Eduardo ran what was called a physician-based infusion clinic, and had to abide by a whole list of requirements, from maintaining sterile conditions to monitoring patients for adverse reactions. However, it didn't look like the regulations governing their payment were strictly enforced.

Cubans and Cuban-Americans were often at the center of health care fraud, I discovered from reading a number of different news reports online. Cuban immigrants were immediately eligible for government health care benefits as soon as they landed in the U.S. I was stunned by the statistic that people born in Cuba represented less than 1% of the U.S. population but committed 41% of Medicare fraud. Many of them were alleged to be funneling those profits back to the island.

One very organized crime ring had opened a home health-care agency in Miami in 2010 and within three days had submitted $1.5 million in fraudulent claims to Medicare – and that was just a small bit of an empire that was draining billions of dollars from the U.S. health care system.

Was the Center for Infusion Therapy committing similar crimes? I'd heard Lili mention once or twice that Cubans considered themselves the "Jews of the Caribbean," because like Israel, their country was a fierce and independent nation, small in size but huge in ambition, surrounded by historical enemies who sought to bring about their ruin. Cubans saw themselves as hard-working and determined to be successful, as Jews did. But somehow those islanders had used that determination for criminal means.

I began channeling my sadness over Doug's death into anger that someone at the clinic had been exploiting the sick and needy. I went back to Facebook and checked Tiffany's page. "Looks like I am out of a job, AGAIN," she had posted earlier that day. "What is it with me and jobs? Back to waitressing I guess."

At least Tiffany had the chance to start over again. Unlike Doug.

As I walked Rochester late that evening, I wondered what it was about me that got me involved in all these dramas. Rick didn't need my help to find out what was up with his ex-wife. I was sure he had plenty of official ways to search.

And Doug Guilfoyle? I hardly knew him. Sure, we had gone to college together, but only been casual acquaintances. Somehow, though, I had gotten involved in both situations. Lili had her own ideas why – she thought I was not only curious, but that growing up Jewish, going to Sunday School and studying Torah, had given me an impulse toward social justice, making things right for those who had been wronged.

Lili had said the night before that she understood my impulses to help people even if they led me into illegal behavior. I couldn't blame that on my upbringing, because my parents had been law-abiding citizens.

By the time Rochester and I got back into the house Lili had gotten over whatever she felt and I was grateful that we could snuggle together. There was so much sadness in the world—divorce, illness, and death—and it was nice to have found my own refuge with my sweetheart and my dog.

15 – INVESTMENT ADVICE

Thursday was quiet at Friar Lake, as if the property was holding its breath waiting for the influx of middle-school students the next day. I spent most of the morning on preparation for Kids Code—signs to print, tables to set out and so on, but eventually I was able to go back to the Excel files Doug had downloaded for me, and the hyperlinked one I'd found the password for. There were twenty properties in the Beauceron REIT portfolio, and I put them in alphabetical order and began examining them.

Absecon Promenade was an outlet mall down the Jersey Shore, anchored by several retailers I recognized and a whole lot I didn't. It was moderately profitable, and the numbers on both spreadsheets matched.

Briarwood Forum was an office complex in northeast New Jersey, showing 98% occupancy and steady revenues. Again, the numbers on both sheets matched. I went through the next four properties on the list, and everything seemed kosher. Maybe the strip center Doug had stumbled on was the anomaly, and the rest of Beauceron's portfolio was performing as advertised.

Then I got to Garden City Center on Long Island, another strip mall on the Jericho Turnpike. It was anchored at one end by Tranny

Man Transmissions and at the other by a Chinese restaurant called Wok This Way. A quick Google search showed that Wok This Way had closed down after repeated health violations, and an article in *Newsday* mentioned a protest against the transmission company by a group of LGBT activists.

The numbers on the public sheet didn't match those on the protected sheet. As with Route One Plaza, there was little income coming in from the property, though Beauceron represented it as a thriving investment.

I was encouraged. So the problems with Beauceron's REIT ran deeper than a single under-performing property. It was only the second piece of evidence, but it encouraged me to continue farther along.

Catherine Guilfoyle called my cell phone late in the morning. "I'm not bothering you, am I?" she asked. "I can call back this evening."

"No, no bother. What's up?"

"Can you do me a favor? I have so many things to take care of, and Hannah and Tammy have been urging me to delegate. Doug's boss told me there's a box of Doug's stuff at the office. Could you could pick it up for me? In case there's important papers or anything the kids should have."

I told her I'd be happy to handle it, then called Shawn and explained about Catherine's request. He said I was welcome to come up as soon as I wanted to.

Rochester put his head on my leg and stared up at me. "Doug mentioned that you bring your dog to work," I said. "I do, too, so I have my golden with me now. Would it be all right if I brought him with me?"

"No problem. Chocolat loves to play with other dogs."

I went back to work on the Beauceron spreadsheets, and by the time I had to leave to meet Shawn I had identified six suspect properties out of the twenty that the fund had invested in. That made this definitely a big problem.

I was eager to see what kind of operation Shawn Brumberger had created, and as Rochester and I drove a zigzag route through the countryside, I wondered how he'd let things go so far. When the first property tanked, why not just take the loss and move on?

Then I remembered the way that he'd named both his kids after himself—Shawna and Shawn Jr. Somebody with an ego that big probably could not handle failure well. I knew from my own experience how easy it could be to ignore reality and push forward— in my case until I landed behind bars. Would Shawn end up the same way?

The office park where Beauceron rented space was about a mile off I-95, in a two-story building set back off the road and surrounded by trees sprouting new leaves. It resembled the kind of barns that were still around when I was a kid – slat siding, peaked roof, little windows under the eaves.

I introduced myself and Rochester to the receptionist, and a few minutes later, Shawn came out with a big black shepherd by his side. "It's always best for Chocolat to meet new dogs outside of his own territory," he said, as the two dogs sniffed each other.

Chocolat was alert and confident-looking, with reddish tan socks and half-pricked ears. Rochester went down on his front paws in the play position, and Chocolat woofed once, then sniffed Rochester's ear.

"Good, they're going to get along," Shawn said as we watched the dogs.

"How long have you guys been here?" I asked.

"Five years," he said. "And business gets better and better every year."

Since it was almost five o'clock the stock markets were closed, so maybe that was why the Beauceron suite was as quiet as a mortuary. No phones ringing, no voices coming from the other offices. "You probably do a lot of your business online," I said.

"Nope. We do things the old-fashioned way. If you're our client, we walk you through all your decisions. Our reps give their customers their personal cell numbers, and they can reach us any time for investment advice or to make new purchases."

"That sounds like the kind of company I'd want to do business with." As I said it, I realized that talking with Shawn might give me some further insight into what kind of shady stuff was going on at Beauceron—which I could feed to Rick.

He looked at me. "You interested in investing?"

"Doug's seminar motivated me," I said. "I was going to ask him for some advice, but maybe you could help me out instead."

"Certainly. Why don't you look through Doug's stuff, and when you're finished Vanessa can buzz me."

He led me into a pretty barren office just behind the reception area. "I had my assistant put together Doug's things. Not much, but there might be something there his kids want."

"Thanks. I'm sure they'll appreciate it."

He and the dog left, and I sat behind Doug's desk. There was no computer, and I wondered if the laptop he'd brought to Friar Lake was the only one he used. It was clear that Shawn's assistant had cleared out any material that might have been confidential, leaving behind only a fancy multi-line phone, an empty in-and-out box, and assorted office supplies.

Rochester walked around the office as I looked through the box Shawn's assistant had packed. A leatherette folder of business cards, a day planner, and a coffee mug with #1 Dad on it. A couple of expensive pens with commemorative inscriptions, and a sterling silver picture frame with a photo of Ethan and Madison in it. Not much to sum up a career.

I flipped through the card holder. A lot of the cards were from folks in Manhattan, Westchester County and North Jersey. They were a mixed bag, from a community college professor to Wall Street types to the manager of a car wash. I was about to flip past that one when I read the name – Alex Vargas.

Was it the same Alex Tiffany was dating? Wouldn't that be weird?

I looked at the address of the operation—it was in Hoboken, and I knew Doug had lived there for a while. Maybe he'd just picked up the card when he got his car washed one day. How could I find out if it was the same guy?

Rochester was nosing around the garbage can beside Doug's desk. A couple of crumpled pieces of paper sat at the bottom, and I picked them up. They were from a notepad with the Beauceron logo, in what looked like Doug's handwriting. I smoothed them out but rather than read them right there I put them in the box with the rest of Doug's stuff.

I went back to the receptionist and she buzzed Shawn, then led me and Rochester to his office, which was larger and more impressive than Doug's, with a big picture window that looked out at the wooded area behind the complex.

The dogs sniffed each other once more, then Rochester rolled onto his back, his legs up in the air. Chocolat stood on top of him, preparing to hump him, but Rochester wriggled out from underneath and they began to romp around the office.

"Tell me about your investment strategy in the past," Shawn said, after we'd watched the dogs for a moment or two.

"I haven't really had one," I said, thinking as fast as I could. "But listening to Doug speak at the seminar got me thinking, and then over the weekend I was talking to someone I know, a guy named

Alex Vargas, and he said he invested with Doug and the fund he was in was doing well."

"You remember which fund?"

I shook my head. "Any way you can find out which one? If it's such a good one I might want to put some money into it."

"Let me look in our client base and see where he's invested. What was the name again?"

"Either Alex or Alejandro Vargas."

He typed and then said, "He's in our REIT. You're right, we've been getting excellent returns on that fund."

It was an interesting fact, but I had no idea what it meant, if it was relevant at all. I listened with only half my brain as Shawn made a pitch for the fund, and accepted a glossy folder about Beauceron and all its funds. "If you have a blank check with you, we can get your account set up right now," Shawn said.

"I need to talk to my fiancée," I said. Though Lili and I had no immediate plans for marriage, it gave her opinion more weight than calling her a girlfriend.

"No hurry," Shawn said. "But remember, time is money! You can't start earning those excellent returns until you make your first investment."

It was interesting the way that Shawn had slipped into his slick pitch from our previous conversation about Doug. And he hadn't mentioned anything about losing Doug, or needing to replace him.

On my way home, I thought about the potential profits Shawn

had mentioned. Were they real, or just illusory? I'd have to finish my analysis of the spreadsheets and properties before I could make that judgment, though certainly six properties with suspicious returns indicated real problems.

It was interesting to learn that Tiffany's boyfriend had invested with Doug—but did it mean anything? If I told Rick, would he think it was important, or would he say my imagination was running away again?

When I got home, I carried the box of Doug's stuff inside with me and set it down on the dining room table. After Rochester and I had both kissed Lili hello, I said, "Catherine called me today and asked me to pick up Doug's effects from his office. I talked to his boss for a few minutes, too."

"That was nice of you," she said. "I was talking to Tamsen today. Catherine's kids are broken up over their father's death. She said the kids really liked Rochester and she wanted to know if we could come over this weekend with him. Give the kids something to think about besides their dad."

"That's a great idea," I said. "We can drop off this stuff then."

I was curious to talk to Catherine anyway. She certainly had a reason to want Doug dead. What if Doug had called her from the bar, after he finished with Shawn? He wouldn't be the first guy to drunk-dial an ex—after all, Tiffany had done that with Rick a few months before. Suppose she agreed to meet him at the canal, and then, knowing his fear of water, pushed him in?

It was a big step to kill anyone, no less someone you'd once loved, who had fathered your children. I figured I ought to be grateful Mary had walked away from me when I went into prison. Was Catherine that angry, that extreme?

Lili and I talked as we threw together dinner, then ate. The students in her photography class had compiled portfolios of their best shots, then had to write critical essays about which photographers they'd studied during the term had most influenced them. It was slow going because she was not only reviewing their photos and their papers, she was comparing their work to their influences to see if they were on target.

"Can I do anything to help you?"

"Find somebody to grade the rest of these papers. Any bum on the street will do."

"Come on. They aren't that bad."

"Let me read you a couple of excerpts." She opened the messenger bag she took back and forth to Eastern with her. "I printed some out specially for you. Here's a good one. 'I didn't read any of the essays on Dorothea Lange because they were all written in the past, and I believe in looking ahead, not backwards.' Or 'I chose to photograph animals for my project because they have been around for a while'."

"I can top that. One of my students once wrote, 'Moses and Steve Jobs are the same thing because they both came up with tablets and started revolutions.'"

She shook her head and laughed. "That is wrong on so many levels."

After she went upstairs to continue grading, I cleaned up the kitchen. That Lady Gaga song had become an earworm, and I kept hearing that phrase again and again about Alejandro.

That made me wonder if there were more connections between Doug Guilfoyle and Alex Vargas. I opened my laptop and put their names together in quotes, but nothing came up. I went back to Tiffany's Facebook page and scanned through all her photos again, looking for Doug's face, in case he'd been in the background of one of her bar shots.

No luck there either. The idea that the connection had to matter kept tantalizing me, though. But how could I get Rick to ask Tiffany about it? Would he believe there was a connection?

16 – KIDS CODE

Soon after Rochester and I arrived at Friar Lake on Friday morning, the first of two yellow school buses pulled up. I put Rochester on his leash and walked out to greet the clusters of chattering excited kids, a mix of boys and girls from around ten to twelve, predominantly white, but with a couple of Asian, Indian and African-Americans as well.

With a pang, I realized that if Mary's first pregnancy had come to term, I'd have a child of about that age. Would he have been a boy like that one there, with floppy brown hair like I'd had as a kid? I'd been skinny then, awkward in my own skin, but these kids seemed supremely confident, talking and laughing with each other. Would Doug's kids grow up that way, or had his death scarred them too much?

Rochester tugged on his leash, straining to back away from the buses, and I was surprised. He normally loved kids and attention, but maybe the presence of so many of them was freaking him out.

"I guess you don't want to be part of the welcoming committee," I said. "Fine, be that way." I took him back to the gatehouse, where he took up a position under my desk.

Once he was settled, I walked out to the computer classroom, where I found Joey had already opened the door and was helping Yesenia make sure everything was working properly. I stood in the doorway and scanned the crowd of kids. Some had brought their own laptops, while others carried thick books about programming. A couple of them were talking eagerly about Boolean data, the basics of if/then statements in computer languages. Another boy was explaining the concept of reverse ciphers to a small group – the way that the letters of the alphabet were reversed – A swapped for Z and so on.

Yesenia had opened a presentation about Python, an open-source programming language, on the screen beside the podium. I was impressed. These kids were way more advanced than I'd been at their ages.

I sat through most of Yesenia's introduction to Python, and it was cute to see the kids taking notes so industriously, writing down maxims of the language like "simple is better than complex" and "beautiful is better than ugly."

It reminded me of my own training in HTML, where I'd been taught to make my code as readable as possible, indenting tables and rows so that it was easy to follow the structure visually.

I missed doing that kind of coding, and I wondered how I could get back to it. In my Silicon Valley days, I'd been able to go deep into the zone as I coded, shutting out everything else as I typed and visualized, tested and corrected.

After an hour or so, I slipped out to the chapel, where I helped one of the volunteer moms set up mid-morning snacks and box lunches, but I kept thinking about how I could return to the simple coding I had enjoyed so much.

I'd done some freelance web design work back in the day, before the advent of the more complicated technology. It was doubtful that I'd be able to go back to school and learn all that, but maybe I could do some work on the Friar Lake website myself instead of relying on the college's programming team.

It was nearly eleven o'clock by the time I returned to my office, where Rochester was skittering around the room anxiously. "What's the matter, puppy?" I sat on the floor beside him and scratched under his neck. "Too much excitement for you?"

He nuzzled my face and I laughed. After I rubbed his belly for a while he spread out on the floor and went to sleep, and I got up, my joints creaking, and sat at my desk. But Rochester's fidgetiness had infected me, and I worried about all those kids using the brand-new computers the college had sprung for in setting up Friar Lake.

I walked back to the classroom and peered through the window. The kids were all working industriously, some typing on their own, others clustered in small groups.

Was Yesenia training the next generation of hackers? She'd been born in Cuba, after all, and I remembered all the material I'd read about how many Cuban-Americans were involved in illicit activities.

I shook my head. I was stereotyping and letting my imagination run away with me. Yesenia Cruz was simply a mom with computer skills who wanted to pass her knowledge on to the next generation. I ought to be praising her, not suspecting her motives.

As I watched, she called a lunch break, and I followed the kids over to the chapel, where I sat with Yesenia at one of the small round tables we used for cocktail receptions. "You have such a pretty name," I said. "Does Yesenia mean something in Spanish?"

She shook her head. "When I was born, during the Cold War, lots of parents used Russian-inspired names starting with Y, like Yuri and Yulia," she said. "And then the trend spread, so that when I was in school almost everyone I knew had a name that began with Y. My best friends were a boy called Yadinnis and a girl called Yoani."

That name rang a bell, and it took me a moment to remember that Yoani was the name of the woman who had preceded Tiffany at the Center for Infusion Therapy. "So someone named Yoani would be Cuban?" I asked. I didn't know why that mattered—after all, the CIT was in Union City so it wouldn't be unusual if there were Cuban-Americans working there.

"Almost certainly," she said. "You know someone by that name?"

"Not directly. A friend of a friend." I picked up my sandwich. "I think it's awesome that you're providing this opportunity for kids. Are you a programmer?"

"I have my own computer consulting business," she said. "I present a lot of seminars to corporations about email security. You'd be astonished how many computer savvy people still click on links that can install malware on their networks."

I wouldn't be surprised at all, because I'd taken advantage of that myself, but I wasn't going to come clean about it to Yesenia.

"For one client, I send out a message every month or two that has a link in it that downloads a program, and even though I've lectured and lectured, still about five to ten percent of the staff click on it."

"Did you learn all that in Cuba?" I asked.

"At first, yes. I went to a special school where a teacher from Moscow taught us how to use Russian ES EVM computers. When I came to Philadelphia as a teenager, I tried to sign up for an advanced course. I was told girls did not use computers. Especially not Latina girls."

I heard the gentle lilt in her voice, the lack of contractions that was often typical of a second-language learner. "Wow. Someone actually told you that?"

She nodded. "The principal of the Catholic school thought I was Puerto Rican, because most of the Latins in Philadelphia come from there. He said I was just going to get pregnant before I even graduated so why bother? I had to tell him that I am Cuban, that my people are smart and hard-working. Eventually he let me take a very basic course. It was hard because it was in English but I already understood how computers operated so I was able to do very well. By the time I graduated I knew several languages and a lot of very high-level math."

"Sounds like you got a good preparation," I said. "And you had good mentors."

"It's a shame, because in many places Cubans have a bad reputation," she said. "There is a lot of economic fraud committed by my people, so Anglos are still suspicious of Cuban programmers. I hope to make good changes with Kids Code."

"I've been a high school teacher and an adjunct professor, so I'm all in favor of education," I said. "If you need to, I hope you'll come back to Friar Lake in the future. Maybe we can even involve some of our students as mentors to yours."

"This afternoon they are going to put together their own routines in Python, and it would be great in the future to have a peer to check them."

"What kind of routines?"

"I give them about two dozen choices, everything from simply adding two numbers to checking to see if a phrase is a palindrome or not, depending on if their interests are in math or in computer language in general."

After lunch I went back to my office and opened up a web browser to look at the Friar Lake webpage. It was laid out like every other page on the Eastern College site—same header and footer, same links down the left side.

I had written the text, and the programmer I'd worked with had put together the list of courses and online registration forms. But the overall effect was bland and corporate, and I started brainstorming ways to make it more interactive. Once I had a roster of programs behind me, I could include seminar photos and testimonials.

I needed to beef up the information on faculty I had recruited to lead programs. Right now the links simply led to their computer-generated faculty pages, which listed their credentials and the courses they taught.

It was great to get so involved in my work again, in a way I hadn't felt since I'd begun creating the programs for Friar Lake to offer. I enjoyed focusing my attention on something other than mortality and malfeasance, though Doug Guilfoyle and the circumstances of his death still floated in the back of my mind.

17 – SKID MARKS

Rick called me that night soon after I got home. "This morning we got a call from one of the store owners at the Old Mill," he said. "There was a break-in last night, and some cash and small items were stolen from a couple of the stores."

I wondered why Rick was calling to tell me. Surely he didn't think I knew anything about such an event?

"While I was there, I walked back to the canal. I watched the current for a while and then back-tracked from where Doug Guilfoyle's body surfaced. I found the place where it looks like he slipped into the water. I talked to the chief and based on Mr. Guilfoyle's personal situation, the comments about his mental state from his boss, and the consumption of alcohol at the bar, we're calling this a suicide."

"I don't believe that." It just didn't make sense to me that he'd kill himself while he was right in the middle of figuring out what was going on at Beauceron, just as he'd moved to town and reestablished his relationship with his kids.

"Believe what you want, pal. That's the official line. I'm sorry for what this might do to Catherine and her kids, but I can't help it."

I couldn't just let it go, though. If someone had killed Doug because of what was going on at Beauceron, I owed it to him to follow through on his suspicions. And even if he'd killed himself, or slipped into the canal by accident, what I discovered, and the possibility that innocent people could be protected from nefarious actions, would give Doug's death some meaning.

I was about to bring up those points, but Rick surprised me by asking, "Say, are you busy on Sunday?"

"Not as far as I know. Why?"

"Tiffany wants to get together, and honestly, I don't want to see her on my own. I'd ask Tamsen to go but she's helping Catherine with the funeral arrangements."

I was intrigued. I'd heard about Tiffany ever since Rick and I reconnected and I was curious to meet her in person. "Sure. When and where?"

"She wants me to come up to this place where she's living in Weehawken," he said. "Suppose I pick you up at eleven?"

"We taking the dogs?"

"Not a chance. Tiffany hates dogs. I was hoping I could leave Rascal with Lili."

"That's something I need to clear with her," I said. "Hold on."

Lili said she could manage Rascal for a couple of hours on Sunday, and I relayed that information back to Rick.

"Good deal. Catch you on the flip side."

He hung up, and I wondered what kind of drama he was about to get into. At least I'd have a front row seat to it.

Lili motioned to a place on the sofa beside her and put down the book she'd been reading, a mystery novel I'd recommended to her, about a policeman determined to do his job in the face of an oncoming asteroid that was going to destroy the planet. "Where are you and Rick going? Investigating something?"

"Not really." I told her that Tiffany wanted to see Rick in person, and that he'd asked me to go along.

"Is he scared of her? He doesn't want to see her by himself?" she asked.

"How would you feel if I said I was going to see Mary?"

"You're a different story," Lili said. "You're over Mary, and she's over you."

I turned sideways to face her, and we twined our legs together. "You don't think Rick is over Tiffany?"

"Rick and Tiffany are tied together in a co-dependent relationship," she said. "At least that's what I get from talking to him, and to Tamsen. Tiffany sounds like one of those heroines from a telenovela who's always getting into trouble. I wouldn't be surprised if she tried something with Rick."

"Rick's a good guy. And he's too smart to get tangled up with Tiffany again."

Rochester settled on the floor beside us. "Rick's a guy," Lili said. "And Tiffany's pretty, and needy. Guys like Rick fall for that damsel in distress business. I just hope Tamsen's willing to put up with the occasional interference from the ex."

My mind was racing. "How do you know that Tiffany's pretty?"

I'd seen her photo on Facebook, but hadn't paid much attention to it.

"Rick has a picture of the two of them in his house. You never saw it?"

"Oh, yeah. That one where they're at the Grand Canyon." I shrugged. "Honestly, she's not my type so I never noticed her."

"Really?" she asked, stroking my thigh with her bare foot. "What is your type?"

I smiled. "Tall. Beautiful. Smart."

She pulled her foot back in mock anger. "Like Tamsen?"

I reached across and moved her foot onto my thigh again. "Tamsen's great. But she can't hold a candle to a certain woman I know." I began massaging her foot, and she sighed with pleasure.

Then Rochester jumped up on the couch between us, settling his big hulk over our legs. We extricated our limbs from beneath him, and he woofed once and then rested his head on my lap. "You want your dinner, boy?" I asked.

He jumped up and raced across the floor to the kitchen. "There's my answer." I leaned down to kiss Lili. "We'll have to continue this conversation later."

"I'll look forward to it," she said, and picked up her book again.

We were willing to accept neediness from Rochester—his desire to cuddle with us, his demands for food and walks. But we frowned at such overt demands from the others in our lives. Would Tiffany always have a hold on Rick because of her personality and his need to take care of her?

Honest to Dog

***

Saturday morning Rochester and I walked into downtown Stewart's Crossing, pausing at the Chocolate Ear for a grande raspberry mocha and a dog biscuit to go. Then we continued down Main Street to the corner of Ferry, where the Drunken Hessian occupied the northeast corner. The bar wouldn't open until eleven, so its parking lot was empty, just a few cars spilling over from the drugstore and the IGA grocery. So Rochester and I took a shortcut through the lot, down to the water's edge.

If I were Doug, out for a walk to clear my head, where would I go? It would have been dark on Tuesday night, and there were no street lights down by the canal. The only illumination would have come from the windows of the bar and the houses on the other side of the canal.

Rochester and I walked along the far edge of the parking lot toward the Old Mill. When Rick and I were kids, the fieldstone grist mill in the center of Stewart's Crossing had been a wreck, but during the Eighties a developer had renovated it into a mini-mall. I'd been inside once, years before, but since I didn't need handmade jewelry, postcards of ducks crossing Main Street or tie-dyed T-shirts, I'd never been back.

A thin screen of sassafras and skinny maples just coming into leaf stood between us and the water. A weeping willow marked the boundary between the Drunken Hessian's lot and the one belonging to the Old Mill.

157

Rochester pulled forward until we reached a break in the tree line, where he sat down and scratched his flank with his hind leg. Just beyond him, the pavement disintegrated into a rough scree of tiny pebbles and dirt, and when I looked closely I saw faint footprints, a bit elongated, as if someone had slipped through. That must have been what Rick found.

Satisfied that he'd scratched that itch, Rochester stood up and nosed around the area, keeping well away from the canal and its fast current. The water was too murky to see the bottom clearly but it was pretty deep there as the mill race spilled into the canal.

The water continued to flow over a mossy lip, tumbling into a tiny waterfall. If Doug had slipped a few feet either way, he might have fallen down the slope to the stream below, rather than into the canal. He might have broken an arm or leg, but he wouldn't have drowned.

Was it just bad luck that he'd lost his balance right there? Why hadn't he heard the noise of the water, as I did? Had there had been music coming out of the Drunken Hessian that masked it?

Doug was skittish around water, so he wouldn't have gotten that close to the edge of the mill race. Could he have lost his way in the darkness, not realized he was so close? He might have felt he was far enough from the canal to be safe.

When I looked around for Rochester, he was sitting on his haunches once again, this time chewing something. "No sticks or rocks," I said. I reached down and pried his jaws open, and retrieved a small plastic llama, about two inches wide. It was such an odd thing to find that I was surprised, and I turned it around in my hand. He hadn't had a chance to destroy it—there were just a couple of teeth marks on the llama's legs.

The llama's back legs were hinged, and when I pressed on them a USB port popped out of the animal's butt. I laughed. I'd seen jump drives in all kinds of shapes from dogs to dice, but I'd never seen a llama. The text on the animal's flank read "Phone Llama – unlocked GSM cells."

Had Rochester found another clue, as he often did? I pocketed the drive so I could check out its contents at home.

Then he and I walked back to where I'd parked. I wasn't convinced that Doug had committed suicide, or that he had fallen into the canal accidentally. To me, it looked like murder, and I was determined to find the truth, for Doug's sake, and so his kids would know, too.

Neil S. Plakcy

18 – HAZARD ZONE

When I got home, I checked the box of stuff I'd brought home from Doug's office, looking for clues to his mental state, and once again I was struck by how little he'd left behind.

His day planner was a thick leather-bound book the size of a hefty paperback novel, with metal rings inside so he could add or remove pages. I started at the beginning of the year, flipping through lists of prospects he met with, noting the way he had marked off the alternate Tuesdays and Saturdays he had with his kids.

There were no ominous notes, nothing worrying about anyone he met with. There were occasional scribbled messages but nothing that indicated his state of mind, or an inclination toward suicide.

I went back through his collection of business cards, and then pulled out the pieces of crumpled paper I'd picked up from Doug's wastebasket. It was a list of upcoming events—his kids' birthdays, Ethan's high school graduation in June, a Broadway play he wanted to take Madison to.

Was that the list of a man about to commit suicide? I didn't think so. He was looking forward to the future, coming up with ways to connect better with his kids.

An hour later, Rochester and I headed over to Catherine's house. I was dreading the grief I would find there, but I knew it was my responsibility to deliver the box, and to provide whatever comfort I could to the grieving. That tradition had been built into me as a kid, going to family funerals and sitting shiva—the process Jews go through after a death, when family and friends gather to mourn together.

At the last minute, Lili had to back out of accompanying me. Grading those student portfolios was taking way more time than she had expected, and the clock was ticking on getting her final grades in. "Kiss them for me and tell them I'll see them at the funeral on Monday," she said. "And that we'll all get together after graduation, when life is easier."

I promised to do so. As I drove toward Catherine's, I marveled once again at how much the area had changed since I was a kid. When I was born, most of the area around Stewart's Crossing was farmland. The opening of the section of I-95 to the Scudder Falls Bridge eased a commute from Lower Bucks County to Philadelphia, and as I grew up, more and more of those farms were converted to housing developments.

Valley Heights, the development where Catherine had bought a house, had sprung up in the eighties, and all the streets were named after famous mountains. Catherine's house was a three-bedroom split level at the corner of Everest Drive and Denali Way.

Madison answered the door, her shoulders drooping and her head down. Only when she saw Rochester did she smile. He stepped forward and nuzzled her. "I like your dog," she said, as she scratched him behind the ears. "Ethan has Pixie up in his room and he won't let me see her. Can I take Rochester for a walk?"

"Sure. Just hold on to his leash." I handed the lead to her and Rochester tugged her forward down the driveway. Catherine appeared in front of us as I heard Madison begin what I was sure would be a long, one-sided conversation with the dog.

I tried to hand the box of Doug's stuff to Catherine, but she looked at it like it was nuclear contamination. "Unless there's something in there I need to know about, I don't want any of it," she said, backing away. She wore a pair of jeans and a dark blue T-shirt, a probable compromise against the all-black of mourning.

"No papers of note," I said. "How about if I give it to Ethan? He might want something of his dad's."

"If you want. He's up in his room sulking with Pixie."

I couldn't blame him; I used Rochester for comfort a lot myself. "How are you holding up?" I asked.

"I didn't expect to feel so much grief," she said, as we walked into the living room. "I was so angry at Doug for so long, before and after the divorce, and now I realize I was using that anger to shield myself from the pain. Now that I can't be angry at him anymore, it's all coming home."

I hugged her, and she rested her head on my shoulder for a moment. "I know it's hard," I said. "I was a zombie for a while after my father died." I backed away. "I was in prison then, and all I could think of was how much I had disappointed him."

"I'm trying to hold it together," Catherine said. "For the kids' sake. But it's even harder than pretending everything was all right as my marriage was falling apart."

"How about the kids. How are they doing?" I asked, as we sat.

"They've been through the wringer, I'll tell you. First the divorce, then the move away from all their friends. Now this. Thank God I have Jimmy. He's been a rock the last few days. I can see how good he must be in his classroom because he's great with Ethan and Maddie."

"Jimmy?"

"Jimmy Burns. One of the first things I did when we moved here was look for a writers' critique group. Jimmy teaches English at George School and he writes kids' books. He's been running this group for a while. We really connected."

So he was the new boyfriend Madison had told her father about, and who Tamsen had also mentioned—the one who didn't have two nickels to rub together. "I'm glad," I said. "I want you to know that you can count on Lili and me, too. If you want to send Maddie and Ethan over to us sometime to play with Rochester so you can have some time to yourself."

"That's very sweet of you," she said. "I had to stop writing when all this started happening, and I need to get going again. But it's tough to find the time. I can manage about an hour in the morning while the kids are in school, but then there's laundry and shopping and running them around to sports."

"Other writers I know say it's important to set up a schedule."

She nodded. "Tammy says the same thing. Doug used to take the kids every other Tuesday night, and she volunteered to have them over for dinner on the nights they weren't with him, so I could focus for a couple of hours. Fortunately Ethan got his license a few months ago so he can drive them over there."

Tuesday night. "So they were at Tamsen's the night Doug died?"

She nodded. "Maddy said that if she and Ethan had been with Daddy he wouldn't have fallen in the water. I haven't told them that the police think it was suicide. They're upset enough already."

With Ethan and Madison out of the house on the night Doug died, Catherine probably did not have an alibi. Suppose Doug had been feeling maudlin after all the alcohol, and he'd called to talk to the kids. Could Catherine have agreed to come out and meet him by the canal, then seized the opportunity to push him in? Was she that terrible a person?

Once again, I was letting my imagination get away from me. I pushed that thought ahead as Madison came back into the house with Rochester. "Your dog is strong," she said. "He pulls a lot more than Pixie does."

"You think Pixie would want to play with Rochester?" I asked.

Madison twirled a couple of plastic bands around her wrist. "I dunno."

"Come on. Why don't we see if Ethan will let Pixie out."

I followed her up the stairs, where she stopped in front of a door with a nuclear hazard sign on it. "My mom got Ethan that sign because he doesn't like to clean up his room," Madison said. "I clean mine every day."

"I'm sure your mom appreciates that." I knocked on the door. "Ethan? It's Steve Levitan and Rochester."

Rochester put his nose down to the doorsill and sniffed, and from inside we heard the Yorkie's shrill bark.

Ethan opened the door. His hair was unkempt and it looked like he hadn't washed his face in a while. A few dark hairs sprouted from his chin, and my heart choked up as I realized Doug wouldn't be around to teach him to shave.

"You can't come in," Ethan said, but Rochester didn't pay him any attention, just shoved right past him to romp around with Pixie.

The knuckles of Ethan's right hand were scraped, as if he'd been hitting something, or someone. Had he been hitting his father? Fighting with him?

Behind Ethan I saw a pile of T-shirts and jeans on the floor, an open backpack with school books spilling out of it, a pair of barbells in the corner. "You want to come out to the back yard and let the dogs play?" I asked. "We could toss around a Frisbee or a tennis ball."

"I'm in the middle of a game," he said, nodding back toward his computer.

Pixie dashed out into the hallway, followed by Rochester. "This is a box of your dad's stuff from his office," I said. I held the box out, embarrassed at its lack of contents, but Ethan glanced at it and took it from me. Then he stepped back and slammed his door shut.

"My mom says Ethan is acting out," Madison said, as the two dogs raced down the stairs.

"Sometimes it's hard to come right out and say what we're feeling," I said. "Especially when we're sad, or angry. So we do things to distract us from what hurts. That's probably what your mom means."

"Every time I think about my dad, it makes me sad. But my dad always told me and Ethan that we had to be nice to Mommy because the divorce was hard for her, so I try not to cry in front of her."

"That's brave of you," I said. "But I'm sure that your mom wants to know how you're feeling, so it's okay to cry when you feel bad. Maybe she needs to cry sometimes too, and she's afraid to show you. If you cry together it will make both of you feel better."

She didn't say anything, but I could see from her face that she was processing the information. "Now let's go play with Rochester and Pixie," I said.

She and I took the dogs into the back yard, threw balls for them, and watched them romp around. It was funny to see my big dog cowed by the Yorkie, who yipped sharply whenever he did something she didn't like. I looked up at the back of the house once and noticed Ethan watching us, but as soon as he saw me he turned back into the room and pulled down the shade.

When Madison and the dogs were tired out, we all went back

inside. I wanted to leave, but Catherine had brewed a pot of coffee and brought out an Entenmann's cake. It reminded me of when I was a kid and my aunts and uncles, or my mother's cousins, would drop by for coffee, conversation and a piece of Entenmann's.

Madison took her piece of cake up to her room, and I joined Catherine at the table. "Are you going to be able to stay here in Stewart's Crossing?" I asked, between bites of coffee cake. "It would be tough for the kids to have to move again."

"I can't imagine giving up my support network here," she said. "It's great to have cousins like Tammy and Hannah so close. I should be able to manage, though I'm going to have to look for a job."

She picked up her coffee cup but waited to take a sip. "Back when Doug and I were divorcing, my attorney fought for Doug to take out a five-million-dollar life insurance policy. The interest on the payout was supposed to replace my alimony and child support in case anything happened to him."

She sipped her coffee. "Back then I was worried that Doug worked so hard he might give himself a heart attack. I had no idea something like this would happen."

Five million dollars. That was a seven-figure-motive for murder, especially if Catherine wanted to remarry and knew that would cause her to lose her alimony.

"You're coming to the Meeting for Worship on Monday, aren't you?" Catherine asked. "That's the Quaker equivalent of a funeral. Even though Doug didn't have any religious belief, it will be good for the kids. It would be nice to have someone there who knew Doug when he was younger. Maybe you could say a few words about him."

Lili had already said she wanted to go to the funeral, so I'd been planning on it. I was touched that Catherine asked me to speak. I couldn't tell the story of our drunken, naked romp around Birthday House, and I didn't want to speak about Doug's suspicions about Beauceron. "I'll think of something," I said.

Ethan and Maddy were both suffering the loss of their father. I wanted his children to remember Doug well. I'd truly have to consider what I wanted to say, knowing that the memory of that service would be with them for the rest of their lives.

When Rochester and I got home, I was feeling the weight of grief, and I spent some time on the floor playing tug-a-rope with him. At one point, he backed away from me, tugging hard, his tail wagging like mad. It brushed something off the coffee table, which landed on the tile floor with a clatter.

I let Rochester have the rope and leaned down to pick it up. It was the jump drive he had found by the canal, the one from a company called Phone Llama. Since I wasn't sure what was on the drive I didn't want to risk sticking it into my regular computer, so I pulled Caroline's laptop from the closet. Because of the kind of sites I surfed with it, I'd installed a lot of extra security provisions on it.

I got no malware warnings, so I clicked on the directory to see what was on it. I was disappointed that all it appeared to hold were a bunch of pictures of someone's kids. A boy in a baseball uniform stood at home plate holding a bat. A younger girl in a princess dress. Family parties, kids at play. No one in the photos looked familiar, and even the backgrounds didn't ring a bell with me.

Where had the drive come from? I Googled the company name, and came up with a website in Spanish. The left column contained a cartoon of a llama like the one the jump drive resembled. The animal held a cell phone against one ear with his front leg. A speech bubble coming its mouth read "*Llámame!*"

I used the automatic translate feature from my browser, but all I could find was what I expected. They sold unlocked GSM phones. Since I didn't know that Doug was planning an overseas trip, or needed to make calls to foreign countries, I figured it was a dead end.

Well, not all the clues Rochester found could be good ones, right? Sometimes he was just a dog looking for something to chew, or something that smelled good. Even so, I'd hold onto the drive in case it came to matter.

19 – WHAT RICKY LIKES

Sunday morning Rick picked me up and we headed up I-95 to where it connected with the Jersey turnpike.

"How did you end up marrying Tiffany, anyway?" I asked, as we rode. "Was she as much of a train wreck back then?"

"She's not a train wreck. She's just – got issues." He swerved around a slow-moving car driven by an old man so short his head didn't make it over the seat back. "I dated girls in high school," he said after a while. "And they were okay, but Tiffany was in a whole other league. She was gorgeous and lively and so sexy. I couldn't figure out what she saw in me. We'd go out dancing and man, the way she moved when she was next to me. And she spoke this thing she called Spanglish, mostly English but throwing in all these Spanish words and phrases. We went to a party in North Philly once, and stayed until it was almost dawn, and then she convinced me to drive into Center City and run up the steps of the Art Museum like Rocky."

He turned to me. "She made me feel alive, like the whole world was out there for the taking. She encouraged me to go to the police academy in Philadelphia. We moved in with her parents while I did, and she was so excited when I got a job in the city."

"You worked for the Philly police?" I asked. "I didn't know that."

"Just for a year, walking a beat in Market East, around the Reading Terminal. I hated the noise and grime and congestion in the city, though, and when I got the chance to come back to Stewart's Crossing I took it."

He shook his head. "That was probably the beginning of the end for me and Tiff. She couldn't find the food she liked in the grocery. Didn't make any friends, said people looked down at her because of her Philly accent and her Spanglish. Then I got my detective's shield and she said I'd turned into a boring old man, and she couldn't take it anymore."

It was the first time Rick had ever talked in any detail about his marriage. It was a good sign, that he was finally able to speak about it and put it in the past.

We hopped on the turnpike, through the area that most people think of when you say New Jersey – oil refineries and run-down apartment buildings jammed up against the roadway, a permanent smoggy haze in the air. I crossed my arms over my chest and looked out the window.

Rick handed me his phone. "She messaged me the directions. Can you read them?"

I told him to take I-495 toward the Lincoln Tunnel. Tiffany had ended her message with a bunch of emoticons—little hearts and kisses. Guess she wasn't bitter about their divorce, or at least she wasn't anymore.

We got off the highway at John F. Kennedy Boulevard and headed south, toward the border of Hoboken and Union City. Since I had Rick's phone in my hand, I used it to check the address for the Center for Infusion Therapy.

"The clinic where Tiffany worked is up ahead on the right," I said, as we approached it. "That low white building with the yellow ramp in front."

The signs were in both English and Spanish, and small decals pasted beside the front door advertised the insurance they accepted.

"Small building," I said. "They must not see a lot of patients."

Rick didn't even look over. "Tiffany says most of the building is office space—there are just two exam rooms."

We continued about a half-mile down the street to the restaurant where we were meeting Tiffany. It was like driving through a foreign country—signs were embellished with the flags of various Latin American countries, the wording in Spanish and Portuguese.

We found the café but the narrow street was crowded with parked cars, and we had to travel an extra block to find a space. A church up the street was letting out, and the sidewalk was busy with people in their Sunday best. The women wore low-cut dresses in bright colors, the men natty suits with wide lapels or white guayaberas.

I heard a woman's high-pitched voice call, "Ricky!"

Tiffany was ahead of us. She was shorter than I expected from her online photos, and more buxom – but maybe it was just the low cut dress, a silky red number that was way too tight for a woman of her age and her endowments. She clattered up to us on three-inch heels and wrapped her arms around Rick.

She wasn't as pretty as she'd been in the older photos I'd found online. She had a couple of lines across her forehead, and her skin was sallow.

"I'm so glad you came!" she said. "You're the only one I could ever count on." Her voice had an odd accent, a combination of Spanish and North Philly.

She kissed his cheek, leaving a smear of red lipstick. She wet her finger and wiped it off, and Rick blushed. "This is my friend Steve," he said.

She turned to me. "You're the one with the dog, right?"

I nodded. "Nice to meet you."

She took Rick's hand. "Come on, I'm starving. This place makes the best food in town."

I followed them to a Colombian café. The smell was heady, a mix of cheese and fried foods, and my stomach grumbled.

Rick made a point of sitting across from Tiffany, with me beside him. Even so, she reached across the Formica-topped table to take his hand. "Oh, Ricky. What am I going to do?"

A plump young waitress with dark hair in a net and a big mole on her cheek came over with a coffee pot in her hand and spoke to Tiffany in Spanish. "You don't mind if I order for you, do you?"

Tiffany said to me. "I know what Ricky likes."

"Sure, I eat anything," I said.

Tiffany rattled off an order to the waitress, who poured coffee for all three of us. "Colombian coffee, it's the best," Tiffany said.

"So what's up, Tiff?" Rick asked, when the waitress was gone. "You said the police don't think you knew what was going on. So what do you need from me?"

"You need a reason to see me?" she said, pouting.

Rick crossed his arms over his chest and stared at her. I'd seen that stare before, when he wanted information from someone, and Tiffany wasn't immune to it.

"You've got to help me, Ricky. I can't go to prison."

"Then tell me exactly what you know," he said. "I can't do anything until I hear the whole story."

She took a deep breath. "It wasn't until a couple of weeks after I started that I figured out that something was wrong. People were calling to complain that their insurance was billed for appointments they didn't make and services they didn't get. My boss, Maria Jose, she told me just to apologize and say that it was the fault of the girl before me, Yoani, and that I would fix it for them."

I remembered her Facebook posts, and then what Yesenia Cruz had told me about those names that began with Y. It wasn't surprising that a Cuban would be working at an office in Union City.

"And did you?"

"Sometimes I could withdraw the claim, but other times the

insurance had already rejected it. Usually they just paid."

"How often did you get these complaints?" I asked.

She shrugged. "Only once or twice a week. Most of the patients, they're too old, or they didn't speak enough English to realize what was wrong. But it was strange, I was processing tons of claims but there were almost never any patients in the building."

Suddenly she looked down and whispered "Holy shit."

"What's the matter? Rick asked.

Without raising her head, Tiffany said, "My boss just walked in."

I shifted around so I could see the front door of the restaurant, expecting to see an elderly man. But the Latin guy speaking with the hostess was in his forties, wearing a white soccer shirt advertising Emirates Air.

"Is that Eduardo de la Fe?" I asked Tiffany, when I turned back to her.

"Yeah. I really don't want him to see me."

No luck there. A moment later the guy was standing beside our table. "*Hola*, Tiffany," he said, pronouncing her name Tee-fah-nee.

She looked up. "Hi, Eddie." She introduced Rick as her ex-husband, and me as his friend, and we all shook hands.

"I'm sorry we had to close the office so quickly," he said. "I hope you'll be able to find a new job soon. If you need a reference, please let me know."

She thanked him, and then the hostess led a boy and a girl up. "I have your table now," she said to de la Fe, and he followed her and the kids to the back of the restaurant.

"He seems like a nice guy," I said.

"He can be a jerk sometimes," she said. "I kind of, you know." Her voice trailed off.

Rick and I shared a glance, and I knew what he was going to ask.

"Were you dating him?" Rick asked. "I thought you had a boyfriend. This Alex guy."

"It wasn't dating," Tiffany said, still not making eye contact. "We just, you know, fooled around. He has a lot of money. He took me to way nicer places than Alex."

Because I knew Rick so well, I could tell that he was getting angry. Was this the same way Tiffany had behaved when they were married? Why else would he care?

To diffuse the tension, I shifted the conversation back to why we'd come. "Did you ever talk to him about the strange stuff you saw at the clinic?" I asked.

"I asked him about it one day. That's when he offered to take me out to dinner and explain."

Rick looked at me, and Tiffany must have noticed, and kicked him, because he said, "Ouch!"

"I know what you're thinking, Rick Stemper. You think he had sex with me to shut me up."

"And?" Rick asked.

"It wasn't like that. He was nice to me. He used to give me little things."

Rick shook his head. "You're dating one guy and cheating on him with another. Is he married, this de la Fe?"

"Separated," Tiffany said defiantly. "That's why he's here with his kids. He has them every other weekend."

Like Doug Guilfoyle. A dad struggling to do right by his kids. But I wasn't ready to assume de la Fe was a good guy. "Did he ever tell you that the clinic was filing false claims?" I asked.

She shook her head. "Never."

I pressed on. "Did he ever say anything specific that would lead you to believe he was breaking the law?"

She looked from me to Rick. "Is he a cop now too?"

"Answer him, Tiffany," Rick said.

"No. The first time I knew that something was seriously wrong was when those FBI agents came to the clinic last week." She looked closely at me. "Ricky's talked about you before," she said. "You were in prison, weren't you? You don't look like the type."

"Everybody makes mistakes," I said. "Some of us get caught, some don't."

20 – EASY LIES

The waitress arrived a few minutes later with our platters spread out along her arm. "This is *bandeja paisa*," Tiffany said, as the waitress laid the plates in front of us. She pointed to each of the dishes. "Red beans with pork, fried egg, fried sweet plantains, and chorizo sausage." There was also a big lump of white rice and some ground beef in a red sauce. It was an awful lot of food for a Sunday brunch, but I dug in.

We ate in silence for a while, but Rick didn't seem to have much appetite. Finally he pushed the plate away and said, "You shouldn't be in trouble. If the FBI ask you more questions, just tell them what you told us. You didn't know anything was wrong."

"But what if they find out about Eddy and me?"

"It's not illegal to date somebody," Rick said.

She looked down at the table again. "Eddy and Alex are friends. If Alex finds out he'll be really mad."

I could see Rick had finally gotten fed up with Tiffany when he said, "Again, not illegal. Sleazy, maybe, but nothing the FBI will care about."

"When did you get so mean?" she asked.

"Maybe when you walked out on me?" Rick asked.

Tiffany pouted and I wondered if she'd start to cry. Clearly he wasn't as over her as he'd pretended to be, but maybe this meeting would help him push her into his past and move forward.

The waitress came over and asked if we wanted anything else. I was almost afraid of what Rick might say next, but he said, "Just the check, please."

"Let's keep focused on the problem," I said, trying once again to shut down the emotion that kept building. "Tiffany, you said you asked Eddy what was going on, and he took you out to dinner. What was his explanation?"

"He said that the whole insurance and Medicare system was screwed up, and I shouldn't worry about it."

"Then that's what you tell the FBI."

"But what if Alex finds out about me and Eddy?"

"That's easy," I said.

Rick's head swiveled toward me. "Easy?" he asked.

"If Alex finds out, you say that Eddy forced you. That he threatened to fire you if you didn't go out with him. But you drew the line at having sex, because you wouldn't do that to Alex. Fortunately, the FBI came in before Eddy could force you."

"But we…" She stopped. "Oh, I get it. Yeah. I can say that."

"You know how to lie way too easily," Rick said to me.

"It's just a little white lie," Tiffany said. "Because I wouldn't want to hurt Alex. Or get him mad at me."

"Would Alex hurt you if he found out?" Rick demanded. "He

hasn't pushed you around, has he, Tiff? Hit you or anything?"

"No!" she said. "I mean, yeah, he has a temper, but that's just because he's Latin, like me. You know how it is."

I could see from Rick's face that he knew. By then, I was tired of refereeing between them. We'd learned everything we needed to know, so I slid out of the booth. "I'm just going to wash my hands," I said. "Be right back."

Because I was at that age where the sight of a men's room made my body want to take advantage of it, I used the urinal and then turned to wash my hands as Eduardo de la Fe walked in. He stepped up to the urinal, unzipped and began to pee. Then he turned to me. "So Tiffany is seeing her ex-husband now?"

"He's a police detective," I said, as I turned off the faucet. "She's worried about this FBI business." As long as I had de la Fe in front of me, I thought I'd see what I could find out. I turned to face him as he finished at the urinal. "Any reason why she should be?"

"Just a misunderstanding," he said. "This insurance billing is very complicated. And it's hard to get good people to do the work. Mistakes get made."

Yeah, right. Blame it on the staff, you sleazy bastard.

I stepped away from the sink and dried my hands. "I hope it all works out," I said. Then I walked out.

When I got back to the table, it looked like Tiffany had emptied her purse in search of the bright red lipstick she was applying to her lips. The debris in front of her reminded me of all the crap Mary had carried in her purse, and I wondered for a moment how come Lili never had so much junk with her.

I looked at the pile in front Tiffany – tissues, a compact, a couple of hair scrunchies in bright colors, a key chain with a little llama on the end of it.

A llama. I looked closer and saw the same logo on it as the one that Rochester had found by the canal. "Cute jump drive," I said to her.

"What?"

"The little llama on your key chain. It's a jump drive. You didn't know?"

She shook her head.

I leaned over and pressed the llama's back legs, and the USB port popped out of its butt.

"How cute!" she said. "I never knew that was in there. And I can use one of these. I have a ton of pictures on my phone I want to copy off."

"You got that from the phone store?" I asked.

"No, I found it at work, behind my desk. I was changing my shoes and I accidentally kicked my sneaker back there, so I had to crawl down and get it. The llama was back there, and I just thought it was a cute little thing, so I took it and put it on my keychain."

She put all her stuff back in her purse and looked out the window. "Oh, there's Alex. He's early." She squeezed out of the booth. "I've gotta go, Ricky. Thanks for coming to see me."

She was heading toward the door before Rick or I could react. We watched her go out to the sidewalk and jump into the arms of a tall, muscular Latin guy in his late thirties wearing a tight black T-shirt stretched across his chest, showing off impressive biceps.

She kissed him, and then put her hand in his and steered him back the way he'd come.

"Some things never change," Rick said.

I couldn't tell how Rick felt at that moment. Was he glad Tiffany was gone? That she was someone else's problem?

"I didn't expect her to pay the bill, but I did think she'd stick around for dessert," he said. "What was up with that jump drive?"

"I found one just like it when Rochester and I were walking out along the canal about where Doug went into the water. I checked what was on it, and it definitely wasn't Doug's – just a bunch of photos of somebody's kids."

He shook his head. "You won't be able to let this go, will you?"

"Nope."

"Speaking of kids, I promised Justin I'd get him a jump drive for his computer. He needs to be able to carry his homework back and forth to school. You think he'd like one shaped like a llama?"

"Why not? I think he'd get a kick out of the way the USB comes out of the llama's butt. The store's somewhere around here. Want to and see if you can buy one for him?"

"Sure. I guess you can say we're off to see the llama," Rick said.

Neil S. Plakcy

21 – PHONE LLAMA

I checked the company's website on my phone, and discovered that the Phone Llama store was only a few blocks beyond where Rick had parked his truck, wedged between a bar called Las Iguanas and a karate dojo with signs in both Spanish and Japanese. It was bright and sunny and the temperature was just in the low seventies. We strolled past trees and fire hydrants and trash cans, and I wished I had Rochester with me so he could enjoy all the different smells.

Up ahead was the Phone Llama store, a single bay in the middle of a block. A big banner over the door announced unlocked GSM phones, and signs in English and Spanish promised you could call Cuba and Latin America.

We walked inside, and while Rick went up to the counter I browsed around the store. It was so easy to be connected with anyone in the world. When I was a teenager, my parents had sent me on a study abroad program to France, and I'd only been able to call them once the whole time, because it was so expensive. Now as long as you had a computer and internet access you could call anywhere in the world.

"No luck," Rick said, when he returned. "The only way to get one of those drives is to buy a phone, and it's not worth that much to me."

"I can give you the one I found," I said. "If Justin doesn't mind a couple of teeth marks on the llama."

"There are plenty of different kinds of drives," he said. "I'll find him one." He looked around. "But you know what? I should have hit the can when you did. Something in that food didn't agree with me."

"There's a bar next door," I said. "We can stop over there."

We walked back outside, up to the bar's front door. The logo was an iguana with its tail curled around a map of Cuba, and from inside we heard laughter and cheering in Spanish.

Inside the cool, dim bar a mostly-male crowd clustered around a TV showing a soccer match. Rick headed for the door marked "caballeros," and I wandered around the bar. I stopped at a wall of candid photos of bar patrons. I was surprised to spot Doug Guilfoyle in one of the photos.

When Rick came out of the men's room I called him over, and pointed to the picture. "That's Doug."

"That's a weird coincidence. But didn't he live around here for a while?"

"He told me he lived around here for a while after leaving the house in Westchester, while he was still working in the city," I said. "There's a direct train on the PATH line from here to Wall Street."

I peered at the photo. One of the men with Doug looked familiar but I couldn't place him. Was he another classmate? I pulled out my cell phone and took a picture of the photo. Fortunately there was a light right above the photo so the image came through clearly. I didn't know why, but I had a hunch there was a clue in that picture.

We drove back to Stewart's Crossing, neither of us saying much. I kept thinking about the jump drive Rochester had found by the canal. Knowing that Doug Guilfoyle had been to the bar next door to the phone store rang bells in my head. Was there more of a connection than I had thought?

Maybe someone had given it to Doug, and he hadn't cleaned it out. Or maybe someone dropped it while pushing Doug into the canal. But who?

I had a couple of suspects in mind.

Suppose while they were at the Drunken Hessian, Doug had confronted Shawn about the financial irregularities at Beauceron? What if Shawn had accompanied Doug down to the canal? What kind of cell phone did he have? If he traveled a lot, he might have needed one of those GSM phones.

Who else had reason to be angry at Doug?

His son Ethan came to mind. I'd seen barbells on Ethan Guilfoyle's bedroom floor. He was working out—which meant he was strong enough to give his father a push into the water. He was angry with his father, and he could have easily met Doug by the canal and argued with him. Catherine had said that Ethan had his driver's license, so he could have gotten down to the center of town on his own. His knuckles had been skinned, too. But hadn't he been with his sister at Tamsen's?

When I'd seen him the day before, he was troubled. Just by the fact of his father's death? Or because he had caused it?

I'd already considered the possibility that Catherine might have met Doug outside the bar. And all the murder statistics pointed to someone close to the victim, a friend or family member.

"Do you know if Catherine has an alibi for Tuesday night?" I asked Rick.

"You think I'm that much of a slacker? She says she was home alone that night. But I already told you that I'm considering Guilfoyle's death an suicide, so it doesn't matter where she was."

"And you know about the five-million-dollar life insurance policy?"

"Again. You are not following me. Where she was, what she inherits, whether she was mad at him or still loved him, doesn't matter. It's not my decision anymore – the chief looked over the evidence with me, heard about the guy's mental state, and he's the one who said suicide. After those problems at the nursing home during Christmas he's freaked out about the possibility of a murder happening in our charming little town. So I have my marching orders and they don't include continuing to snoop into Guilfoyle's death unless some new evidence pops up that indicates something other than suicide."

He turned toward me. "Look, Steve. I know you liked the guy, and you feel bad that he died. You want to keep looking into what happened? Feel free as long you don't break any laws yourself, and if you find something, by all means bring it to me."

He was giving me permission to investigate. I could handle that.

Later that evening, after dinner and a long walk around the lake with Rochester, I remembered the picture I'd taken of the photo on the wall at Las Iguanas. I emailed it to myself from the phone and then opened it up in Photoshop. I was curious to see if I could figure out who was with Doug Guilfoyle.

I reduced the size of the photo so I could see the whole thing on one screen, and leaned forward to stare at the two men with Doug. One was swarthy, with dark hair in tight curls and a heavy five o'clock shadow. He didn't look familiar to me at all.

I recognized the third man, though. Tiffany's boyfriend, Alex Vargas.

Rick had told me that Alex Vargas was living in Hoboken, though I couldn't find any record of his current address. Was it a weird coincidence that two men I knew from different parts of my life would know each other?

I was curious to see if there were other connections between Alex Vargas and Doug Guilfoyle. I began by Googling the two names together, with quotation marks around first and last names.

Nothing.

Back to Facebook, then. Were they "friends" there? Nope. Alex didn't have an account of his own, and Doug's showed little activity other than a bunch of birthday wishes from a few months before.

I fancied myself as some kind of super sleuth, determined to seek out truth, justice and the American way. Well, maybe not all of that. But I did like looking for clues and solving puzzles.

Lili was in the living room when I found her. "You're as excited as Rochester with a new rawhide," she said. "What's up?"

I told her how Doug had lived in North Jersey for a while after he moved out of the house in Westchester. "Single guys often hang out in bars, and Doug was the kind of guy who talked to people, especially once he had the job at Beauceron and needed to find clients to invest with him."

"It's that whole six degrees of separation thing," Lili said. "I'm sure that if you picked any random group of people and quizzed them about everyone they knew, you'd find all kinds of connections."

Perhaps that was true, but pursuing these leads with only the occasional result felt like putting together a jigsaw puzzle without knowing what the image looks like, just hoping that the big picture would fill in eventually.

Rochester was underfoot, and when I sat down on the carpet he hunkered down beside me. I stroked his soft, golden head, and told him what a good boy he was. At least in that, I was sure I knew what I was doing.

22 – THE GRACE OF GOD

As Lili and I walked up the half-moon driveway in front of the Friends' Meeting House, I felt an overwhelming sadness. The oaks and maples beside the single-story building were coming into leaf, and some early forsythias gleamed yellow along one side of the front door. It would be full spring soon, and Doug Guilfoyle would not be among us to enjoy it.

I'd taken the day off from work to attend Doug's funeral, and left Rochester home alone. The melancholy of the afternoon made me miss his happy smile, and accentuated my determination to find out what had happened to my old friend.

The sign out front read "Meeting for Worship in Thanksgiving for the Grace of God in the Life of Douglas Oliver Guilfoyle."

"I never realized Doug's initials spell out DOG," I said. "No wonder Rochester liked him."

Lili put her arm in mine and we walked into the large, low-ceilinged room, then down the central aisle. The decor was plain and spare in a way that reminded me of colonial America. Rows of ancient wooden pews were parallel to each of the four walls, forming a square with an empty space in the center. Since Quaker worship involved silent waiting for God with no ritual, there was no need for an altar. Instead, a framed photograph of Doug sat on small wooden table with carved legs.

Catherine walked up the aisle to meet us. She wore a white knee-length dress, with short sleeves and big red and black poppies spangled across it. She kissed our cheeks and thanked us for coming.

"I feel like I have to explain what I'm wearing to everyone," she said. "Quakers don't wear black to services like this. We consider them a way to celebrate the person who's passed, not mourn." She smiled. "Doug loved this dress, and I haven't worn it since the divorce."

As we moved toward a pew, I saw Shawn Brumberger, and Lili and I stopped beside him. "Steve, good to see you," he said. He stood up and shook my hand. "Sorry it's under sad circumstances, though."

"I agree. Lili, this is Shawn, Doug's boss at Beauceron."

"The fiancée," Shawn said. "Congratulations." I saw him look down at Lili's ring finger, which was conspicuously empty.

"Thank you," Lili said, twining her arm in mine. "I never met Doug myself, but from what I understand he was a great guy."

"He was," Shawn said. "We'll miss him at Beauceron."

Shawn sat down and Lili and I walked ahead to a pew a few rows from the center. "Fiancée?" she whispered as we sat down. "Does he know something I don't?"

"I wanted to learn more about the kind of business they do, and Shawn ended up trying to get me to open an investment account. I told him I'd have to talk to you first."

"And a fiancée carries more weight than a girlfriend," Lili said.

"Well, yes. And there isn't a word in English that conveys everything you mean to me."

She suppressed a laugh. "Smooth, Levitan."

I looked around but didn't see Rick; I was surprised that he wasn't there with Tamsen, but perhaps because he believed the case of Doug's death was closed, he had decided to stay away. The presence of a police detective at the funeral might convey the wrong impression.

Tamsen sat in the front row with her son, her nephew, and Catherine's kids. Madison looked uncomfortable in a pink tulle dress that looked more appropriate for a birthday party and her brother, in jeans and a plaid shirt, toed the floor nervously. There were about two dozen other people in the room, and I assumed they were Doug's friends and relatives.

After a few minutes, Tamsen's sister Hannah, the Clerk of the Meeting, stood up and walked to the table, introduced herself and explained the way Quaker services were run. "I'm going to speak for a few minutes and then we'll move into Open Worship, a period of contemplation."

Her voice carried in the half-empty room. "During that time, anyone who has a memory of Doug, or wants to say something on his behalf, can speak up," she continued. "We believe that the spirit of God speaks through all of us. After everyone has spoken who wishes, we'll sing Doug's favorite hymn together."

She picked up a piece of paper and began to read. "Rudyard Kipling wrote the poem 'If' in memory of his friend Leander Jameson," she said. "It's in the form of paternal advice to Jameson's son, and I think it's fitting to hear it today, because of Doug's love for Ethan and Madison."

I glanced at Ethan, who was hunched over, his head hung.

Hannah read beautifully, pausing at the right points, her voice clear and strong.

"If you can bear to hear the truth you've spoken
Twisted by knaves to make a trap for fools,
Or watch the things you gave your life to broken
And stoop and build 'em up with worn-out tools."

I was moved by that line, because Doug had tried to tell the truth about what was going on at Beauceron. He'd also seen his marriage and family broken, and been struggling to build up his relationship with his kids again.

When she finished the poem, Hannah spoke of Doug's life – his childhood, education, marriage to Catherine. "Doug often said that the greatest gifts Catherine gave him were their two children, Ethan and Madison." She looked directly at the kids. "Ethan, your father was proud of everything about you, from your success at Little League to the way you passed your driver's test the first time. Madison, you were Daddy's girl, and from the moment he first held you as a tiny baby, nothing gave him more pleasure than to spend time with you and your brother."

Ahead of us, Catherine put her arms around her kids, one on each side of her. Madison leaned into her mother's shoulder, but Ethan remained upright.

I began to tear up, and I could tell from the hitch in Hannah's voice that she was, too. I squeezed Lili's hand.

"All of us are here today because of our love for Doug Guilfoyle, and I hope each of us will pledge to keep his memory in our hearts and help Ethan and Madison in the ways that Doug would have wanted."

She sat down beside her son, and the room was quiet for a moment. Then Tamsen spoke, followed by Doug's father. After he sat down, the spirit moved in me, and I stood up.

"I met Doug during our freshman year at Eastern College. I didn't know him well, but he was one of those guys I saw throughout my four years—in dorms, in classes, as a friend of friends. I had the opportunity to get to know him again when he moved to Stewart's Crossing, and he told me how determined he was to stay in his children's lives. Ethan and Madison, don't ever forget that your father loved you both very much."

I sat down. My heart was racing and I was overcome with emotion.

"That was lovely," Lili whispered into my ear.

A few other people told stories about their experiences with Doug. One man, with olive skin and a slight accent I couldn't place, said, "I didn't know Doug as well as you all did. But he and I shared a rough period in our lives and I'll be forever grateful for his support after my divorce, when I was struggling to put my life back together."

He sat down, and then Shawn stood. "I first met Doug at a financial conference two years ago. I was impressed with his intelligence and his financial acumen. When he contacted me last year about moving to Bucks County to be closer to his kids, we began a series of conversations that culminated in him coming to work with me at Beauceron."

I watched Shawn carefully as he spoke. Would he say something that would betray a rift between him and Doug? They'd argued at Friar Lake, just before the seminar began, and he'd asked Doug some probing questions about Doug's snooping in company files.

"Doug did not disappoint us," Shawn continued. "He worked hard to learn everything he needed in order to make a career change, and all of us at Beauceron are sorry we will not have the benefit of his expertise in the future."

Shawn sat, and the room was silent for few more minutes. Then Hannah stood up and walked back to the center table. "Doug's family has chosen to have his remains cremated, so there will be no interment ceremony. Those of you who wish to can accompany us back to Catherine's home."

The crowd rustled, and Hannah said, "Before we go, please join us in singing one of Doug's favorite hymns, 'Amazing Grace'."

We all stood, and Hannah began to sing. The crowd joined in. I knew there was a meaning for Doug's life – he had been blind to the importance of his family while he worked on Wall Street, and then had learned to see.

But for me, the most meaningful lines were

"Through many dangers, toils, and snares

I have already come

'Tis grace hath brought me safe thus far,

And grace will lead me home."

I had been through my share of dangers and snares, and grace had brought me back to my home town, and had brought Rochester and Lili into my life.

After the last lines of the hymn, Hannah turned to Catherine and shook her hand, which seemed an odd gesture until I remembered that was the traditional way for Quaker services to end. Others began to follow suit, shaking hands with their neighbors. People began to filter out of the service.

I was curious to speak to the olive-skinned man who said he'd shared a rough period in his life with Doug, and I went up to him. "I'm Steve Levitan," I said. Up close, I recognized him as the third man in the photo of Doug and Alex at the bar.

"Hari Kozoglu. Pleased to meet you."

"Doug shared some of the pain of his divorce with me," I said. "I went through a lot of the same experiences he did. Sounds like you did, too."

He nodded. "My wife left me about a year ago and I began to

drink too much. I spent a lot of time at a bar in Hoboken, where I live. Doug was living nearby while he worked on Wall Street and we got to be friends. You knew him in college?"

"I did, though like I said, we weren't friends. When he moved here, I reconnected with him, and he helped me out with a financial planning seminar at the conference center I manage."

"Doug was such a smart man, with a great sense of humor," Hari said. "A bunch of us guys, all divorced, used to hang out together. Doug called us the First Husbands Club. He even gave us investment advice."

"That's tricky. Sometimes people get angry when the advice doesn't work out." I hoped Hari might agree with that idea, and mention someone with a specific gripe, but I was disappointed.

"I guess we were lucky then," he said. "Even though a couple of the guys could be hot-headed, we all got along." He reached out to shake my hand. "It was good to talk to you. I've got to head back to North Jersey and I want to miss some of the rush hour traffic."

I wished him well. As I walked back to Lili, I marveled again at the weird coincidence that Alex and Doug, two guys from separate parts of my life, had known each other. Was it just the shared bonding of their divorces that had brought together a Wall Street whiz with and a muscle-bound guy arrested for drug dealing? I didn't suspect Doug had been using drugs, and Rick hadn't mentioned the presence of any drugs in his system.

But the same curiosity I'd had in Hoboken the day before

niggled at the back of my brain.

Just what had gotten me into trouble before.

Neil S. Plakcy

23 – Making a Splash

Catherine's house was crowded with friends and family, and though a few people I recognized from the funeral stood talking in small groups, the only people I knew were Tamsen and Hannah and their sons.

Lili joined the women in the kitchen and I walked into the living room. Madison sat on the sofa with her grandmother, but I didn't see Ethan until I glanced through the sliding glass doors to the back yard. He threw a worn tennis ball for Pixie. The little dog raced ahead and jumped up to grab it with her teeth, then trotted back to him and dropped it at his feet.

I stepped up to the door beside a sandy-haired guy in his late thirties and we watched Ethan throw the ball to Pixie again. It was sad to see Ethan on his own out there, while everyone else was inside sharing their memories, eating and drinking.

"Ethan's been going through a tough time," I said to the man beside me. "Poor kid. I wish there was more I could do for him."

I turned to him. "I'm Steve Levitan. Went to college with Catherine and Doug."

"Jimmy Burns. I'm, well, I'm a friend of Catherine's."

The boyfriend. His eyeglasses had broken above the nose, and were kept together with duct tape. My father had always said there wasn't anything damaged that couldn't be fixed with duct tape except a broken heart.

Then I thought of Ethan's bruised knuckles. Maybe he hadn't hit his father, but his mother's boyfriend?

Jimmy wore khakis, a light blue shirt with a skinny black tie and light brown wool blazer with the George School logo on the breast. "I taught for a while at Eastern College, where I had a bunch of kids from George School." I pointed to the logo on his jacket.

"It's a good school," he said. "I want Catherine to send Ethan and Madison there next year. But finances have been a problem." He looked around at the house, the crowd. "Without the money from Doug, she'll probably have to sell this house. Don't know where the kids will end up."

So Catherine hadn't shared the five-million-dollar payout with him. Or maybe he was just making conversation.

"Catherine told me she met you in a writers' group," I said. "She and I were in some creative writing courses together back in college. She mentioned you're writing kids' books?"

He nodded. "A middle-school series about two boys who get into trouble and use what they learn in class to solve their problems."

"Sounds clever." Catherine joined us as Jimmy and I swapped business cards. His was quite colorful, showing five book covers.

"I'm so glad you could come, Jimmy," Catherine said, as she squeezed his hand. "The kids will be happy to see you."

The three of us looked out to the back yard, where Ethan was now sitting on the ground, Pixie on his lap. "I should go out and say something to him," Jimmy said.

"And I should rescue Maddie from her grandmother." She turned to me. "Thank you for what you said at the service, Steve. Ethan and Maddie are going to need all the reassurance I can give them that their dad loved them."

I said goodbye to them, and Jimmy headed out to the back yard while Catherine went back into the living room. Lili and I left a short while later, and in the car on the way home, I told her about meeting Jimmy Burns, and that he at least pretended to be unaware of Doug's life insurance.

"You are so suspicious," Lili said. "Do you go around analyzing everything I say?"

"Only as it relates to murder," I said. "And so far I don't consider you a suspect for any unexplained deaths."

"That's good to know," she said drily.

I took Rochester for a long walk around the lake to make up for being away from him all afternoon. He acted like he'd been a prisoner starved for fresh air the way he kept dragging me forward from smell to smell, wagging his tail and bouncing on the balls of his paws. Being with him made me feel better. I hoped Pixie would do the same thing for Ethan and Madison.

Lili left for her evening class, the last one of the spring semester, and I put some water up to boil for pasta. Rochester jumped up on me, reminding me it was his dinner time, too, and Jimmy Burns' business card tipped out of my pocket.

I poured some chow for Rochester and looked at the card. Jimmy seemed like a nice guy, and I was curious to see what he wrote. I used my Kindle to download a sample chapter of his first book, *Making a Splash*, and read while I ate.

As Jimmy had said, the two main characters were middle-school boys, Noah and Boogie, best friends who got into one scrape after another. The book was lively and well-written, and my impression of Catherine's boyfriend went up a notch.

I was almost at the end of the free sample when Noah and Boogie began fooling around down by the banks of a river much like the Delaware, though it wasn't named. Boogie confessed that he was afraid of the water, and I wondered if Jimmy had known about Doug's fear. Then Boogie slipped and fell into the river.

Whoa. Shades of Doug Guilfoyle. I flipped ahead eagerly to see what happened and realized I'd come to the end of the sample.

One of the great things about e-books is instant gratification. After a couple of clicks, I had the whole book on my Kindle, and I went upstairs to read. Rochester followed me to the bedroom and jumped up on the bed as I plumped up the pillows for reading. He circled twice, and with a gentle thump landed beside me. His head rested on his paws and he stared at me.

"Okay, okay, I won't ignore you." I held the Kindle with one and with the other I scratched behind his big floppy ears until he put his head down on the spread and went to sleep.

Making a Splash was a quick read, and I enjoyed it. I was almost disappointed that there were no other parallel's to Doug's situation in the book. But then I checked the copyright, and realized that the book had been written and published long before Doug and Catherine divorced.

Rochester and I heard Lili's car in the driveway and he jumped off the bed and charged downstairs to bark a welcome. I put a kettle of water up to boil as Lili greeted Rochester at the door. "How was your class?" I asked, after kissing her hello.

"I am so glad to see the end of this semester," she said, as she collapsed theatrically on the sofa. "I've been talking to other faculty and it's not just my imagination. Students this term are worse than ever before."

"You say that every semester."

The teakettle whistled, and I went into the kitchen to make Lili a big mug of green tea. It was her favorite way of relaxing after a long day. I stirred in a drip of organic honey from New Zealand, then carried it out to her.

She put the mug up to her nose and sniffed. "That's heavenly," she said. "What did you boys do while I was gone?"

"I read a book by Catherine's boyfriend Jimmy Burns," I said. "About a boy named Boogie who falls into a canal a lot like the one in the center of Stewart's Crossing."

"Boogie?"

I nodded. "It's a nickname, obviously. But it reminds me a lot of

Dougie, which is what we called Doug Guilfoyle at Eastern."

"Boogie, whose name reminds you of Dougie, falls into a canal like the one Doug fell into."

I nodded, and she sipped her tea. After a moment she asked, "Does Boogie die like Doug did?"

"That's where the story changes. Boogie's friend Noah runs down along the river bank as Boogie gets swept along in the current. Noah remembers a science experiment they did where they learned that wood floats because it weighs less than the amount of water it would have to push away if it sank. He sees a bunch of sticks on the ground ahead of him and he throws them into the water for Boogie to hold onto."

"Smart kid. How does Boogie get out of the river?"

"Apparently they studied beavers the year before, so Boogie uses the sticks that Noah throws him to divert himself into a narrow channel, and then piles them up as a makeshift dam. Then Noah helps him climb out of the water."

"Doesn't sound like best-seller material to me," Lili said.

"It's pretty funny – lots of silly jokes and puns. At first I was kind of freaked out by the parallels to Doug, but then I realized it had to have been written long before he met Catherine."

"And it would be a pretty iffy connection to Doug's death even if it was recent."

"But Catherine still could have read the book and been inspired by it. Could she have killed Doug?"

"Steve. Your imagination is working overtime tonight."

"You're right. I just keep thinking there's something about Doug's death I should be figuring out."

"The only thing you need to figure out is what we can do to help Catherine and her kids," Lili said. She reached out and took my hand.

"As usual," I said. "You are right on target." I kissed her hand, and then we went upstairs and I put that imagination of mine to a more productive use.

Neil S. Plakcy

24 – ETHAN'S CONFESSION

Tuesday morning was busy, filled with answering emails and making phone calls as I made up for my day off. I had to drive down to Eastern around lunchtime to hand in some paper forms, and Rochester and I stopped by Lili's office to check in with her.

Her office was on the second floor of Harrow Hall, a modern building shaped like a giant pill capsule, with wrap-around windows. She was sitting on the wood floor with a portfolio of student photos in front of her, and I had to rein Rochester in to keep him from trampling the pictures.

She stood up and brushed herself off. "Thank you for rescuing me from some of the most banal, ordinary photographs I have ever had submitted for a class."

Behind her desk, Lili had hung a montage of photos she had taken. A young Afghan girl played jacks with a female U.S. soldier in camo gear; the Baghdad skyline lit by a tracery of what looked almost like fireworks; a tiny monkey, looking almost human, stared at the camera from the safety of a tree in a tropical rain forest. The grim beauty of a panoramic shot of a refugee camp in Darfur, taken from a helicopter.

Lili was passionate about photography, and was often frank with students who she felt weren't putting their all into their work. I looked down at the pictures. "They don't look that bad." They were pretty shots of the Eastern campus, the old stone buildings, the tall trees and the grassy lawns.

"They look like promotional shots for the college," Lili said. "The student who took them has a good eye for perspective, but that's about it. She takes her pictures, develops them and submits them."

She pointed at one of a girl in an Eastern sweatshirt reading a glossy brochure about the college. "Look at this picture," she said. "No current student would ever read that thing—it's just to entice potential students to come here. So that means the photo was staged, and to me that makes it a dishonest picture."

Honesty was a tricky concept for me—I'd done some things in my hacking career that most people would consider dishonest, like breaking into protected websites, but I had always justified my behavior because I was pursuing a greater good. "It's not believable, but does that make it dishonest?"

She walked to her desk and sat down. "There is a difference, at least to me. I don't believe that the girl was reading that brochure, and my student found her and took her picture because she thought it was an interesting statement about college. So it's not believable. But it's also dishonest, because it was staged, and she's trying to convince her audience – in this case, just me, but think about newspapers and websites – that this was a true photo, when it's not."

She riffled through the pile of photos on her desk and picked up a shot of an old tombstone in a cemetery. "This is an honest photo, in my opinion," she said. "First there's the inscription – beloved husband and father– and the dates. This man lived from 1840 to 1861."

"He died when he was twenty-one," I said. "That had to be young, even back then."

"And he was already married and a father."

My mind flashed back to Doug Guilfoyle. Older than this man, certainly, but still leaving behind young children.

"It's a sad photo, and it's an interesting choice because this guy was about the age of the student. But the photographer also paid attention to the light and either waited or worked his way around until the shadow fell over the stone." She pointed at the picture. "So there's a deeper element here, about the shadow that someone's death leaves over those left behind."

"Interesting."

"And see in the background? There were lots of tombstones to choose from, if the kid just wanted to take a gloomy picture. He paid attention to what was on the stone, to the lighting, to the meaning. There's an honesty in this picture that says something to me."

We talked for a few more minutes, and then I kissed her goodbye and drove back to Eastern. On the way, I kept thinking about honesty. In Sunday school, I'd learned about the basics of Judaism, and always been fond of the quote Rabbi Hillel had given, when asked to provide the essence of Judaism while standing on one foot.

"Love thy neighbor as thyself," he had said. I also liked the bit from the Hippocratic Oath, "First, do no harm." It was the way I'd tried to live my life, though not always with success. In trying to protect my ex-wife, I had hacked into the three major credit bureaus. In retrospect it was a stupid move, of course, but at the time I'd thought I was doing it to protect her, and myself, from falling back into debt after her second miscarriage.

The state of California had judged that a dishonest act, one that went against the common standards of behavior, and I had been punished with a year in prison, and another two years on parole.

I had broken a few more laws since then as a hacker, always justifying my acts because I was pursuing justice in some way. I wanted to create a particular result, so I manipulated data and information. Was that any different from the student who'd posed her subject?

On my way back to Friar Lake, I thought about the research I had begun for Doug. Maybe if I finished it, there would be something in the data that would give someone a motive to murder Doug, and that would allow Rick to reopen his investigation. I spent the rest of the afternoon on the rest of the suspect properties, looking through public records for ownership, bankruptcy, tax liens and other proceedings. Each property that had two spreadsheets was in trouble, some worse than others.

I put what I had found into a short, simple report. The unusually high returns Beauceron promised, the discrepancies between the income on the real spreadsheets and the fake. I was convinced that someone was manipulating the numbers at Beauceron. But was it Shawn? The fact that Doug was on the trail of this information when he died ought to be enough to raise some suspicion. I emailed the report to Rick, then closed down my computer.

On my way back to River Bend I called Lili and offered to pick up dinner, and I brought home a pair of big chicken Caesar salads for us. We were just finishing when my cell rang with a number I didn't recognize. "Can I speak to Mr. Levitan?"

"That's me. Who's calling?"

"It's Ethan. Ethan Guilfoyle."

Ethan? Why was he calling me? I'd only met him a couple of times, and if he needed an older guy to speak with, he knew Rick or Jimmy much better.

"I was wondering. Um. Do you think, uh, that I could... you know."

"Do you need help with something, Ethan? I'm happy to help out if I can."

"Can I come talk to you sometime?" he said, in a rush. "I won't take too much time, but I just kind of need to talk to somebody and you knew my dad."

When he stopped to take a breath I said, "Absolutely. You want to come over to my house? Meet somewhere?"

"I have my mom's car. I could come to your house. You live in

StewCross, don't you?"

It was funny to think that today's kids used the same nickname for our hometown that my classmates and I had, twenty or thirty years before. I gave him my address and he said he'd come right over.

I found Lili in the kitchen, cleaning up after our take-out dinner. "What do you think he wants?" she asked, after I told her about the call.

"He said something about how I knew his dad. So maybe he wants to talk about his father for some reason."

The gate called to announce Ethan's arrival, and I opened the door to his knock. In the glow of the light over my front door, Ethan appeared younger than sixteen. He had a light sprinkle of acne on his forehead, and he kept his arms close to his body, as if he was trying to take up as little space as possible.

He looked behind me to see Lili and Rochester, then took a couple of steps backward. "If this isn't a good time," he said.

"I was about to take Rochester for a walk. You want to come with us?"

"Sure." He reached down to scratch Rochester under his chin.

I got the golden's leash and we walked out into the cool evening. Rochester led the way, sniffing and peeing, and Ethan and I followed, neither of us speaking. In the glow of a street lamp, I looked at Ethan. He wore no jacket, just a T-shirt, and I could see that lifting those barbells in his room was building muscles.

Was he strong enough to have pushed his father into the canal after an argument? Was that why he'd come to see me, to confess?

My brain was racing toward what I could say, how I'd have to call Rick, when Ethan said, "You and my dad were friends, right?"

"Back in college," I said.

"But you were talking to him over the last couple of weeks, right? Before he, you know, died."

"That's true. We hadn't seen in each other in a long time and we had a lot to catch up on."

"Did he... was he..."

I didn't know where Ethan was going, so I couldn't prompt him. I just waited for him to spit it out.

"Was he mad at me?"

That wasn't what I was expecting, and it took me a moment to gather my thoughts. "Not at all," I said. "Every time your dad and I talked about you or your sister, it was always that he loved you both, that he'd moved down here to be closer to you."

"But I was mean to him. I wanted to go to a concert at this club in Greenwich Village with some of my friends from home, and he said I was too young to go into the city by myself. I got really mad at him and I told him I hoped he died. What if he killed himself because of what I said?"

Ethan was on the edge of crying, so I put my arm around his shoulder. "Sometimes we say things to people that we love that we don't mean. You should have heard some of the things I said to my father when I was your age."

I remembered those screaming matches when I was a teenager and I only wanted to do the exact opposite of whatever he asked. "I used to tell my dad that I hated him, that he was mean, that he didn't care about me."

Ethan sniffled. "What did he say?"

"Back then? Usually something like 'go to your room' or 'you're grounded.' It wasn't until I was older that I started to see that my dad hadn't just been mean or hateful. That whatever he did was because he loved me and wanted to protect me."

Rochester tugged me forward and I let go of Ethan's shoulder. "That's probably why he didn't want you to go into the city by yourself. He wanted to make sure you didn't get lost or confused or have somebody take advantage of you."

"My friends are taking a train into Grand Central," he said. "But the train I'd have to take from Trenton goes to Penn Station, and he said it would be too confusing to get from there to the Village."

"That's true," I said. "I lived in Manhattan for a couple of years and I still have trouble getting around sometimes."

Rochester suddenly stopped, turned around, and put his paws up on Ethan's waist.

"Rochester! Get down!" I said.

Ethan laughed, and said it was all right. He petted Rochester's head, and then the dog went back to the ground and continued forward.

"Did you apologize to your father?" Ethan said, after a moment or two. "For all the times you were mean to him?"

"All the time. The older I got the more I understood what my father was getting at. I used to call him up, when he was here in Stewart's Crossing and I was living in California, and tell him things I'd seen, tell him how I heard things he used to say coming out of my mouth. He just laughed." We reached the end of the street and turned around to head for home. "Parents know that their children love them, and they don't mean the bad things they say."

"But I can't apologize to my dad."

"Sure you can," I said. "Listen, Ethan, do you believe in God?"

He shrugged. "I guess so. My mom and dad never made us go to church or anything. Just to the Quaker meeting once in a while."

"Well, I believe in God," I said. "And I believe we each have a soul that survives after our body is gone. So that means your dad's soul is out there, keeping watch over you and Madison. He can't be here in person, but I know he'd hope that you thought about the lessons he tried to teach you, that you were trying to be a good person."

"So you think I could, like, pray to him?"

"I don't know if prayer is the right word," I said. "More like talk to him. Sit down on your bed at home, close your eyes, and see your dad in your mind. And then tell him whatever you want to say."

We followed Rochester on a circular route through River Bend, back to where Ethan had parked his mother's car. "Thanks, Mr. Levitan," he said.

"Call me anytime you need to talk." I hugged him, feeling his damp face against my shoulder. I felt that old familiar ache—if the first child Mary lost had lived, he or she would have been close to Madison's age, and I'd have a lot more experience as a parent than I had.

I was glad that Ethan hadn't admitted to an argument by the canal the night his father died, and sad that Doug couldn't be here with his son. I wasn't the boy's father, but I vowed to do my best to help when I could.

25 – WHEELS OF THE WORLD

Wednesday morning dawned sunny and warm enough that I could sit outside the Chocolate Ear to wait for Rick, who'd emailed the night before about the report I had sent him. So much had happened since I'd had breakfast there with Doug and I couldn't help thinking of him as I sipped my cappuccino, sitting on a white wrought-iron chair under the dark green awning with Rochester at my feet.

Rick came out of the café with a cup of coffee in one hand and a dog biscuit in the other. Rochester jumped up and took the biscuit from Rick's hand, then slumped at my feet, chewing industriously.

"Remember that picture we saw on the wall at Las Iguanas?" I asked, as Rick sat down across from me.

"The one with Guilfoyle and a couple of his friends," Rick said.

"Yup. One of those friends was Alex Vargas."

"Tiffany's Alex Vargas?"

"One and the same. Isn't that a weird coincidence? I met a guy at the funeral who said they were all close—him, Doug, and Alex. Doug called them the First Husbands Club. Can you find out if Vargas has an alibi for the night Doug was killed?"

"I told you. The chief has ruled Guilfoyle's death a suicide. Case closed. Nothing more to investigate. Plus, there is no way I'm going to drag Tiffany into this. She's already enough of a mess over this business at the clinic."

"Can you at least look into that report I sent you? Doug thought someone was fiddling with money at Beauceron, and I owe it to him to follow through."

"You have this idea that the law is something you can twist around to your own advantage," Rick said. "How'd you get this information, anyway? Hack into their system? You think the end justifies the means, pal, and you're wrong. You want justice but if you don't obey the law, then what's the point?"

"Doug gave me that set of spreadsheets to look at. I owe it to him to follow up."

When I taught college level writing, I insisted that my students pay attention to their language, using exactly the right words to say what they wanted. The corollary to that was that you could also choose your words to convey different levels of meaning, to clarify or obscure it. Doug had indeed given me the original spreadsheets, so I wasn't lying, just omitting that I had indeed hacked into the Beauceron server in order to download the locked spreadsheet with the real numbers.

"You want to open this can of worms, be my guest," Rick said. "You met Hank Quillian at the FBI when that neighbor of yours was involved in the online art theft. Give him a call and show him what you have. But don't come crying to me if things backfire."

"Great to see you have so much faith in me." I stood up, scraping the wrought-iron chair on the pavement and leaving my half-empty coffee cup on the table. "Come on, Rochester, let's go."

"Be that way," Rick grumbled, but he didn't say anything to convince me to stay.

By the time I checked my email, later that day at work, Rick had sent me Agent Quillian's email address and direct phone number. I called Quillian and explained what I'd discovered about Beauceron in broad terms, and we made an appointment for me to come to his office the next morning. I was lucky that it was a slow time at Friar Lake and I could take off two days in one week.

I spent the rest of the day on Beauceron, checking and double-checking everything. I amplified the simple report I had prepared for Rick, adding details and printing out both the real and fake spreadsheets. I had an old one-gig jump drive and I put all the documents on that as well.

That evening, as I followed Lili into the kitchen, I told her I was going to Philadelphia the next day. Rochester was right behind us, because the kitchen was where the food was kept. "Do you remember that FBI agent I talked to about that guy who was stealing from Mark Figueroa? I'm going to show him the information I found on Beauceron."

"You can't just email it to him?"

"I want to explain it."

"Uh-huh." She stared into the refrigerator, then closed the door.

"Since no elves appear to have made a grocery run and stocked our fridge without us knowing, what shall we do for dinner?"

Rochester knew the word "dinner," and it made him crazy that we didn't appear to be doing anything about his. "How about hoagies?" I asked as I opened the container of Rochester's chow. "I can run down to DeLorenzo's and pick them up."

I'd grown up on DeLorenzo's hoagies, made on fresh-baked rolls with hand-sliced meat and cheese, and I was pleased that the Thai couple who had bought the place after Mr. D died had kept up the traditions.

I fed Rochester, called in our order to the sandwich shop, then drove into downtown. DeLorenzo's was behind the post office on a narrow street that ran parallel to the canal. A line of shotgun houses spanned the narrow chunk of land between street and water.

I was surprised to find Catherine in line at the deli counter when I walked in. "You're clued in to all the local spots," I said to her.

"Yeah, Tammy turned me on to this place. The kids got tired of eating the stuff people brought us, so I thought I'd treat them to sub sandwiches. Plus I like the fact that everything here is fresh."

It was funny how using a single word could mark someone as a native, or not. In the greater Philadelphia area, we called them hoagies; subs and hero sandwiches were indicative of an outsider. I wondered for a moment how Ethan and Maddie would grow up— still rooted in New York? Or would they accept Stewart's Crossing as home?

"I have to admit, sometimes I come here just so I can walk along the canal," Catherine said, as the clerk was wrapping up her last sandwich. "It clears my head, especially when the kids are acting up or I've been fighting with Doug."

Her smile was sad. "Guess I won't have that to worry about anymore."

She paid for her sandwiches and I stepped up and got the ones I'd ordered on the phone. As I walked out, I saw Catherine's car driving slowly down Canal Street and I remembered what she'd said. She was familiar with the canal and the towpath, and of course she must have known that Doug couldn't swim.

I pushed those thoughts aside. Catherine had a reason to want Doug dead, but I couldn't believe that girl I'd known back at Eastern was capable of murder. And there was the whole Beauceron issue.

Not to mention the fact that Rick had already made up his mind that Doug's death was no one's fault but Doug's own.

Over dinner, Lili said, "I spoke to Tamsen this afternoon, and she invited me to join her and Catherine for a girls' morning out on Saturday," she said. "Catherine needs cheering up, so Tamsen booked us appointments for manicures and pedicures, and then we'll go out to lunch."

"I'm sure that'll be good for Catherine," I said. I was glad that Lili got along so well with Tamsen, too, because if she and Rick ended up together it was important for them to be friends, too.

"You think you could watch the kids for a while?" she asked. "I kind of volunteered you."

"Me?"

"It would be good for you to spend some time with Ethan and Madison, since you knew their dad," she said. "You said you had a good conversation with Ethan last night. And I know you get mopey sometimes over not having kids. This'll be a wake up call for you."

I snorted, but I agreed.

***

I slept badly that night, worrying about my meeting with Special Agent Quillian the next morning. What if he didn't believe me? Suppose he confiscated my computers and tracked where I had been and what I had done?

I kept reminding myself that I had a very reasonable explanation for where I got the material, and there was no reason for Quillian to challenge me. With luck, he'd already have heard rumors of illicit operations at Beauceron and would thank me for my help and send me on my way.

Rochester was unhappy that I was leaving without him, and he stood by the sliding glass doors and watched me walk out through the courtyard and close the gate behind me, an expression of desolation on his face.

I caught the Septa train from the Yardley station into the Reading Terminal in center city. As I walked out to Market Street I remembered that Rick had walked this beat in his first job as a cop. That was one of the many things I loved about being back home—

the connections to my past, and my friends, that were all around me.

It was only a few blocks to the FBI office at 6th and Arch, on the edge of Chinatown. It was a tall, glassy office building and as a convicted felon, it gave me the creeps to enter such a bastion of law enforcement.

Hank Quillian was in his early thirties, with the kind of weathered, wary look I'd come to associate with ex-military guys. He had a bristly crew cut and wore a dark suit, blue tie and white shirt, what I'd come to consider the standard attire for G-Men. But then, he was the only one I'd met, so maybe it was just him.

A year or so before, Mark Figueroa had hired the son of one of my neighbors to help out at his antique store. I didn't trust the guy, partly because Rochester didn't like him. He'd gone on to seduce Mark and steal from him, and my investigation had led me to the FBI. I'd liked Hank Quillian then and I trusted that he'd do the right thing with my information.

"Rick Stemper says you've been messing around in one of his cases again," Quillian said, as he sat down across from me in one of the Bureau's interview rooms. "But he told me I ought to see what you've got."

"I'll tell him I appreciate his referral." I went through how I'd reconnected with Doug, and how after the seminar was over he had come to my room with his laptop and showed me the first spreadsheet, from the defunct shopping center. "We looked at the numbers together and I agreed with him, that they didn't look right."

He held up a hand to stop me. "If this is going to be important to an investigation, I'd like to record our interview, so I make sure to get everything correct. Do you mind?"

I agreed, though my stomach jumped a couple of times. He clicked a couple of buttons on a tape and introduced himself, adding my name and the date, time and location of our conversation, and then asked me to recap what I had just told him, for the record.

I did, then continued. "The spreadsheet showed that the owner of the shopping center was receiving rental income on each of the spaces, but Doug knew the two anchors were both closed. Most of the other storefronts were empty, and the few that remained looked like they were struggling."

"What led you to believe there was anything illegal in that?" Quillian asked. "Could have just been bad bookkeeping."

"That was my first thought," I said. "But then while I had my hands on the keyboard my dog knocked my elbow, and I accidentally hit a couple of keys that took me to the last cell in the worksheet, where there was a hyperlink to another sheet."

"The amazing Rochester," Quillian said.

I was impressed that he remembered my dog's name. But Rochester had played a part in that previous investigation, though Rick had tried to minimize it so that neither of us would look too wacky in front of the FBI.

"That's right, Rochester." I paused. Here was where I was going to deviate from the truth, and I knew I had to keep the details simple.

"The link took us to a master spreadsheet that had separate sheets for each of the company's investments. When we compared the numbers for the shopping center on both sheets, we realized that the numbers on the second sheet were much more realistic. They represented that the shopping center owner had stopped making payments on his loan months before."

Quillian looked at me. "So you found some financial irregularities. Why do you think this is a case for the FBI?"

"Beauceron is a financial advisory firm. They put together investment funds like REITs and solicit consumers to invest in them. If the numbers they present on potential income are doctored, isn't that fraud? And if Beauceron has clients in multiple states, that would be interstate fraud. Isn't that covered by the FBI?"

"It is. But let's step back for a minute. Why did Mr. Guilfoyle come to you for help? You're not an accountant, are you?"

"I'm not. But Doug and I went to college together, and when we reconnected I told him about my computer background. He was looking for some way to compile and analyze all the data he had found, and he thought I could help with that. I was able to write and then run a couple of macros in Excel to pull all the data together into one place."

I opened the manila folder I'd brought with printouts of the Beauceron spreadsheets, and then flipped through them. "As you can see, there were a lot of spreadsheets, and Doug didn't have the time or the computer skill to go through them all."

"How many of the properties did you find that had anomalies?"

"About a dozen." I closed the folder and pushed it toward him, then pulled the one-gig jump drive from my pocket and passed it across the table to him. "All the data is on this drive as well." I took a deep breath. "The true spreadsheet is password protected. The password is in a document on the drive."

"Where'd you get the password?"

Time to massage the truth. "Doug supplied it. I don't know where he got it from."

"You didn't break the password yourself?"

I knew that Quillian had learned about my hacking background previously, and now I was sure that he remembered it. And I had learned enough about legal procedure to know that if the FBI knew I'd hacked the password, anything I found after that would be inadmissible in court.

"I didn't have to. Like I said, Doug gave it to me."

He raised his eyebrows, but all he said was, "Why didn't Mr. Guilfoyle come to us himself?"

"He was hesitant to raise any alarms at Beauceron because he needed his job," I said. "He wanted to stay until the end of the month to collect his commission check. We talked about passing the information on the authorities after he got a new job."

"Do you believe that his death is connected to this information?" Quillian asked.

"I don't know," I said. "Rick Stemper has already decided that

Doug's death was a suicide – he had too much to drink, he was depressed, and he went into the canal. With him gone, I contacted you. Doug was an honest guy and he'd have wanted the victimization to stop."

Quillian ended the recording, then slid the jump drive into his computer and checked it for viruses. When he was sure it was clean, he downloaded the information from it. "I'll take a look at this material," he said. "If I have any further questions I'll be back in touch."

He ejected the jump drive and handed it back to me. I figured that was my cue to leave. I shook his hand, thanked him, and walked out into the spring sunshine.

I was satisfied. I'd passed on the research Doug and I had done to the FBI. It was time for me to step back and let the wheels of the world move on. At least I'd try to.

I walked back to Reading Terminal, where I walked around the market picking up donuts from one of the Pennsylvania Dutch stalls, fresh artichokes and asparagus from a farm stand, and a big head of spinach.

When the West Trenton local arrived, I climbed on board. As the train racketed over the ancient tracks, passing mile after mile of industrial parks and commercial buildings behind a narrow screen of trees, I was transported back to my childhood.

My mother had a cancer scare when I was young, and she felt that the hospital at Penn had saved her life, so every time we needed to see a doctor we went down there, often on the train. I remembered shopping trips with her to long-defunct stores like Nan Duskin and Blum's, which had a mezzanine level with a railing that looked over the first floor, and when I was little I'd curl up under a rack of dresses and stare out at the people below me.

Lili and I had agreed that we were too old to have kids. Risks to her health, and the health of any children she bore, grew much greater after forty, and we recognized that even a healthy child would require major life adjustments. So all those rituals of childhood would never to be relayed to my own kids. I'd never develop new rituals that would bond me to them, that would leave someone behind to remember me after I was gone.

It was sad, but I knew plenty of couples of all ages who lived happy childless lives. I had Rochester, too, and he was such a source of love that between him and Lili I knew I'd manage.

It was nearly five o'clock by the time I got home. I logged into my college email and did some work until it was time to fix dinner. I boiled the artichokes and made a quick oil and vinegar dressing for them, then sprinkled the asparagus with kosher salt, wrapped the stalks in a damp paper towel, and stuck them in the microwave. I put a couple of chicken breasts under the broiler and sautéed the spinach with garlic, salt and pepper until it was wilted.

"This is a treat," Lili said, as she sat down at the table across from me. I had to admit the food smelled great.

"I had some time to kill at Reading Terminal," I said. "Are you still on for your mani-pedi on Saturday?"

"Yes. Catherine needs more cheering up than we thought. You remember that life insurance policy her divorce attorney had Doug take out?"

"The one for five million dollars?"

"Yup. It had a suicide clause for the first two years of the policy term. Because the police ruled Doug's death a suicide, she won't be able to collect a penny."

"Wow. That's terrible."

It also effectively ruled her out as a suspect in Doug's death. I was sure that her attorney had gotten her a copy of the policy as part of her settlement, so she had to have known about that clause. Unless she'd believed Doug's death would be ruled an accident?

I had to stop. Doug was dead, and nothing was going to change that.

"You and I will meet Tamsen and Hannah at Catherine's at ten," she said. "Ethan's going out with friends, but you'll have Madison, Justin and Nathaniel to wrangle. You'll be okay with that, won't you?"

"What am I supposed to do with them all?"

"You're a teacher," she said. "You're accustomed to dealing with a whole classroom of kids. You'll figure something out."

"My students are older," I protested. "And I have lesson plans."

"So wing it. I have faith in you."

I looked down at Rochester, who sat eagerly beside me hoping for a tidbit. "Will you help me, puppy?" I asked him.

He woofed and nodded his head.

"See, there you go," Lili said. "You'll be fine."

Lili volunteered to do the dishes, since I'd cooked, and I fed Rochester and took him out for his walk. I still felt unsettled about my trip to the FBI office. I'd done what I intended, and passed on the information about Beauceron. Hank Quillian had been polite and accepted what I had to offer, but I still worried. Was there some way he could figure out what I had done? Would he call me back and grill me about the password? If I had to admit that I'd broken the cipher myself, how could I justify that?

As usual, I'd pushed forward without fully thinking through the consequences of my actions – first in breaking into the Beauceron server, then in cracking the password. I'd done what I had in order to help Doug, but now he was dead, and it might be my ass on the line.

What stupid impulse had sent me to the FBI? Why couldn't I do what Rick had suggested, and just forget about all of it?

"What do you think, boy?" I asked Rochester, as we walked around the lake. "Have I made a huge mistake?"

He didn't answer, just kept pulling forward on his leash.

26 – CUCKOO

Time moved slowly on Friday. I was still unsettled from my visit to the FBI the day before. Joey and I were the only ones at Friar Lake, and every time I heard a scrape on the gravel outside, or the phone rang, I worried it was the FBI coming for me. I spent a lot of time with Rochester, playing with him in the office and walking him around the property, but even though his presence usually comforted me I couldn't get over the sense of impending doom.

It was early afternoon when Rick called. "Can you do me a huge favor? I just heard from Tiffany and she's completely freaked out. She went out on a job interview this morning and while she was gone, somebody broke into her apartment. She called the local cops right away and they came and took fingerprints, but she needs somebody to hold her hand and help her clean up."

"What about Alex Vargas? Why doesn't she call him?"

"I asked her about Vargas and she said he gets angry if she calls him at work."

"So she calls you instead. Like being a cop is less important than running a car wash."

"Well, this cop has to give a deposition in Doylestown this afternoon so I can't go up there. You think you could?"

"How are you ever going to get her to stand on her own two

feet if you keep running whenever she calls? Or getting your friends to run?"

"Whatever. I'll figure something out."

"Hold on," I said. "I can go. But I have Rochester with me. Will she be all right with him?"

"She'll have to be." He hesitated, then added, "Thanks, Steve. I know I have to do something about Tiffany but I can't while she's in the middle of a crisis. It's just not in me."

"I know. You've stood by me enough times."

After we hung up, I stared out the window and wondered what kind of trouble Tiffany had gotten herself into now. She didn't seem to have a lot of money, so why would someone break into her apartment—especially during day? Because of the kind of guy he was, I was sure Rick had been generous with her when they were married, so she might own some expensive jewelry or electronics. With the price of gold so high, even small earrings or pinky rings could be enough motivation for a junkie or other low-life to break in.

Rochester and I left Friar Lake a few minutes later. Instead of driving all the way back downriver to Yardley to get onto I-95, I took route 611 north through the Pennsylvania countryside. Cliffs butted up against the tight curves of the winding roads and I was surprised there could be so much wilderness right in the middle of one of the most populated parts of the United States.

As I navigated the interchange for I-95, I ran into a sun shower, that weird combination of sun glaring at my windshield through a screen of rain. A few minutes later I passed through it and into brilliant sunshine, and a fuzzy rainbow stretched over the industrial landscape. It reminded me of the line from Springsteen's "Glory Days" about the gas fires of the refineries. Something kind of trouble was clearly brewing in Tiffany's life, and I hoped Rick and I would be able to figure it out before it exploded.

When I got close to Tiffany's address I snagged an on-street parking space. Rochester was loving the urban smells and I had to keep tugging him forward, past a mattress outlet, a carpet shop called Sav-on-a-Roll-A, and a convenience store selling international phone calling cards, the front window a hodgepodge of flags from Latin American countries.

Tiffany's apartment was over a frozen yogurt store on a cross street a few blocks from downtown Union City. The lock on the exterior door to her building was rusty and looked like it hadn't worked in years. No need to buzz her to let us in.

The entrance lobby was dim and Rochester balked at having to walk up the narrow staircase to the second floor, but I tugged him along. When we got to apartment 2-C I stopped and looked at the knob and the jamb. There were no scrapes or pry marks around the lock, though I could see smudges of what looked like fingerprint powder.

Rochester sat on his haunches as I knocked. When Tiffany opened the door, her hair was a mess and she looked like she'd been crying. She was wearing a pair of capri pants and a low-cut blouse that showed off her impressive bust. She was barefoot and without her heels on I was surprised at how short she was.

"Rick couldn't make it, huh?" she asked, as she stepped back to let me in. "The dog isn't going to take a dump in here, is he?"

I wanted to say that it wouldn't matter, but I said, "He'll be fine. What happened?"

"Eddy arranged a job interview for me this morning so I was out for a couple of hours." She was shaking, and her voice quavered.

An interview? In what she was wearing? Then I remembered Rick had told me she'd worked as a cocktail waitress before getting the job at The Center for Infusion Therapy.

"When I got home from the bar it was like this." She sniffed once, then waved her arm to encompass the apartment. It looked like a whirlwind had struck, tossing sofa cushions, fashion magazines and kitschy knickknacks into random piles on the floor.

From the hallway, I pointed at the door. "Do you know how they got in? It doesn't look like they broke anything here."

"That's a cheap lock," Tiffany said. "Alex showed me once how you could get it open by sliding a credit card alongside it. He's been after the landlord to replace it for me."

"Could it have been Alex?" I asked as I followed her inside. "Looking for something you have?"

"Why wouldn't he just ask me? It isn't like we got any big secrets from each other."

Not like the one she was keeping from him, that she was seeing

Eduardo de la Fe on the side. "You know about his drug arrest?"

Rochester walked beside me and began sniffing around.

"That was a frame job," Tiffany said. "He told me all about it."

"He still hanging out with those people? Maybe he's holding something out on them, and they think you have it."

Tiffany didn't have an answer for that. She closed the door behind me and pressed the button on the knob to lock it.

"Anybody else have a key to that lock?" I asked. "Old boyfriends, somebody to water your plants or take care of your cat?"

"I don't have any plants and I don't have a cat. And even Alex doesn't have a key to my place." She rubbed her upper arms. "I'm scared. What if I'd gotten home early and whoever broke in was still here? What if someone wants to hurt me?"

She started to cry, and I put my arm around her shoulders. Ordinarily when someone was upset, Rochester would try to comfort them, but he recognized she wasn't a dog person, and he found a place to lie down on the floor.

"It's okay," I said. Her perfume was strong and reminded me of bug spray, though I was sure it was something well-advertised and expensive. "We'll figure things out." I looked around the mess. "Can you tell what was stolen?"

"My jewelry is all here, and the only stuff I have worth any money is my TV and my laptop. The TV's still here, and I my laptop was in my car when I went out."

Interesting. So the intruder hadn't been after something to sell.

What else did Tiffany have?

She sniffled, and wiped her eyes with the back of her arm. "What am I going to do?"

The best thing would be to get Tiffany working, take her mind off what had happened until she could think more calmly. I looked around the room and realized that once again, I couldn't help snooping. I was curious not only to see what the intruder had done, but how Tiffany had lived.

A couch sat in front of two double-hung windows that looked out at the street, with a scarred wooden coffee table in front of it. The cushions had been tossed aside, and all the knickknacks from a wire stand had been thrown to the floor.

No books.

A galley kitchen was along one wall, with a Formica-topped table and two chairs, which had been knocked over. The intruder had sliced open a bag of flour and spilled it on the table along with a plastic container of rice. A couple of jars of jam and hot sauce had been smashed in the sink and I could already see tiny ants climbing around.

"Let's clean up," I said. "You have a broom and a dustpan? Some big garbage bags?"

I put the cushions back on her couch, picked up the chairs and set them by the table. I hung up a couple of pictures the burglar had taken down from the wall, including the same photo of her and Rick at the Grand Canyon that I'd seen at his place.

Rochester kept getting underfoot as I swept the floor and filled a garbage bag. While I worked, my brain kept ticking. Why open all those jars and boxes? That implied the guy was looking for something small. What could it be?"

While Tiffany was rinsing the plastic containers, I asked, "This guy, whoever he was, he was looking for something small enough to hide in a box of rice or under a sofa cushion. What do you think it could be?"

"No idea." Her hands were full of dish soap and she used the back of her arm to wipe her forehead.

When the dishes were done she joined me in the living room. "Ricky gave me this," she said, picking up a miniature cuckoo clock that had been smashed in half. "He said it reminded me of him."

She tossed it into a half-full trash bag. "He probably tells you he can't get rid of me," she said. "Like today. I did call Alex, you know. First. It's just that he couldn't leave work."

"Yeah. A car wash manager's job is more important than a cop's."

"It's not like that," she protested. "Rick doesn't have to clock in or out like Alex does. And all my girlfriends have to work, too. But you know something? I don't need him, or anybody else."

She glared at me, then her whole body sagged. "I appreciate your help, though. I mean, look at me? My life gets wrecked and I'm stuck depending on some guy I hardly know. What's wrong with this picture?"

I realized that I'd been too snarky with Tiffany. I didn't like her because she took advantage of Rick, but she was still a person in trouble. "I know what it's like to start from nothing," I said. "I had exactly one friend who stood by me when I was in prison. My wife divorced me and threw out most of my stuff. By the time I got out my dad had died and I had no family left besides some cousins. I was lucky he left me his townhouse or I'd have been living in a homeless shelter."

"But you picked yourself up."

"I did. I was lucky that people helped me but I had to do the work myself."

"I can see why Ricky likes you," she said. "He's got this thing, he wants to fix the world. All the time we were married, he kept trying to get me to take college classes, to be like the other cops' wives. But I didn't fit in there and eventually we both knew it."

That was a different story than the one I'd heard from Rick. He had said Tiffany was an adrenaline junkie, that she got off on the idea that he might get shot on patrol. When he moved up to detective, she'd left him for a fireman. Now, she was dating a felon and cheating on him with a guy under investigation by the FBI.

Which was the real story?

Tiffany dusted her hands off. "I'd better get into the bedroom. I don't need any more strangers looking through my undies today."

I took a quick look from the doorway and saw the same kind of turmoil there. The mattress on the queen-sized bed had been turned on its side, and her clothes were strewn across the box spring. A couple of handbags had been turned out as well, leaving a detritus of lipsticks, makeup and tissues.

I left her to clean up and returned to the living room. I called a locksmith to replace the cheap lock, and while I waited for him to show up I ran the vacuum and finished tidying up. By the time Tiffany joined me there, Rochester was sitting on her couch, sniffing for something between the cushions.

"Hey, make him get down. I don't need dog hair everywhere on top of everything else."

"Rochester! Down, boy."

He wouldn't obey, and I had to walk over to him and tug on his collar. When he lifted his head I saw that he had Tiffany's keychain in his mouth. He let me take it from him, and then he scrambled back down to the floor.

"Is there anything on this jump drive?" I asked her. "It's small enough to hide in a box of rice. Where did you say you got it anyway?"

"I found it at work. I wanted to put some of my pictures on it but it's full of junk and I don't know how to clean it up."

What Tiffany thought was junk might have been worth breaking into her apartment for. "Can I use your laptop? I'll see what's on it and free up some space for you."

I pulled the llama off her key chain as she turned on her laptop. She didn't have any virus protection software on it, so I quickly downloaded a free version and ran a scan before I did anything else. Nothing harmful on the laptop, or on the jump drive either.

When I was able to look at the contents of the drive, I saw that a huge zipped file took up most of the available space. Fortunately I had the little jump drive I'd taken to Philly with me with the information I'd passed on to the FBI, and I was able to move everything on her llama drive to mine.

"The drive is empty now," I said. "So you can put whatever you want onto it."

"Can you help me download some pictures from Facebook onto it?" she asked. "I always seem to screw that kind of thing up."

We still had a while before the locksmith was due, so I showed her what to do. She had made a Facebook post the day before about the little llama, how she'd found it at work but hadn't realized until then that it was a drive for her computer. She clearly had a lot of time on her hands.

If indeed someone was after the jump drive, she'd committed the number one sin on social media—admitting to having something that might be valuable to someone out there. But it could have been something else entirely – maybe records from the CIT? Could one of her co-workers have been victimized too?

Along the left side of the screen, I saw her list of friends. "Any of these the people you worked with?" I asked.

"Yeah. That's Maria Jose there, she's my boss."

"Can you call and ask her if anyone broke into her place?"

She picked up her cell phone and dialed. I leaned down and scratched Rochester's belly.

After a moment Tiffany said, "Voice mail."

"Can you message her through Facebook?" I asked.

"I guess." She clicked on the head shot of a pretty Latina, and Maria Jose Rodriguez's page popped up.

"That's weird," she said, leaning forward to the screen. She pointed at Maria Jose's latest message, from almost a week before.

Mama huevos, America. Voy a volver a Colombia.

My command of Spanish was pretty basic, limited to ordering food and beer. "Mother eggs?" I asked Tiffany.

"It doesn't make sense." She pointed. "See this? *Mama huevos?* That's Cuban slang for suck my balls. Maria Jose is a real lady. She would never talk that way."

"Not even if she was mad?"

Tiffany shook her head. "She would say something in Colombian Spanish if she was. And it wouldn't be crude, like this."

The locksmith arrived, and I had a good, strong lock put on the door and paid the bill myself. I knew Rick would reimburse me, if only for the peace of mind it would bring him.

"You think you'll be okay now?" I asked Tiffany as he was finishing.

"Yeah, I'm going to stay over at Alex's for a few days. Who knows, maybe I'll move in there for good."

Didn't sound like the greatest idea to me, but it wasn't my

business what she did.

Rochester and I walked back to my car, stopping every few feet so he could sniff and pee. I called Rick and got his voice mail. I figured he was still at that deposition in Doylestown so I left him a message that Tiffany was taken care of and he could call me for more details.

As I drove home, I remembered that Tiffany had said that Rick liked to fix people. Sure, I'd seen that he was a caretaker, the way he looked after Tiffany, the way he was so good with Tamsen and her son.

Tamsen didn't seem broken in the same way that Tiffany was. She was smart and successful and a good mother to her son. But had Rick been attracted to her because of some inner core of sadness he detected?

But me? Was that why he was my friend, because he thought he could fix me?

I'd never thought of our friendship that way. We had initially bonded over our divorces. Then after he got Rascal, we were both dog guys. Sure, he had scolded me about my hacking tendencies, encouraged me to get help, to stay within the lines of the law. But I'd just thought that was the cop in him.

Did I still need to be repaired in some way? Would Rick stop being my friend if I didn't?

27 – CHILD MINDER

By the time I got home, I had to fix dinner, eat and feed Rochester, and then walk him, so it wasn't until early evening that I had the chance to see what was in the zipped file on the llama jump drive that Tiffany had found. Probably somebody else's pictures, just as there had been on the one Rochester found by the canal.

Fortunately this file hadn't been encrypted, and it was easy to unzip it. It was a lot harder to figure out what it meant.

Hundreds of PDF files of what looked like patient records from the Center for Infusion Therapy. And then a .pst file, which took me a minute to remember was the backup format used for Microsoft Outlook. The file was dated two weeks before, a date I recognized clearly because it was the start of my very first program at Friar Lake, the one that Doug had taken over for me.

The only way to view the contents of that file was to use Outlook's restore function. I set up a dummy account on my laptop, then went through the steps to import all the contacts and emails.

When the import was complete, I discovered it had restored an account connected to the address cubamerica1964@gmail.com. I couldn't find any indication in the file headers of who owned the address, so I started opening messages. It took four of them to discover the name Eduardo de la Fe as a signature.

Tiffany had said she'd found the llama at work, thinking it was a toy without realizing it was a flash drive. I believed her, because I didn't think she had the tech savvy to have backed up someone else's email account.

Was Eduardo the one who had been looking for the flash drive? He knew that Tiffany would be out that morning, because he'd set up the interview for her. Tiffany had made a post that indicated she'd found the llama drive at her office, so it was quite possible Eduardo would have seen the post. That gave him a great reason to break into her apartment and look for it. That's why the apartment had been trashed—because the thief was looking for something so small it could have been hidden anywhere.

I called Rick, but once again went straight to voice mail. "I need to talk to you about Tiffany," I said. "Call me when you can."

I kept looking through the PDF files, but there was so much there it was hard to make sense of it all. Most were medical records for Center patients, but some were copies of bank statements for the Center.

It was almost bedtime before I got a text message from Rick. *Long, long day. Going to crash. Talk to you tomorrow.*

Not what I wanted to hear, but I could imagine that after a bad day the last thing he wanted was more of Tiffany's drama. I hoped that she was with Alex, and that he was able to take care of her.

The next morning I tried Rick again but my call went to voice mail. He was probably out walking Rascal, so I left him another message. I still hadn't heard back from him by the time Lili, Rochester and I left for Catherine's house.

I wanted to try Rick again after the women left house for the beauty salon, but I had to deal with the kids first. I sat on the sofa and asked them what they wanted to do.

Madison was absorbed in her cell phone, while Nathaniel and Justin sat on the floor and stared at me. Rochester was no help; he was off in the corner rolling around on the floor with Pixie.

"Why don't we take the dogs outside and play with them?" I asked. That had worked with Madison a few days before.

In front of her cousins, though, she was too cool for school. "Bo-ring," she said.

"How about cartoons on TV?" I asked. "I used to spend whole Saturday mornings watching cartoons when I was a kid."

"Cartoons are for babies," Madison said. She listed a bunch of TV shows she liked, and I was surprised her mother let her watch shows with so much sex, violence and drug use, even if the main characters were teenagers.

"I'm hungry," Nathaniel said. "Can you make me a snack?"

I used the flashlight on my key chain as a wand and said, "Zap! You're a snack! You're a … granola bar!"

He looked at me like I was the stupidest adult in the entire world. Too bad I didn't know where anything was in Catherine's kitchen, or if Hannah would want her son eating in the middle of the morning.

Rochester abandoned Pixie and began roughhousing with Justin, the big dog jumping up and trying to knock him down like a bowling pin. They ended up on the floor wriggling and laughing. I was trying to keep my eye on them, telling Nathaniel he wouldn't starve, and trying to get Madison to put down the cell phone and pay attention when Justin raced around the living room with Rochester and knocked a lamp off the table.

I picked up my phone and called Rick. At last, he answered.

"Is this 911? I have an emergency and I need police backup ASAP."

In the background, Pixie began growling, probably because she was being ignored. That made Rochester start barking.

"Tamsen told me you were baby-sitting the kids this morning, which I knew was going to be a huge mistake. How long have you been there? Ten minutes, and the kids are already trampling all over you?"

"More like a half hour. I never should have let Lili talk me into this."

"Ow! Your dog stepped on me!" Nathaniel yelped.

"I can be there in a half an hour," Rick said. "You can fill me in on Tiffany's problems when I get there."

"Use the siren and the lights," I said, before I hung up.

I was tempted to hide in the bathroom until Rick arrived. "Madison, you think you're an adult?" I asked.

"Sort of," she said, barely looking up from her phone.

"Then act like one. This is your house and your cousins are your guests. What does your mother have in the kitchen that you can bring out?"

She groaned theatrically and stood up, still texting. "Come on, dweebs," she said.

"She's talking to you," Justin said, elbowing Nathaniel.

"Anybody's a dweeb it's you," Nathaniel said, pushing on his cousin's shoulder. "Karate kid."

"Computer nerd."

Rochester jumped up and romped between the boys as we trooped into the kitchen. Madison found some packs of crackers and peanut butter and poured each of her cousins a glass of lemonade.

"Aren't I a guest here too?" I asked.

"You're an adult," Madison said with disdain. "You can take care of yourself."

She flounced back into the living room with her phone. In the short time I'd known her, Madison had gone from happy to sad to disdainful. The change probably had to do with her father's death, though for all I knew she could have been prone to these mood swings all her life.

The boys began arguing over which snack pack was bigger, even though they were clearly the same size. Rochester nosed them, hoping for crumbs, and I moved between the kitchen and the living room, where I picked up the lamp, which fortunately hadn't broken.

I asked Madison what she was reading in school and she looked at me like I was from Mars. "We don't read," she said. "We just study for stupid tests." She went back to her phone.

I turned to the boys, who had trailed back into the living room. "What's your favorite class?" I asked Justin.

"Recess."

This was not going well. "How's Little League going?" I asked. Rick had originally met Tamsen when he coached Justin's team.

"Little League doesn't start for another two weeks," he said.

It went on like that for way too long, while I waited for Rick to show up and rescue me. Every question I asked fell flat. The boys argued and Madison pouted and stuck to her phone. I wondered if I'd have been any better if one of these was my own kid, if I'd watched him or her grow, suffering the tantrums and savoring the sweetness. My stomach felt hollow and I redoubled my efforts to communicate with the kids.

Eventually I found out that Nathaniel was a Lego genius and could build any of the kits in his age group in an hour or less. Justin was hoping to pitch when Little League started, and Rick had been practicing with him. Even Madison shared that she was going to be in the school play, an adaptation of *Alice in Wonderland*. She was going to be the Red Queen. "Off with her head!" she said, waving her hand in the air as if she held a scepter.

By the time Rick rang the doorbell, I was feeling better about my child-minding skills but I was still glad to see him. Pixie and

Rochester began barking and Rascal answered them from outside.

As soon as Rascal got inside he herded Justin and Nathaniel and the other two dogs out to the back yard. Madison remained on the sofa, only raising her head to say hi.

"What was the big emergency?" Rick asked as we walked into the kitchen.

"Maybe it's a good thing I never had kids," I said.

"Justin's very lively," Rick said. "Nathaniel is just the opposite. Madison is a tween and her emotions are all over the place. Plus her father, who she adored, just died." He sighed. "So what happened with Tiffany yesterday?"

We sat down in the living room and I told him about helping her clean up, getting the new lock installed, and then about the huge zip file that had been on the llama drive.

"So all that stuff was on the jump drive when Tiffany found it at the office," he said.

"And she made a post about that drive on Facebook the day before the break in. So Eduardo de la Fe could have known she had it. She told me that he arranged the job interview for her, too, so he'd have known she was going to be out then."

"Hold on, cowboy. Facebook is a public site. Anybody could have seen that post. It doesn't mean that de la Fe is the one who broke into her place. Anyone who worked with her at the Clinic could have put together that data and then lost the drive."

"Oh my God," I said. "Maria Jose."

"Who?"

"Tiffany's boss at the Clinic. She could have collected the data and then lost the drive."

"And?"

"And Tiffany showed me something weird on Maria Jose's Facebook page. She made a post about going back to Colombia, but she used the wrong words—something about sucking balls."

"Slow down. You are not making any sense at all."

I went back over everything I'd talked about with Tiffany.

"So if Maria Jose didn't make that post, then who did?" Rick asked.

"Eduardo de la Fe," I said. "It makes sense. He's Cuban, right? His email address is cubamerica. So he'd use Cuban slang, where this Maria Jose wouldn't."

"You're going pretty far out on a limb here," Rick said.

"You have to warn Tiffany."

"You said she was going to stay with Vargas, didn't you?" Rick asked.

"That's what she told me."

"Then let him look after her. If I call her now, it's just going to reinforce the pattern that when anything goes wrong, she comes to me. And I can't risk screwing up what I have with Tamsen."

I couldn't blame him. "But don't you think we should warn her to stay away from de la Fe?"

"If she's with Alex, she won't want to go anywhere near de la Fe because she won't want to set Alex off. In the meantime, you and I can look through that stuff from the jump drive and see if there's anything to worry about."

The boys came back in with the dogs. "We're bored," Justin said.

"I can show you a trick Rascal does," Rick said as he stood up. "Everybody back outside."

I was about to protest. I wanted Rick to call Tiffany right away. But the kids looked like they were ready to mutiny, so I went along with him.

I hoped Tiffany really was with Alex. She needed someone to watch over her.

28 – BALANCING ACT

It was cool and sunny out in Catherine's yard, and the couple of mature maples at the back were coming into leaf. The green grass was spangled with bits of light and shadow. The house had come with a teeter-totter and a ranger tower as well as a fence separating Catherine's house from the one behind. "Rochester can do this trick too, if he wants to," Rick said. "He's kind of spoiled."

I didn't know what trick Rick was thinking of, but I was curious to see what he'd do. He had put up a small agility course in his back yard the year before so that Rascal could play, and had taken his Aussie to a couple of dog shows to participate.

Rick started to lope around the perimeter of the yard, Rascal by his side, and when they approached the teeter-totter, Rick said, "Rascal, up!"

Rascal ran to the teeter-totter and placed one paw on the side on the ground. Carefully he stepped up, pausing at the top as the balance shifted, then scrambled down.

"Cool!" Justin said. "Can I try it with him?"

Before Rick could answer, Rochester ran over to the teeter-totter, but the end Rascal had climbed up was now up in the air. Rochester leaped up and knocked the board down to the ground, then climbed up on it.

"Show off," Rick said to him.

My dog stopped at the balancing point, though, swaying back and forth nervously. I had to walk over to the teeter-totter and coax him down, accompanied by lots of praise.

After that, the boys took turns running around the yard with the dogs, coaxing them up and over the teeter-totter. "Should we get Madison out here?" I asked Rick.

"Let her be. When she realizes all the fun is out here, she'll come out."

He was right, and Madison joined us a few minutes later, insisting on taking her turn with Pixie, who was too scared to try. Madison picked the little dog up and placed her on one end of the teeter totter and Pixie just sat down.

"You have to encourage her," I said. "Let me show you." I walked over to the board and began coaxing Pixie to climb up. She began to inch forward, and Madison joined me. Her face was so alive as she worked with the dog, and I hoped she could keep that little spark going.

Pixie jumped off the board as it started to lift, but we praised her anyway, and then the kids took turns running around the yard with Rochester and Rascal, cheering when they made the board sway. Rick and I sat on the ground with Pixie and watched.

After a chilly wind swept in, we went back inside. The kids and the dogs slumped on the living room floor. "Who wants hot chocolate?" I asked, and I got lots of affirmative answers. "Hang on, then. I'll make some."

Rick followed me into the kitchen. "I almost forgot, because we were so caught up with Tiffany. Did you hear about the suicide clause in Doug's life insurance policy?" I asked him, as I opened the refrigerator.

"Tamsen told me. It's a bear."

"Any way of changing your decision?" I asked. "At least from suicide to accidental death?" I found the milk and heavy cream I was looking for and pulled them out.

"Now that it's gone to the insurance company that's going to be tough," he said. "I told Catherine her best bet was to hire a lawyer and sue the insurance company, which means she has to demonstrate that I made an error in judgment."

"You?"

"I'm the one who made the final decision. There was no suicide note, and I'm sure she could find people to testify to Doug's state of mind. I told you myself I wasn't sure, but it was the chief who pushed me."

I opened the cabinet and foraged until I found a bar of dark chocolate and some vanilla extract.

"You'd testify for her, wouldn't you?" Rick asked. "You never believed it was suicide, and you were sure he wouldn't leave his kids like that."

I didn't like the idea of having to stand up in court and imply that my best friend had made a mistake, but I didn't want Catherine to lose the insurance settlement she was entitled to.

"Isn't there some other way?" I put the milk and the heavy cream in a pot and set it on a low flame, and began to shave the dark chocolate bar.

"Not unless it turns out he was murdered after all," Rick said. "But I can't keep investigating without pissing off my boss. What did Hank Quillian say after you gave him that information? Does he think Guilfoyle could have been murdered?"

As I stirred the shaved chocolate into the milk I told Rick about my meeting with the FBI special agent. "We didn't talk about murder, just about the financial stuff."

"Do you think there's a connection?" Rick asked.

"I don't believe in coincidence," I said. "And there are too many of them floating around. Logic says that if there is illegal activity going on at Beauceron, and Doug found out, that put his life at risk."

"You suspect his boss? Shawn Brumberger?"

"How can you not?" The hot chocolate began bubbling gently, and I poured it into mugs and called the kids in. I gave them a canister of whipped cream and let them serve themselves.

"Wow," Madison said, as soon as she tasted the hot chocolate. "This is awesome. Did this come out of a packet?"

"Nope. I made it."

"You can cook?" Nathaniel asked. "My mom says my dad is so bad at cooking that he burns water."

Justin looked down at his mug. He didn't have a dad to cook, or not. "Rick's a pretty good chef," I said. "He makes awesome hamburgers."

"We have a barbecue in the back yard but we've never used it," Justin said. "My mom says she doesn't know how."

"We'll change that as soon as it warms up enough," Rick said.

We sat around the kitchen table with the kids, talking and drinking our hot chocolate, until the women returned.

Catherine pulled me aside as Rick and I were getting ready to leave. "You're going to hate me," she said. "But I need to ask you another favor."

"I won't hate you at all. What can I do for you?"

"Doug rented a furnished apartment, at Crossing Commons."

I knew the complex, on the other side of Stewart's Crossing.

"Rick went over there after Doug died, just to check it out, and he told me that there's a lot of Doug's personal stuff there. I just can't face it. Do you think you could box up whatever's there so I can hand the keys back to the landlord?"

"I can do that," I said.

"The police gave me his effects." She opened up a drawer and pulled out a set of keys. "Hannah's handling selling his car for me." She pulled a car key from the chain and handed me the rest. "I'm not sure what all these go to."

She gave me the apartment number and I said I'd try to go over there the next day. "I really appreciate this, Steve," she said. "I feel terrible imposing on you when we've been out of touch for so long.

But there's just nobody else I can ask."

"It's not an imposition." If I had to tell the truth, I was gleeful at the chance to snoop through more of Doug's stuff. Maybe there would be a clue there that would point at a murder suspect, and cause the insurance company to change its decision.

29 – CROSSING COMMONS

Saturday night Lili and I sat at opposite ends of the sofa, our legs entwined. Rochester sprawled on the floor beside me, and I used my left hand to move the pages of my Kindle forward and the right to scratch behind his ears.

That clearly wasn't enough for him, because after a while he stood up, yawned, and padded away. He was back a moment later, and he stood over me, drooling on my lap. Then he dropped the llama jump drive I'd found by the canal on me.

"Yuck," I said. "How can I use this with dog slime all over it?"

I held it up and Lili asked, "Is that the drive with all the material from the clinic on it?"

"Nope. This is the one Rochester found. Just a lot of family pictures on it."

"Are you going to return it to whoever it belongs to?"

"No idea who that would be. I don't recognize any of the pictures."

She sat up. "Let's take a look. Maybe there's something in the file information. I know if I lost a drive full of family photos I'd want it back."

We went upstairs and she plugged it into the desktop computer, then opened Windows Explorer. "There's a ton of information in digital pictures that most people don't realize is there," she said. "Let me show you."

She right-clicked on the first photo and then selected Properties. The Details tab came up, which indicated that the picture had been taken with a Nikon D3000 camera, along with the date it had been created. Then she clicked the General tab which showed where on the drive the pictures were located.

So far nothing that interesting or useful. But then she clicked on Details, and at the very bottom, in the Owner field, were the initials EDLF. "Oh my God," I said. "Look at that."

I pointed to the screen. "EDLF. Eduardo de la Fe."

"And that is?"

"Tiffany's boss at the clinic. How could a drive that belongs to him end up at the Delaware Canal in Stewart's Crossing?"

"Hold on, Steve. Don't you think you're jumping to a big conclusion? Those initials could stand for something completely different."

"There's an easy way to check," I said. "Go to Facebook and let's see if Eduardo put up any pictures of his kids on his wall. Then we can compare them to the pictures on the drive."

It took a couple of minutes of typing and scanning, but eventually we found a match. Eduardo had posted several pictures from his son's softball game, and they were the same photos as on the drive.

"I have to tell Rick," I said.

"Steve. It's Saturday night. Give the guy a night off. If you're right, you'll have to explain it all to him. And aren't you going to see him tomorrow evening anyway?"

"Yeah, he's spending the day tomorrow with Tamsen and Justin. He said he'll bring Rascal over after dinner."

"You can show it to him then."

"As usual, you have the best ideas," I said.

We went back to the sofa and our reading, and Rochester was finally content to doze by my side.

Sunday morning, after taking Rochester for a long walk, I bundled him into the car and we drove over to look at Doug's apartment at Crossing Commons. It was one of the first apartment complexes in Stewart's Crossing, and had been around since I was a teenager. Back then, it attracted what people called "the lower classes," which meant somebody who couldn't afford to buy a house.

It had been completely renovated a few years before and now advertised "apartment homes." If I hadn't inherited my father's townhouse, I might have ended up there – it was a haven for the recently divorced and those who'd lost houses during the great recession.

Long rectangular buildings were punctuated with doors to first-floor units, and to staircases to the second floor. Faux-colonial touches decorated the otherwise bland exteriors – spread-winged eagles over each door, classical pediments and square light fixtures.

Dark blue wood shutters surrounded each window against white siding.

I parked in front of building fourteen, by the door that led to Doug's second floor unit. As soon as I got out of the car, Rochester jumped across my seat and hurried over to a bush and peed, as if he'd been holding it through the ten-minute drive.

A woman watched us from the first floor window. She waved her finger in a "no" gesture, and I waved back and smiled.

Rochester didn't like the claustrophobic staircase up to the second floor, but I flicked on the light switch and pushed against his rump, and he scampered up to the small landing, then sat on his butt and barked once. "I'm coming," I grumbled. "I only have two legs, remember?"

The smell of trash and spoiled food assaulted us as I opened the door. I guessed Rick hadn't done any clean up when he'd been in the place. Rochester rushed immediately to the garbage can in the kitchen and I had to hurry behind him to keep him from eating anything.

The kitchen trash can was nearly overflowing with fast-food wrappers and soda cups. I sealed up the bag and put it on top of a plastic table on Doug's small balcony, which looked out at a narrow hedgerow of oaks and maples that shielded the complex from the gas station next door. I left the sliding glass door open to air the place out and began cleaning up.

The apartment was clearly a bachelor pad, and the only personal touches were a couple of photos of Ethan and Madison. I remembered the photos of Eduardo de la Fe's kids on the jump drive, and got excited all over again about showing them to Rick later that day.

I packed up Doug's wardrobe of dark suits and white shirts and his few pieces of casual clothing into a pair of suitcases from the bottom of the closet, threw away the half-opened bottles of hotel shampoo and body wash. He had a good quality Eastern sweater, maybe a relic of his student years, and it might fit Ethan.

Rochester sprawled out on the balcony while I worked. At least he wasn't getting underfoot. I ferried trash out to the dumpster and stacked the luggage and a box of Doug's personal stuff in my trunk.

I left his laptop for last. Doug had kept a handwritten page with all his passwords beside it, so I didn't have to hack in order to snoop around. The passwords were all combinations of his kids' names and what I assumed were their birthdates.

The laptop was one of the few things Catherine would want; perhaps one of her kids could use it. But I couldn't hand over a computer without knowing what was on it, right? Suppose Doug had a collection of porn, for example? Imagine the horror a kid could experience. So I had an excuse to snoop around.

And of course, there might be some clue to Doug's death. If there was a suicide note, I was sure that Rick would have found it. But there might be some evidence of a connection between him and Eduardo de la Fe, some reason why de la Fe's jump drive showed up at the place where Doug died.

I logged into his Gmail account and began to sort through the mail there, deleting the junk and putting aside anything I wanted to look more closely at.

There were several messages with red flags, and I clicked through to the first, from ucwashwax@yahoo.com.

Dude. You promised I could get my $$ back anytime. Why are you stalling?

There was no signature, and no indication that Doug had answered the email. I right-clicked on the address to see if it had a person's name attached, but there was none.

The second message was stronger.

Dude. I know people who will hurt you if you don't get me my $$ ASAP.

Someone was threatening Doug about getting money back. Was it money this person had lent him? Or invested with him at Beauceron?

I sat back to think about how I could trace that address and heard the sound of paper crumpling from the second bedroom, which I presumed Doug had kept so that his kids would have a place to stay over.

Rochester was on the floor with a Jersey map beneath him, and he'd dripped a big glob of saliva right over Hudson County, just west of Manhattan. As I pulled the map out from beneath him I spotted Union City.

"Hold on," I said to Rochester. "Union City. UC."

He scratched his head with his back leg. "Once again, you're a genius, boy." I scratched the place he'd been trying to get at then went back to Doug's laptop. There was no website for Union City Wash and Wax, but there was a Facebook page, with a bunch of likes and positive reviews. One of them was from Tiffany Lopez, who praised the staff for their attention to detail. "Ask for Alex and he'll give you a good deal," she wrote.

Shawn Brumberger had let slip that Alex had invested money in Beauceron's REIT. The messages demonstrated that he was angry he couldn't get his investment back, and he'd threatened Doug. There was a clear motive for murder.

I doubted that Rick had bothered to look at Doug's email, so I forwarded the two messages to him. Maybe this evidence would be enough to allow him to reopen the investigation into Doug's death. At least we'd talk about it that evening.

I used Doug's password to access his bank and investment accounts, though I knew I was overstepping my bounds. But once again, I justified my actions because I was in pursuit of a greater good.

The news there was grim. He had gotten a big cash payout when he left Tor's firm, but he had used that money to pay off the mortgage on the house in Westchester. He had gone several months without any income, and after a while had cashed in one of his retirement accounts to pay alimony and child support. Then a month earlier, he had zeroed out the remaining account. There wasn't much left, and without that commission check from Beauceron there was no way he could have continued to support Catherine and the kids.

That was going to be even tougher financially on Catherine. All the more reason to do what I could to get Doug's death changed from suicide to something else.

There wasn't much else on Doug's laptop, but I zipped up the files on the hard drive and emailed that file to myself. When I was satisfied I'd looked at everything I could, I closed the laptop down and carried it out to the car. As I opened the door and Rochester jumped in, the woman who'd been watching me stepped out of the first floor unit. "Is he moving?" she asked.

She was in her forties, with a hard edge to her that came out in her messy hair, sweatpants and T-shirt that read *New Jersey: Where the weak are killed and eaten.*

"He's dead," I said. "I'm cleaning out his apartment."

"I'm not surprised," she said. "There was something not right about him." She peered at me. "You a friend of his?"

"Sort of. I'm doing this as a favor for his ex-wife." Rochester stayed in the car as I walked up to her, extending my hand. "I'm Steve."

She shook my hand reluctantly. "Marissa. The ex have a new man?"

I nodded.

"Wonder if that was him, then," she said. "Came around banging on the door yelling for your friend. This is a nice complex. We don't need that kind of thing."

It was hard to imagine Jimmy Burns banging and yelling, but you never know. "When was this?" I asked.

"Maybe two weeks ago?" she asked. "Come to think of it, I hadn't seen him around since then. I was going to complain to him."

"You remember what day?" I asked.

She shook her head. "Just that it was a weeknight, kind of late."

"Did you see the guy who was yelling?"

"Nope. I was already in bed and I didn't appreciate the noise." She pointed behind me. "Your dog is going again. He needs to be on a leash, you know. It's the law."

I looked behind me. Rochester had jumped back out of the car and was peeing on an azalea bush. "Thank you," I said. "Come on, Rochester, in the car."

He jumped in, and I backed out of the space and drove away. I wondered who had been banging on Doug's door. Had it been Alex Vargas? Had he then managed to track Doug down to the parking lot behind the Drunken Hessian? Why would he have had a jump drive that belonged to Eduardo de la Fe—had he stolen it? I didn't trust the guy, but it was hard to imagine a motive for stealing a drive full of someone's family pictures.

Or could it have been Eduardo who met Doug by the canal? What connection could there be between them? Maybe Rick would have some insights.

Or Rochester. He seemed to be providing most of the clues.

Neil S. Plakcy

30 – TROUBLEMAKERS

I was at home that evening when Rick pulled up in my driveway with Rascal, who rushed past me to greet Rochester. "This a good time?" Rick asked.

"Sure." I stepped back to let him in the house. "You got the emails I sent you?"

"I figured they came from you, since dead men don't forward emails."

Lili was behind me. "Give Rick a chance to get in the door before you attack him, Steve," she said. "You want a beer, Rick?"

"I'd love one. I spent the day with Tamsen and Justin. Mostly with Justin—in the back yard teaching him to throw a fast ball. It's been a long time since I used those muscles and they're reminding me of it."

"I'll let you boys chat," Lili said. "I still have a couple more projects to grade." She went upstairs.

I got a Dogfish Head 60-Minute IPA for Rick and one for me, and we sat in the living room. "I assume you got the message that I left you about the man who came by Doug's apartment. Did you know that Doug was living in Crossing Commons?"

"Yup. I checked the place out after he died, looking for evidence of his state of mind. Didn't find anything."

"It's a lot nicer than it was when we were younger," I said.

He sipped his beer. "I agree. Remember Marie Brown from high school? She lived there."

I nodded. In high school, I'd ridden a bus that passed by Crossing Commons on its way to Fairless Hills. Marie was a skinny girl with bad skin and a worse attitude. I remembered once the bus driver closed the door on her face because she was such a troublemaker, and Marie just stood there rubbing her face to make sure all the parts were still there. "If we'd had a chapter of Future Crack Whores of America in high school Marie would have been the president," I said. "I wonder what happened to her."

Rick sipped his beer. "She teaches kindergarten at Crossing Elementary," he said.

I nearly choked. "We're talking about the same Marie Brown?"

"Yup. Single mom at sixteen. Got her GED and started at the community college, but she got picked up for drug trafficking and sentenced to pre-trial intervention. The investigating officer was Jerry Vickers."

I'd met Vickers once or twice; he was the other detective on the SCPD.

"He took a personal interest in Marie," Rick said. "Got her to finish her associate's degree and keep her nose clean. Then he married her and put her through Penn State for her bachelor's."

Just what Rick had tried to do for Tiffany, though it hadn't worked out. "Wow. I did not see all this coming in high school."

"Yeah, and I'll bet if we'd put up you and Marie and asked 'Which one of these two will serve a year in prison,' most people would have been wrong. Or even 'Which one of these two will not learn from their mistakes.'"

"I get it, Ricky," I said, using Tiffany's nickname for him.

He took a pull of his beer. "So. Crossing Commons. Is that where you were when you hacked into Guilfoyle's email account?"

"I didn't have to hack it," I said. "Catherine asked me to clean out his apartment, and his passwords were sitting right there next to the computer."

"I saw them. Checked for any recent documents and emails but nothing that said he was depressed or suicidal. Of course, for you they'd be like an engraved invitation."

"Ha. So what are you going to do with what I sent you?"

"It's tough. I can't start looking into Guilfoyle's death again without something a lot stronger than some veiled threats. That would get me in hot water with the chief. And if he found out that the guy involved is my ex-wife's boyfriend? I'd get fried by both him and Tiffany."

"There's something else. You remember the llama drive Rochester found by the canal?"

"The one that was completely unrelated to Guilfoyle's death?"

"Maybe not so unrelated. Lili helped me look through the files last night and we found that the drive belonged to Eduardo de la Fe."

"You've roped her into your activities now? Teaching her to

hack?"

"No. She taught me how to look at the file information. The 'owner' of the files has the initials EDLF—Eduardo de la Fe. We checked his Facebook page and saw the same pictures there as on the drive."

"So now you're saying Tiffany's boss killed Guilfoyle, not her boyfriend?"

"I'm not saying anything," I said. "Just presenting some facts."

"Which still do not add up to anything concrete."

"Then maybe there will be some more evidence in the files on the other llama drive, the one Tiffany found at the office."

We looked over the restored emails from Eduardo de la Fe at the Center for Infusion Therapy, and then the medical records, and in the end we decided we didn't have enough information to make any judgments. "We need to get this to the FBI," Rick said eventually. "The only agent I know is Hank Quillian, so I'll send it to him and him to pass it on to the right people."

"How are you going to phrase it?" I didn't want my name showing up in a second FBI investigation. Speaking to Quillian about the irregularities at Beauceron had been nerve-wracking enough.

"It came from Tiffany, right? She's my ex, she knows I'm a cop, so very reasonable she would have given it to me. We'll just short-circuit things and say she gave me the drive when we met her on Sunday."

Rick sat back. "With that out of the way I can focus on my real job," he said. "Fortunately I was off duty today, so Vickers caught the case. Would have been bad if I was the investigating detective."

"What case?"

"Ethan Guilfoyle," Rick said. "He and two other guys were caught vandalizing the florist's early this morning, before they opened."

"Oh, crap," I said. "What were they doing?"

"They broke one of the panels in the greenhouse, smashed some plants. One of the guys was caught with a hundred bucks from the register in his pocket."

"You think they broke into the Old Mill too?"

"I think they might have. There were a million fingerprints at the crime scene so we couldn't get anything usable. But Vickers will be getting a search warrant for Catherine's house and the homes of the other two boys, and maybe he'll find some evidence linking them. The three of them were released into the custody of their parents pending arraignment."

"Poor kid. I'm sure he's just acting out after his father's death."

"Don't be too sure. Tamsen told me he got into some kind of trouble up in Westchester, but she didn't want to say more. I'm afraid to ask her for the details."

"You want me to?"

"Absolutely not! This isn't my case, it isn't my business, and it isn't yours. Vickers will find out whatever he needs on his own." After a minute, he said, "There is something you could do."

"Name it."

"Talk to Ethan. Tell him what prison's like. Maybe you can scare him straight."

"It wasn't like I was in maximum security lockup. Don't get me wrong, it was tough. But I was a white-collar criminal and most of the time I worked in the library."

"You're good at embellishing stories," Rick said drily. "I'm sure you can come up with something."

"Seems like I'm not too bad at investigating, either," I said. "If you hadn't been so quick to call Doug's death a suicide, if you'd looked through his emails, I wouldn't have to do so much of your work for you."

He opened his mouth, then shut it again.

Had I pissed off my best friend? Yeah, he hadn't done as much to investigate Doug's death as he could have, but he was under pressure from the chief of police, who didn't want another murder registered under his command.

"I'm an asshole," Rick finally said. "Everyone keeps asking you for favors – me, Catherine, Tiffany. And you go ahead and do what you're asked, and I keep snapping at you because I'm pissed that I can't do what I'm supposed to and I have to rely on you."

"You're not an asshole," I said. "You're in a tough situation."

"Yeah, but everybody's life sucks sometimes," he said. "Look at Tamsen. You never hear her complaining about being a single mom, about working her butt off to sell those monogrammed knickknacks in order to put food on the table. Even to myself I sound like a whiny little kid sometimes."

The dogs came galloping in to the kitchen then, and Rascal nuzzled his head against Rick's knee, leaving a big spot of drool on his khaki slacks. Rochester rubbed against me, but at least he wasn't drooling.

"At least Rascal loves you," I said.

"Yeah, because I feed him." He scratched the Aussie behind his black and white ears and Rascal opened his mouth wide in a doggy grin. Then he and Rochester took off at a gallop into the living room.

I raised my fist to bump Rick's. "Hardy Boys forever," I said.

He returned the gesture, then stood up. "I don't say it enough, but I appreciate your help, Steve," he said. "I want to do right by Catherine and with the chief on top of me it's hard to do that without your help."

"I'll do my best."

Neil S. Plakcy

31 – CROSSROADS

One of the great things about being an administrator in academia is the slow pace while everyone else is busy with grading and graduation. Sure, I had to plan my programming for the fall, set up publicity and handle advanced registrations, but most college business was deferred until late August.

That meant I had plenty of time to play with Rochester and walk him around Friar Lake. It also meant I had free time to do more snooping and see if I could find more connections between Doug Guilfoyle, Alex Vargas and Eduardo de la Fe. Rick had made it clear that he couldn't do anything more to investigate Doug's death until there was more concrete evidence. Which left it up to me to do what I could to get justice for Doug, and the insurance payout for Catherine.

By Monday afternoon, I had finished my college work and I turned to Google. I entered my search terms and kept clicking on links, long after they'd had any meaning. I was sure there had to be something there, but I just couldn't find it.

Rochester came nosing up to me. "What do you have in your mouth, boy?" I asked. The links of an old choke-chain collar dangled from his mouth.

When I inherited Rochester from Caroline Kelly he came with a collar made of metal links that closed tight around his neck when he pulled too hard. As he got older, I'd replaced it with a dark green cloth one with a snap latch, patterned with tiny white paw prints. I'd lost track of where the choke chain had ended up, but obviously I must have left it at Friar Lake.

I pried his jaws open and said, "Does this mean you want to go for another walk?"

He wagged his tail, but instead of rushing for the door he went down on his front paws, then settled his butt to the floor and looked up at me.

I held the cold metal links in my hand. Links. Of course. LinkedIn. Doug would have had a profile on that business-oriented networking site. I put the collar down on the table, scratched Rochester behind the ears, and told him he was a very good boy.

Then I logged in to my account on LinkedIn and searched for Doug Guilfoyle. Sure enough, Doug had a profile there. I skimmed through his experience and education and looked at his connections.

LinkedIn put up the ones we had in common first—a few Eastern classmates, and Tor Svenson. As I skimmed down, I looked for Alex or Alejandro Vargas.

Instead, I found Eduardo de la Fe.

Was it another coincidence? Or a connection that might lead to de la Fe's jump drive landing in the dirt by the Delaware Canal?

It made sense that Doug would know de la Fe; they both hung around at that same bar, Las Iguanas. Tiffany had said that Eduardo was separated from his wife—could he have been a part of that First Husbands Club that Doug had created with Alex and Hari? Plus Doug was hustling for new clients all the time, so he'd be collecting business cards and then connecting through social media.

The LinkedIn connection still wasn't enough to indict Eduardo, though. I'd have to have something more concrete before Rick would be able to do anything.

I looked at the clock. It was tempting to stay at Friar Lake for a while and keep snooping, but I had promised Rick I'd talk to Ethan Guilfoyle and I was planning that visit for the evening.

After dinner, I called Catherine. "I have some stuff from Doug's apartment," I said when she answered. "Can I drop it off?"

"I don't want any of it," she said.

"Catherine. There are some good photos of the kids. And Doug's laptop."

"You're right, I should take those. Ethan's been bugging me for a new laptop. And if you can bring back the key, I'll go past the landlord's office and return it."

"I can drop off Doug's clothes at one of the thrift shops for you," I said. "Rick also suggested maybe I could talk to Ethan."

"Ethan has been grounded, possibly for the rest of his life. Why did Rick want you to talk to him? He didn't steal anything from you, did he?"

"I'll explain when I see you later," I said.

I left Rochester at home this time when I drove to Catherine's, where Madison answered the door. "My brother is grounded," she announced. "He's been very bad."

"Yeah, I heard," I said, juggling the big box full of Doug's stuff. "Can I come in?"

She stepped back and hollered, "Mom! Rochester's dad is here." She turned her back on me and walked upstairs, leaving me standing there. I put the box on the floor and closed the front door.

Catherine came in from the kitchen, wiping her hands on a dish towel. "Sorry, I was just cleaning up from dinner. Can I get you anything?"

"No thanks." I looked down at the floor. It never got easier to explain my past. "So, listen. I guess Rick hasn't told you what I've been up to since we graduated."

"I thought you were teaching and working at Eastern all this time."

I shook my head. "Can we sit down for a minute?"

"Of course."

We sat on the sofa and I gave her the short version. Marriage, miscarriage, retail therapy, hacking, prison. "Rick thought I might be able to speak to Ethan about my experience," I said.

Catherine shook her head. "I don't think so. No offense, Steve, but a felon is the last person I want talking to my son right now."

"With all due respect, I *am* the kind of person he needs to talk to. I know he's been acting out since the divorce, but he needs to understand that his actions have consequences, and that they can turn out to be very bad."

"Do you think he'll have to go to jail?" she asked. "He's a kid."

"I'm not an attorney, and I don't know the specifics of what he's been charged with. But I do know that I met a lot of guys in prison who started out the way Ethan has. And you don't want him to go that route."

"I just don't know what I'm doing anymore," Catherine said, and she began to cry. "I thought I'd put the divorce behind me and the kids and I were doing okay. Then Doug died, and everything was miserable again." I moved over closer to her on the sofa and put my arm around her, and she cried against my shoulder.

After a moment or two she straightened up and dried her eyes with a tissue from her pocket. "Sorry. I try not to break down in front of the kids but it's been very hard lately. Especially now with this insurance business. I had been figuring we'd be able to stay here in the house, but now I have no idea what we'll do. Hannah has been helping me put together a resume, but I have to face the fact that I have absolutely no skills."

"I'm sure you do," I said. "You're a writer, right? So you have creativity, and you know how to put words together. You can probably type pretty well, too."

She nodded.

"I helped a bunch of guys with resume writing when I was in prison. It's all about figuring out the skills you've gained in life, even if you don't have a lot of paid work. You have to be good at time management to raise kids, for example. You can work under pressure. If you need me to look over what you put together with Hannah, just ask."

"Thanks, Steve." She blew her nose. "Sometimes it all gets to be so much, especially with the kids. I love them so much but everything I do only makes things worse."

"Let me help, then. Let me talk to Ethan."

"All right. If he'll even let you into his room."

I picked up the box and climbed the stairs, then knocked on the door with the hazardous waste sign. "It's Steve Levitan," I said. "I have some stuff of your dad's that you might want."

"Go away," Ethan said from behind the door.

"He left a pretty good laptop. I'm sure he would have wanted you to have it."

No response.

"Okay, then, I'll give it to Madison. She'll probably break it in a couple of days, but if you don't want it…"

I heard some movement inside the room and Ethan opened the door. He looked even worse than the last time I'd seen him – his hair stringy and unwashed, the few hairs on his chin looking more like dirt than a beard.

"If you let me come in I'll show you what he left."

He didn't say anything, but he did step back to allow me to walk in. I put the big box on his bed and pulled out the laptop, which I'd left on top. "Why don't you set this up?" I asked, handing it to him.

"Over there on your desk would be good."

"This is the same one he had when he lived with us," Ethan said. "It's not that new."

He carried it over to the desk and turned it on. I pulled out the college sweater I'd found in Doug's closet and held it up. "You think you might like this?" I asked. It was a lightweight wool in an off-white color, with the rising sun logo and the word EASTERN in light blue stitching.

"I don't know why my dad kept that," Ethan said. "He couldn't fit into it anymore."

"Maybe he kept it for you," I said.

"He was a loser," Ethan said. "He told my mom that he was running out of money, even with his new job. And now my mom says we're going to have to move again, to somewhere smaller and cheaper, because his insurance isn't going to pay out."

"He wasn't a loser at all," I said. "Just a grownup. We make mistakes sometimes, just like everybody else. Did he ever tell you about the night he and I and a bunch of our buddies got arrested?"

Ethan sniffled and looked up at me. "He got arrested? He was such a goody-goody."

I told him the story of our naked romp around the exercise course, embellishing with details. I gave Doug all the best lines, and by the time I was finished Ethan was laughing.

"That doesn't mean that what we did was right," I said. "The police called our parents and we got into a lot of trouble. Instead of working to earn money that summer I had to volunteer to clean up along the Delaware. A hundred hours."

"You think that's what they'll make me do? Clean up?"

I shrugged. "I'm not the judge, and I don't know what you did. Do you want to talk about it?"

"Not really." The laptop was on by then, and Ethan began to fiddle with it.

"That wasn't the only time I got in trouble," I said, after a while. "I didn't learn my lesson so quickly. Maybe you'll be smarter than I was." I leaned back against a poster of a soccer player on Ethan's wall. "Or maybe you'll end up in prison, like I did."

He turned around quickly. "You were in prison? For what?"

"Mostly for being an arrogant prick who thought I was smarter than everyone else." I skipped over the motivation for my crime and focused on the time I spent in prison. "I was scared every day. There were guys there who had killed people. Crazy guys who should have been in a mental hospital instead of a lockup."

Ethan's mouth was open but he wasn't saying anything.

"I was lucky, though, because I had a college education and I can speak well and write well. I got assigned to work in the library, and I helped a couple of very bad guys work on their parole applications."

I crossed my arms over my chest. I hated talking about this part, but it was important that Ethan hear it. "Another guy wasn't so lucky. He was a lot like me, white, college graduate, in for only a couple of years for fraud. He thought the best way to succeed in prison was to mouth off to everybody about how much better he was than they were."

"That doesn't sound too smart," Ethan said.

"It wasn't. One day we were out in the exercise yard and somebody stuck a shank in him. You know what a shank is?"

He shook his head.

"In his case, it was a toothbrush with a razor blade in the end. Somebody stuck it in the back of his neck as he was walking past. He stumbled and the guards kicked him and told him to get up. It wasn't until they saw the blood that they realized."

"What happened to him?"

"He died. They never found out who killed him." I looked down at my lap. "I knew, because I saw it happen. But I didn't say anything, because I didn't want to be next."

"Wow."

"So you see, Ethan, you're at a crossroads now. Things have been tough for you—your parents getting a divorce, then your dad dying. You can go two ways from here."

He didn't say anything.

"You can step up and be the man of the family," I said. "Be nice to your mother and your sister. Both of them are in as much pain as you are. It's tough, but you have to believe in yourself, that you're strong enough to get through this, and anything else that life throws at you." I took a breath. "Or you can give in to the pain. Do things you know are wrong just because they help you forget for a while, or because they give you a little jolt of pleasure."

I stood up. "Take a look through the rest of the box when you get a chance. And if you ever want somebody to talk to, call me. Or Rick. We both care about you, and your mom and Madison, and we're here to help you when things get tough."

Ethan mumbled something, and I walked out.

32 – TEMPTATIONS

I was drained after my conversation with Ethan, but even after Lili went to bed, I couldn't sleep. I was obsessed with the connection between Doug Guilfoyle, Alex Vargas and Eduardo de la Fe.

Did de la Fe have an account with Beauceron, too? I'd already established that he and Doug knew each other, through the bar and LinkedIn. It wasn't a big leap to de la Fe investing some money with Beauceron.

I had already gotten Shawn Brumberger to reveal that Alex had an account and I didn't think I could fool him twice. I didn't know how to find that out other than to hack into Beauceron's server.

I pulled out Caroline's laptop and fired it up. My fingers tingled at the thought of snooping around where I didn't belong. The neurons in my brain started firing as I remembered how easily I'd hacked into it before, how great it had felt when I had taken control of that elderly professor's computer, how I'd used my wits and tools to defeat the meager security measures in place at Beauceron.

I had admitted to Ethan that before I was arrested, I'd been an arrogant prick who thought he knew more than anybody else. Despite what I had said to him, I was still that guy.

How could I pretend to advise a teenager if I had so little

impulse control myself? I took a deep breath. I'd hacked into the Beauceron server so that I could download the hyperlinked spreadsheet. There was no other way to get hold of it, and it was the cornerstone of the investigation I'd begun for Doug.

But now I was just on a fishing expedition, struggling to find some connection between Doug and Eduardo de la Fe. Even the Feds weren't allowed to do that, so there was no way I could assert that I was better than they were, above the law. I remembered what Rick had said, that I thought I could twist the law around to my own advantage.

I closed the laptop, probably with more force than I had intended. I had promised Rick and Lili that I would try to control my impulses, that I would control my arrogance and my curiosity. It was time to remove the temptation from my grasp.

From the garage, I fetched a short ladder, then carried it up to the second-floor hallway. With the computer in one hand, I climbed a couple of rungs, and pushed aside the access panel to the attic.

Right after Caroline died, I'd made a place up there to hide the laptop so that my parole officer couldn't find it, between the plastic tub of wrapping paper and the box of half-chewed dog toys I couldn't bear to throw away. I slid the laptop back into place, and before I could change my mind, I replaced the access panel, climbed down, and put the ladder back in the garage.

My fingers were still tingling and my brain racing, so I opened my own laptop and logged into the hacker support group I had joined a few months before, at Rick and Lili's suggestion. I scanned through the recent messages, then searched the group archives. When I couldn't find what I wanted to know, I asked the question: "Have any of you been arrested? Spent time in prison for hacking? I have."

I wrote about my conversation with a friend's son and how I wanted to show him, through my own experience, that if he didn't change his behavior he was on the road to more and more trouble. But how could I say that, when I was having such a hard time avoiding temptation?

I posted the message and thought about Eduardo de la Fe. I was a smart guy—or so I kept telling myself. I had to be able to find out what I wanted to know without hacking.

Could I find something shady in his past, the way I'd discovered Shawn Brumberger had worked for that boiler room operation early in his career? Had de la Fe mentioned something on social media that might indicate he had given some money to Doug to invest?

I started to research Eduardo de la Fe. He had quite a digital footprint on social media. Since separating from his wife, he had begun hanging out at bars and ball games and car races, often accompanied by pretty women. His "likes" included Macallan Scotch whiskey, H. Uppmann Cuban cigars, and a shirt manufacturer called "The King of the Guayabera."

He had expensive tastes. Did that mean he had little left over to invest? I kept looking and it was frustrating that I couldn't find any connection to Doug Guilfoyle or Beauceron.

I went back to Facebook. Tiffany had been active, posting photos of her apartment after the break in and then again after she and I had cleaned up – though she made it sound like she did all the work herself.

A few hours earlier, she had posted that she had managed to get hold of her boss so she could get into the clinic the next day to pick up the personal stuff she had left behind in the flurry of the FBI raid. "I am not abandoning my only pair of Manolos," she wrote.

Shit. If I was right, and Eduardo de la Fe knew she had incriminating evidence against him, then she could not be alone anywhere with him. I had to warn her, but I didn't have her cell phone number.

It was too late to call Rick, so I sent him a message with what I'd learned, and told him to warn Tiffany.

I didn't sleep well that night, my head full of strange dreams about Tiffany swimming in the Delaware Canal and bumping into Doug's dead body floating there. She started waving her arms as if she was drowning and, from the bank, Pixie the Yorkie began barking madly. Ethan sat oblivious, caught up in something on his father's laptop. I dove into the water to save Tiffany but realized I had forgotten how to swim.

When I woke, Lili was staring at me. "You kicked me," she said. "You were flailing around like you were having some kind of fit."

"I was swimming," I said. "Or at least trying not to drown." I told her about my dream and then remembered Tiffany's plan to meet up with Eduardo de la Fe that afternoon. "I have to call Rick."

"I'm going back to sleep," Lili said as I got up. "I don't have to be at graduation until noon."

Since I was only an administrator, my presence wasn't required, and I planned to spend a quiet day at Friar Lake. I took the phone out into the courtyard despite the morning chill, so I wouldn't disturb Lili's sleep.

Rick told me he had already called Tiffany and left her a message, telling her that he would come up that evening and go to the clinic with her. "I said I'd pick her up at five, and she's meeting de la Fe at five-thirty. I didn't want to freak her out so I didn't tell her what you found on that drive."

"You want me to come with you?"

"Probably a good idea." He sighed. "I have to interview a witness in Lumberville this afternoon, so I'll meet you at your office at four and we can drive up to Union City together."

Rochester and I ate breakfast and then walked around River Bend. By the time I finished my shower and got dressed, Lili was still asleep. Her black cap and gown, with the brown-lined hood that signified her degree was in fine arts, were hanging on the back of the bedroom door. I kissed her forehead and left her asleep.

As I drove up to Friar Lake, I thought that perhaps next year I'd volunteer as a marshal for graduation, putting students into neat lines for their procession, making sure that each had a card with his or her name and the proper pronunciation. Or perhaps I'd be teaching again part-time, and I'd be able to march in the academic procession with Lili. I didn't have a cap and gown, but I did still have the hood I'd bought when I graduated from Columbia with my MA in English.

The campus would be buzzing with crowds of happy families, the graduates in their sky-blue gowns and broad smiles. I remembered my own graduation, years before, my parents so proud of me, the enthusiasm I'd felt and all my hopes for the future.

I was restless at Friar Lake, walking Rochester around and around the property until he finally refused to go any further. Early in the afternoon I went back to my hacker support group. Brewski_Bubba, the guy I'd chatted with the other day, had answered my post.

In the past, he hadn't revealed much about himself, just that he had gotten into trouble with credit cards, and his posts were often about the minor irritations of life lived on a cash basis—his inability to make plane reservations online or to rent a car, the way he always had to carry cash for everything from buying gas to groceries. All the little things that we take for granted in our plastic-obsessed society.

"County lockup, three times," he wrote. "No big deal. I'm six-four and weigh close to 300, though a lot of that is in my beer belly, LOL. So nobody messed with me. But then the state got hold of me and shoved me in St. Clair—worst prison in Alabama."

He typed in a link to an online article about the prison, but I skipped that and kept reading his post. "Seriously bad dudes there," he wrote. "Locks didn't work right and the warden didn't give a shit. Dudes were getting shanked all the time while they were sleeping. Swear to God, I had to sleep with one ear open in case anybody broke in."

That made my time in California seem like a picnic. Sure, I'd been scared, but at least I'd felt secure in my cell.

"That's why I won't get myself a credit card again, even though I can," he continued. "Any time I think about it I remember what it was like to be in the middle of pure evil. If you have any temptation, hold off."

I thanked him for his honesty and told him that I'd remember what he wrote. Then I switched over to my own Facebook account. Lili had posted a selfie with a couple of her colleagues, all in their academic regalia. I "liked" it, and added a message about them being the best-looking group of faculty at the graduation.

Just before four, Rick arrived and we headed north. "You get your interview done?" I asked.

"That was the high point," he said. "This morning I spent a couple of hours at the Court of Common Pleas in Doylestown with Catherine and Tamsen, waiting for the hearing for Ethan and the other two boys. Ethan pled no contest to three misdemeanors and the judge sentenced him to a hundred hours of community service."

"He's getting off easy this time. And eventually he can get his juvenile record sealed. I hope it's enough to keep him honest in the future. What about the other two?"

"Their parents hired an attorney who advised them to plead not guilty. A big mistake, in my opinion. Good thing you had that talk with Ethan. It seems to have put some sense into his head."

We chatted off and on through the drive, Rochester occasionally poking his head between the seats. I had just turned onto 495 when Rick's phone rang. "Hey, Tiff," he said. "I'm on my way."

I could hear her screaming through the phone. "Ricky! Oh my God, I was so stupid!"

He put the phone on speaker so I could hear, too.

"What's the matter?" he asked.

"Eddy called me this afternoon and I told him you were going to come with me to pick up my stuff. But he said he had a thing to go to and we had to meet earlier."

Rick looked at me and without him saying anything, I accelerated and began darting around cars. From the back seat, Rochester stirred nervously.

"What happened? You didn't go to the clinic with him, did you? After I told you to wait for me?"

"I didn't think it was a big deal. So I said yeah and I came over here."

"Hold on. You're at the clinic now?"

She had begun to cry and it was tough to make out her words sometimes.

"He started yelling at me and telling me I stole something that belonged to him. The only thing I could think of was that dumb llama thingy—it was the only thing I took from the office that didn't belong to me."

Of course that's what he'd want. It had all that information about clinic billing and his bank accounts.

"I handed it back to him but when he put it in his computer all he saw was the pictures your friend loaded for me. I told him that we had dumped all the stuff that was there but he didn't believe me."

She sobbed again. "He hit me so hard I fell down, and I must have hit my head."

I got off the highway and after looking both ways ran a red light. Rick didn't say anything, just nodded. "It's okay, Tiff. I'm on my way. Is he still there?"

"I don't know. But I can't move. He knocked a desk over me and I can't get out from under it."

Rick reached out and grabbed the dashboard but he didn't say anything to me as I swerved around cars. We were only a few blocks from the clinic by then. "I'm almost there. Just hold on."

I heard her sniffling through the phone, and then she stopped suddenly. "Oh my God, Ricky, I think the building is on fire! I can smell smoke."

I handed him my phone. "I'm calling 911 right now," he said. "Give me the address."

As I navigated through the crowded streets he relayed the information that Tiffany had given him to the dispatcher. At least there were no visible flames coming out of the building. Maybe the fire was a small one.

I pulled up in front of the clinic and Rick jumped out, holding both phones. The last thing I heard him say was, "I'm here, babe. I'm on my way in."

I watched as he ran ahead. "Don't do anything stupid," I called, even though I knew he couldn't hear me by then. Rochester stuck his head between the seats and whimpered.

"It's okay, boy." I peered ahead and saw Rick race up to the front door of the clinic and tug on the handle. When it wouldn't give he looked around frantically.

I was still double-parked, and a car pulled up behind me, beeping. I opened my window and waved the car past as I saw Rick grab a chair from the café next door, then slam it toward the plate glass window into the clinic.

The glass shattered as the car behind me went past. Then Rick disappeared through the opening.

There was no on-street parking I could see ahead of me, so I made a K-turn my high school driver ed teacher would have been proud of and went back down the street until I spotted a space in front of the Phone Llama store.

I parked, but when I tried to leave Rochester in the car he began barking and pawing as if he had to get out and pee. So I put his leash on and led him to a fire hydrant. He ignored it and pulled me toward the clinic. In the distance I heard the approach of a siren. I

The big golden was very agitated, pulling me forward, but I

couldn't let him get too close because of the broken glass on the pavement and the danger that the fire would burst out. I was down on one knee petting him when I looked up and caught sight of Eduardo de la Fe a few feet ahead of me.

He was leaning against a phone pole, half hidden from the street, the bastard. He was waiting there until Tiffany burned. I wasn't going to let him get away with it, though.

The fire engine pulled up, and de la Fe turned away from me. He began to walk quickly toward the clinic. I was so focused on watching him that I didn't realize until it was too late that my big dog had slipped his leash and taken off in the same direction.

Neil S. Plakcy

33 – HARDY BOYS FOREVER

"Rochester! Stop!" I cried, as he raced toward the clinic.

He kept going past the building, and I realized he was after Eduardo de la Fe instead. I hurried after him, but de la Fe had a big head start, and Rochester had four legs to my two, so I trailed far behind.

As I passed the clinic, the fire truck roared up and a couple of firemen jumped out. "It's that building," I said, stopping and pointing to the clinic. "Two people are inside."

When I looked ahead again, I saw that Rochester had caught up to de la Fe. As I watched, he launched himself at the man. The two of them went down, with Rochester on top of him. I ran as fast as I could to catch up, and by the time I got there, Rochester was sitting on de la Fe's back, the man immobilized beneath him.

"Good boy, Rochester," I said.

"Get your dog off me," de la Fe said, panting heavily. He tried to push Rochester off but my dog was too big.

"Not til the cops show up," I said. "I'm sure they'll want to talk to you about setting the clinic on fire while Tiffany was inside."

"You're crazy," he said. "I'm going to sue your ass."

I looked behind me as an EMT pushed a gurney out the front door of the clinic. Most of Tiffany's body was covered with a white blanket, but her head was visible, and she was holding Rick's hand.

I waved to Rick but he was focused on Tiffany and didn't see me.

"I'm serious, *hombre*," de la Fe said, as he struggled to get out from under Rochester's bulk. "You'll be sorry you messed with me."

"Yeah, like Doug Guilfoyle," I said. "And Maria Jose Rodriguez."

"I don't know what you're talking about."

"But the cops do," I said. "You left a jump drive with pictures of your kids by the canal where you pushed Doug into the water."

As the EMTs slid, Tiffany into the ambulance, I saw Rick lean down and kiss her forehead. Then he pulled out his cell phone.

I kept waving my arms like a lunatic until he turned toward me and I caught his attention. He ended his call, stuck his phone in his pocket, and hurried toward me.

As Rick arrived, de la Fe said, "I didn't push him. We were arguing and he stumbled and fell. Not my fault the jerk couldn't swim."

"Eduardo de la Fe," Rick said. "You have the right to remain silent." He leaned down and cuffed de la Fe's wrists as he continued to read his Miranda rights.

"I'm telling you, I didn't do anything," de la Fe insisted, as I called Rochester off. "I was just walking by my place of business when all of a sudden this guy's dog attacked me. You should be arresting him, not me."

"Yeah, well, he didn't hit my ex-wife over the head and then leave her to die in a burning building," Rick said. "Come on, stand up."

I squatted on the pavement, scratching Rochester under his ears, as de la Fe stood up, still arguing.

"I have to know," I said, when I stood up to face him. "So I can tell his children. Why did you kill Doug?"

De la Fe snarled. "That *hijo de puta*," he snarled. "He was a weasel, that one. He pressed me for details of how the clinic operated, of how much money it generated. Then he kept telling me how much money I could make if I invested with his funds."

It all came together, and I understood his motive. "Doug realized you couldn't be making as much money legally as you said you were," I said. "Did he figure out the insurance scams you were running?"

"Scam! His company was the biggest scam of all. I wanted my money back and he kept making excuses. I was sure he reported my clinic to the FBI to get me to back off. He denied it but then he went into the water before I could press him any further."

Behind him, I saw a couple of uniformed officers approaching us. "Then you figured out it was Maria Jose," I said. "She had all that information on her jump drive, but then she lost it."

"I want my lawyer," de la Fe said. "I'm not saying anything more until I can speak to him."

"Doesn't matter," I said. "I already know the whole story. You tracked down Maria Jose, but she told you she'd lost the jump drive with all the information on it. What did you do to her? Kill her, too?"

"I want my lawyer."

"Steve, that's enough," Rick said.

I wouldn't be stopped, though. "You made a strange post on Facebook pretending you were her. Then you realized that Tiffany had the drive, and you lured her here. But she had already given me the contents of the drive, and I passed them on to the FBI. You're done, *hombre*," I said, putting emphasis on that last word. "You're going to jail."

The officers walked up. "Thanks for the use of the cuffs," Rick said to one of them. "You can take this guy away now. I read him his rights, and he's already placed himself at the scene of a murder in my jurisdiction. The woman who went to the hospital, Tiffany Lopez Stemper, will give you a statement confirming that he lured her here, knocked her out, and then left her to burn."

De la Fe continued to argue with the cops as they led him away. Rochester looked at me as if I'd forgotten he was there, and I got down on one knee and kissed his golden head.

"I suppose you want me to say you were right all along," Rick said, as he watched them go. "That Guilfoyle's death was a murder, and the chief was wrong to force me to call it a suicide."

"All I care about is that de la Fe goes to jail, and Catherine gets the insurance payout."

I watched as the cops put de la Fe in the back of a squad car.

There would be justice for Doug, and his family would get the money they were owed, and know that he hadn't committed suicide.

The air was heavy with smoke, the flashing lights of the fire truck and police cars, the sound of car horns stuck in traffic.

"We should go," Rick said. "The local cops have my information, and they can call me when I need to give a deposition."

"What about Tiffany? You don't want to go to the hospital?"

"You know what? I was so worried about Tiffany as we were driving up. But then after I moved the desk off her and got her out of there, I realized that I'd have been a hell of a lot more scared if it had been Tamsen or Justin."

"But I saw you kiss her."

"Yeah. I'm not saying I don't care about her. Of course I do. But to me, that was a kiss goodbye. Then I called Alex Vargas, and he's on his way to the hospital. Let her be someone else's problem for a while."

He reached down to pet Rochester. "You're a good dog, aren't you? Grabbing the bad guys once again." He smiled and looked at me. "You want to stop by Catherine's and give her the news?"

"I think it's right that we do it together," I said. I stuck my fist out to him, and he bumped his against it. "Hardy Boys forever."

He shook his head, but he smiled. "Hardy Boys forever."

Rochester woofed his agreement.

Neil S. Plakcy

34 – CONNECTIONS

Acting on the information Tiffany and I provided, the police went to Maria Jose's Rodriguez's apartment that evening. The next day, I met Rick for a beer at the Drunken Hessian and he explained what they found.

"She was on her living room floor, surrounded by blood," he said. "Dead for at least a couple of days. There was a big gash in the side of her head, and the crime scene team matched it to blood on the edge of a glass coffee table."

"She fell?"

"Or she was pushed."

"Just like Doug," I said.

"You could say that. The police found de la Fe's fingerprints in her apartment, but he says that he was there long before she died. Not my case, but I'm sure they'll find more evidence against him."

"Wow. What an evil guy."

"You said it. I'm not sure who's going to prosecute de la Fe first, either Union City for Miss Rodriguez's murder or the Feds for the health care fraud. I already spoke to the chief, and he's willing to reclassify Guilfoyle's death as an accident."

"An accident!" I said indignantly. "But de la Fe pushed him into the water!"

"De la Fe insists that Guilfoyle slipped into the canal while they were arguing. You and I might call it murder, but it would be nearly impossible to prove beyond reasonable doubt, and calling it an accident keeps the press and the public off the chief's back. Plus it gets Catherine the insurance money sooner rather than later."

I didn't like it, but I understood. "How's Tiffany doing?" I asked. "She didn't have to stay in the hospital, did she?"

"Nope. She just had some bruising from where the desk fell on her, and some smoke inhalation, but they sent her home that night with Vargas."

"Uh-huh," I said.

"I had a long talk with him, while he was waiting for her at the hospital," Rick said. "I know I was suspicious of him, and what Tiffany said about his temper didn't make me happy. But he swore to me that he loves her, and that he's been a good law-abiding citizen ever since that beef for drug possession. Broke away from his old friends, been working steadily at the car wash."

"You believe him?"

"I do. Sure, he's got an edge, and it wouldn't shock me to see him get in trouble again. But I think he'll be good for Tiffany. Stable, but just wild enough to keep her interested."

"Unlike you."

"Hey, I've got my wild side," he said. "But you're right. I'm too boring for Tiffany."

"How about for Tamsen? She was married to a soldier. She have a taste for danger, too?"

"If she had one when she was younger, having Justin took it out of her." He cupped his beer. "This whole business with Tiff helped me see that Tamsen's the right woman for me. I love her and I love Justin, and I think they both feel the same way about me."

"Marriage?"

"In the future, I think. Neither of us is ready to rush into anything. Kind of like you and Lili."

I couldn't argue with that.

"I talked to an agent from the Newark office of the FBI this morning," Rick said. "Hank Quillian sent them all the information from the jump drive Tiffany found and they're adding it to what they already have."

"De la Fe thought that Doug had triggered the investigation into the clinic," I said. "Did the agent you spoke to say anything about that?"

"From what I understand, it was Maria Jose Rodriguez," Rick said. "She passed on a lot of information about the clinic, and she had collected more on that jump drive before she was able to hand it over. The Feds got a subpoena for de la Fe's phone records. He called Guilfoyle's cell phone the night Guilfoyle died. And toll records from the Jersey Turnpike indicated he traveled south early in the evening, and then north again a couple of hours later."

I shook my head. "Two murders and two FBI cases. Been a busy couple of weeks for Frank and Joe Hardy."

Rick smiled, and we clinked our beer glasses together. Then we moved on to happier topics, including getting Rochester and Rascal together for another agility session in Rick's back yard.

A few days later, I spotted an article in the *Bucks County Courier-Times*. The FBI had shut down Beauceron Capital Partners. Shawn Brumberger and several of his employees were facing allegations that they had been running a Ponzi scheme.

That afternoon, Lili and I were invited to a party celebrating Ethan's graduation from Pennsbury High. I still remembered my own graduation, marching in a sea of black gowns from the high school out to the football stadium, the long speeches under the beating sun, the chaos afterward as I found my parents.

When we got to Catherine's house, I let Rochester off his leash and he romped ahead of us, looking for Rascal and Pixie. The room was crowded but I spotted Tamsen with her sister Hannah and Hannah's husband Eric. Through the glass doors I saw Justin and Nathaniel outside with the dogs.

Catherine had decorated the living room with paper decals of caps and gowns and strung a big banner that read "Congratulations Ethan." I didn't see the guest of honor, but Madison was off in a corner with a couple of girls her own age.

Rick walked out from the kitchen and handed me a beer, and we clinked our bottles together. "I heard yesterday that Eduardo de la Fe has pled guilty to eighteen counts of insurance fraud," he said. "All the evidence implicating him in the death of Maria Jose Rodriguez is circumstantial, so the cops in Union City have backed off. They're happy to let de la Fe serve his time in a federal prison."

"Too bad neither of the murders happened in Alabama," I said. Rick looked curiously at me, so I told him what I'd learned from my online hacker friend, Brewski_Bubba. "He made my federal time sound like a cakewalk compared to doing state time." I wondered if de la Fe would be as arrogant as the guy I'd told Ethan about, who'd been killed in the prison yard because of his attitude, and I shivered.

"What about Shawn Brumberger? I saw an article in the newspaper today that said his firm was shut down."

"Hank Quillian has been spearheading an investigation into the financial crimes there. Doug Guilfoyle was smart to recognize he needed to get out—all the other account executives have been charged, too."

We were both quiet for a moment, thinking of Doug.

Then Rick stretched and cracked his back. "You'd think I'd learn," he said. "After Justin figured out how to throw a fast ball he wanted me to teach him the change up, and stupid me, I went along with him. Playing hell with my back. I'm too old for this."

I left him reclining in a chair and walked over to Catherine. "How are you holding up?" I asked her.

"It's tough," she said. "Right after Doug died, when I thought we weren't going to get the insurance money, I started talking to people about doing some freelance writing work, to get something current on my resume. I got a referral to a woman who works for this non-profit that encourages social responsibility in kids, and she asked if I'd be willing to do some writing for them. They need a brochure, a couple of fund-raising letters targeted to different aspects of their programs, and a revamp of their website content."

"That's awesome," I said.

"It's not much money, but having recent experience will give me a leg up on job hunting. And part of the work will be interviewing kids and parents who are doing things to help others, and then writing up their stories."

"You might even find you could write a book based on those stories," I said. "Jimmy should be able to help you with the publishing stuff."

"That's a great idea," she said. "I want to do something in memory of Doug, to celebrate the way he was trying to act honestly, and show Ethan and Maddie that I don't hate him or anything. I could dedicate the book to him."

"Well, don't jump ahead of yourself," I said. "But that's a great goal."

I stood around talking to different people until I saw Ethan come downstairs, wearing his father's Eastern sweater. I walked up to him. "Congratulations on finishing high school," I said. "I like your sweater."

"It makes me think of my dad," he said. "Did my mom tell you? I was on the wait list for Eastern, but I got accepted last week."

"Wow. Double congrats, then."

"Yeah, my mom thinks it's a good idea for me to stay close to home, and she and my dad got good educations there." He looked down and toed the floor. "My mom said you helped figure out who killed my dad."

"I did. I wanted you and Maddie to know that he didn't commit suicide, and that he died trying to do what was right."

"Thank you. I was bummed worrying that it was because of what I'd said to him."

"If you want to meet up on campus and hang out sometime, just let me know," I said. "I can show you the places your dad and I ran around together, back in the day. I can't take his place, but I want you to know that I'll always feel connected to you and Maddie because I knew him."

"Thanks," Ethan said. He shook my hand, and I was impressed at how much growing up he'd gone through in the past couple of months. He stood up straight and spoke well. He was a kid his father would be proud of.

One of the kids opened the sliding door to come inside, and Rochester rushed in between his legs, hurrying up to Ethan. He went up his hind legs and put his front paws on Ethan's waist. "Rochester wants you to know he'll be around too," I said.

Ethan laughed. My big happy golden woofed once, then ran off to play with Rascal and Pixie. I watched him go, once more so happy that he was in my life.

Neil S. Plakcy

I hope you enjoyed spending time with Steve and Rochester! Have you read the previous books in the series?

1. In Dog We Trust

After a bad divorce and a brief prison term for computer hacking, 42-year-old Steve Levitan has returned to his home town of Stewart's Crossing and taken a part-time job as an adjunct professor of English at his alma mater, Eastern College. While walking around his gated community, he becomes friendly with his next-door neighbor, Caroline Kelly, and her golden retriever, Rochester.

When Caroline is shot and killed while walking Rochester, Steve becomes the dog's temporary guardian. Together, these two unlikely sleuths work to uncover the mystery behind Caroline's death.

2. The Kingdom of Dog

After the uncertainty of adjunct teaching, Steve's relieved to have been offered a full-time job in Eastern's alumni relations office, and delighted that Rochester can come to work with him every day. He's still on parole, though, and his parole officer is uncomfortable with Steve's access to computer systems and records.

When his mentor, Joe Dagorian, director of admissions, is murdered during a fund-raising event, Steve feels obliged to investigate. He and Rochester go nose to the ground to dig up clues, including a bloody knife and some curious photographs. But will Steve's curiosity and Rochester's savvy save them when the killer comes calling?

3. Dog Helps Those

It's almost time for graduation, and Eastern College is in trouble. A prominent alumna is dead, and a faulty computer program is jeopardizing student records and financial aid. It's up to Steve and Rochester to dig into the situation and retrieve the culprits!

Rita Gaines wasn't a nice person—but she did love her dogs, and most of her clients respected her financial acumen and her talent in training dogs for agility trials. When she's found dead, there's a long line of potential suspects from Wall Street whiz kids to doting doggie daddies-- including one of Steve's former students.

Felae is an art prodigy now studying with Steve's girlfriend, Lili, chair of Eastern's Fine Arts department, and Rita hated his controversial senior project. When she tried to have his scholarship cancelled, he threatened to kill her. But is he the villain behind her death?

4. Dog Bless You

Autumn has come to Bucks County, and Steve Levitan has a new job: develop a conference center for Eastern College at Friar Lake, a few miles from campus. But on his first visit to the property, his golden retriever Rochester makes a disturbing discovery, a human hand rising from the dirt at the lake's shore.

Whose hand is it? Why was the body buried there? The answers will take Steve, his photographer girlfriend Lili, and the ever-faithful Rochester to a drop-in center for recovering drug addicts on the Lower East Side, a decaying church in Philadelphia's Germantown, and finally to a confrontation with a desperate killer.

5. *Whom Dog Hath Joined*

Steve still gets a thrill from snooping into places online where he shouldn't be. When Rochester discovers a human bone at the Friends Meeting during the Harvest Days festival, these two unlikely sleuths are plunged into another investigation.

They will uncover uncomfortable secrets about their small town's past as they dig deep into the Vietnam War era, when local Quakers helped draft resisters move through Stewart's Crossing on their way to Canada. Does that bone Rochester found belong to one of those young men fleeing conscription? Or to someone who knew the secrets that lurked behind those whitewashed walls?

Steve's got other problems, too. His girlfriend Lili wants to move in with him, and his matchmaking efforts among his friends all seem to be going haywire.

Whether the death was due to natural causes, or murder, someone in the present wants to keep those secrets hidden. And Steve and Rochester may end up in the crosshairs of a very antique rifle if they can't dig up the clues quickly enough.

6. *Dog Have Mercy*

Christmas approaches and Steve Levitan tries to help a fellow ex-con now working at the vet's office in Stewart's Crossing. His curiosity, and Rochester's crime-solving instincts, kick in when liquid potassium ampoules are stolen from the vet and Steve's new friend is a suspect.

Is this theft connected to a drug-running operation in North Philly? Or to a recent spate of deaths at the local nursing home? And can Steve continue to resist his computer-hacking impulses or will his desire to help others continue to lead him into trouble?

If you visit my website at www.goldenretrievermysteries.com and sign up for my newsletter, I promise I won't spam you, but I will let you know about new books in the series.

Neil S. Plakcy

ABOUT THE AUTHOR

Neil Plakcy's golden retriever mysteries have been inspired by his own goldens, Samwise, Brody and Griffin. A native of Bucks County, PA, where the books are set, Neil is a graduate of the University of Pennsylvania, Columbia University and Florida International University, where he received his MFA in creative writing.

He has written and edited many other books; details can be found at his website, http://www.mahubooks.com. Neil, his partner, Brody and Griffin live in South Florida, where Neil is writing and the dogs are undoubtedly getting into mischief.

Made in the USA
Middletown, DE
27 December 2018